SUMMER of SLOANE

Erin L. Schneider

HYPERION

Los Angeles   New York

First Edition, May 2016
10 9 8 7 6 5 4 3 2 1
FAC-020093-16046
Printed in the United States of America

Library of Congress Cataloging-in-Publication Data
Names: Schneider, Erin L., author.
Title: Summer of Sloane / Erin L. Schneider.
Description: First edition. | Los Angeles ; New York : Hyperion, 2016. |
Summary: Seventeen-year-old Sloane McIntyre spends a summer in Hawaii as she deals with being betrayed by both her boyfriend and her best friend, and she and her twin brother, Penn, begin new, complicated romances.
Identifiers: LCCN 2015028795| ISBN 9781484725252 (hardback) | ISBN 1484725255
Subjects: | CYAC: Dating (Social customs)—Fiction. | Brothers and Sisters—Fiction. | Twins—Fiction. | Hawaii—Fiction. | BISAC: JUVENILE FICTION / Love & Romance. | JUVENILE FICTION / Social Issues / Friendship. | JUVENILE FICTION / Social Issues / Dating & Sex.
Classification: LCC PZ7.1.S593 Sum 2016 | DDC [Fic]—dc23
LC record available at http://lccn.loc.gov/2015028795

Reinforced binding
Visit www.hyperionteens.com

For Mom:

Love and miss you. Every. Single. Day.
Me ke aloha. A hui hou kakou.

For Dad:

Thank you for being every reason a book was always in my hands.
Love you.

One

The condom must've broke.

Her words, not mine.

They belong to McKinley—or Mick, as I've called her for as long as I can remember.

We stand together near the swings at our favorite park. Fifteen years, we've known each other. Fifteen years we've been best friends. Our moms met during a playdate at this very park when Mick and I were two, and the rest, as they say, is history.

"Wait, what? How? . . . When? . . . *Who?*" It all stumbles out of my mouth, tripping over my tongue in one incoherent string. But somehow my best friend understands exactly what I'm trying to ask.

"Believe me, I know." She clenches her eyes shut and rubs at a spot on her forehead that creases under her fingertips. "Everything, all of it, it's such a mess. But I need you to understand—*I need you to know*—that I never, ever meant to hurt you."

I start to open my mouth to console her, to tell her everything's going to be okay, that I'm not going to leave her side just because she's pregnant. But something makes me hesitate, just for a second, as her words begin to register in my head.

"What do you mean, you never meant to hurt me?" I stare at her, but now she won't look me in the eye. In fact, she looks everywhere but at me, and it triggers something inside, some mental warning that's shouting for me to run, duck, cover . . . anything.

That's when my surroundings turn fuzzy and the playground and all its toys move in and out of focus. I hear little kids playing, enjoying one of the first sunny days of summer vacation here in Seattle. Everyone so happy to be outside after months and months of nonstop rain. They run around the playground laughing and squealing as they swing on the swings and slide down the slides. But I only stand there. Numb. Frozen in place as I try to understand what Mick is saying.

And that's when she unloads the truth. The real zinger, the stab to the heart, the pièce de résistance.

"It's Tyler's."

Tyler, as in *my* boyfriend.

Oh my God, I can't breathe.

It's such a simple act, mindless even. We learn to do it

the very second we come into this world. But right now it's anything *but* simple.

I press my hands tight to my chest like that will help. It won't. The weight of what Mick has just told me settles heavy on my chest and slowly presses down on my lungs.

"You're kidding, right? This is all some big joke?" I stare at Mick as my vision blurs, creating a second version of her in front of me. "When the hell did this happen?"

She stares up at the sky like some divine intervention is going to save her. "Last month, at one of Jansen's parties. You left early because you weren't feeling well. I think you had the flu or something." She fights back tears of her own but loses, and quickly scrubs at her cheeks to wipe away any trace of them. "I'm so, so sorry—please . . . please don't hate me. Oh God."

"Are you serious? I was there for almost the *entire* party— and afterward, I was literally sick for like an hour!" I close my eyes and try to take in deep, even breaths. But instead, all I get are short, ragged stutters of air. And it's not enough.

Asthma is bad enough on its own, but I'm the lucky victim of these stupid attacks brought on by my own anxiety. There's a mental trick to combating them, something that took several visits to my doctor to figure out and involves visualizing a swimming pool. My home away from home. I have to build the image in my head from scratch, piece by piece, drop of water by drop of water. Right down to the red-and-white plastic lane lines that float effortlessly on the surface, their only job to divide the pool into equally measured sections.

But I'm having a hard enough time focusing on anything, let alone fabricating some pool in my head.

Because Tyler and I slept together for the very first time less than three weeks ago. A few weeks after Jansen's party. Which means Mick and Tyler slept together before that.

Before me.

Panic sets in as the familiar freeze from lack of oxygen takes over my limbs, one creeping inch at a time, and I close my eyes to try to rein it back in. To try to get some sort of handle on a situation that is clearly out of my control.

When my knees hit grass, I know it's too late. And I can't stand how humiliating and out of my control all of this is.

I try to focus on the image in my head. It's blurry at first, but before me is an empty pool, with its cool white cement and painted lane lines that race along the bottom, from one end to the other. As the image begins to take shape, drains form along the floor and caged-in metal lights ring the outer rim.

I force the pool to fill itself with water, and for a moment, it falters and the pool is empty again. I clench my eyes tighter and focus and watch the water level rise and rise, until it's right below the lip of the edge, right where it's supposed to be. Calm turquoise water laps against the side of the pool, the red-and-white lane markers bobbing along the surface.

I build the cement pathway around its edges next, then the bleachers one at a time—filling each bench with a crowd that's silently cheering around me. With every deep, even breath, the scent of chlorine stings my nose, as I focus on the path of water in front of me that's all mine. Light glistens off the surface, rolling with each ripple like beckoning fingers, taunting me to dive in and go.

Fluid. Tranquil. Soothing.

"Where's your inhaler? Mack, your inhaler?"

The image of my pool breaks into a thousand tiny shards and is replaced by Mick standing over me, concern pinching the small space between her eyes. I see her mouth moving, but I can't hear a word she's saying. I stare at her lips and blink. She's swiped my bag off my shoulder, but I have no idea why. Something hard and plastic is pressed into my hand and forced to my mouth.

My autopilot kicks in, and I suck in two long drags and try to inhale a deep breath through my nose. Around me, the park begins to fall into place, one blade of grass at a time, one giggling toddler after another.

After a few more deep breaths, everything snaps back into a hard, sharp focus, and around us, people have stopped and are staring. I can feel the heat flood my cheeks as a few of them ask Mick if we need help. But she only brushes them off. She's been around me long enough to know exactly what to do.

"That's it, Mack. . . . You've got this."

Mack. I'm the other half of Mick and Mack. Nicknames her older brother, Bryson, gave us years ago, a play on her name, McKinley, and my last name, McIntyre. Nicknames given when everyone realized how inseparable we were. When we ourselves realized that while we may look nothing alike, Mick has always been the left to my right. And I the right to her left.

In fifteen years, there hasn't been a single day we haven't been there for each other. When I was in the fourth grade, she brought over her favorite stuffed bear and hugged me tight when I found out my parents were getting a divorce and my mom was moving back home to Hawaii. She stood by my side when I was twelve, as I mumbled to my dad that I needed to go to the store for some, er, female products—and then two weeks later, I stood by her when she had the same conversation with her mom. We were together the first time we ever snuck out to toilet-paper Tyler's house in the ninth grade. And of course as soon as I got my driver's license, I drove us everywhere, from the mall to all things ballet. . . . Not that I minded; it wasn't her fault her mother would never let her get her license, let alone a car.

When I think back to everything we've been through—from the swim meets and the recitals, to the double dates and the dances—there isn't a thing I wouldn't do for Mick. She's my best friend.

But now I can't help but wonder if she feels the same way.

"Why . . ." My voice catches. I can't imagine there's an answer she could give me that would be good enough, but I have to know. Anything that would justify why she slept with my boyfriend of almost a year. Or better yet, explain how she could betray our friendship. "What did I do?"

She shakes her head and covers her mouth with an unsteady hand. When she looks away, I know I'm not going to hear a good reason . . . at least not today. And out of everything, her silence is what makes the biggest impact.

Then she clears her throat.

"Mack, you didn't do anything. I . . . It just sort of . . . I think . . ." When she takes a deep breath and reaches for my arm to help me up, I can't help but flinch, like her touch has somehow become electrified. I rise slowly and move away from her. "Mack, *please.*"

I try to swallow the bitter taste my inhaler has left behind, and I hesitate, just for a moment. A fraction of a second where I remember how many times the two of us have been there for each other, no matter what.

No matter what.

"Tyler and I, we never meant for this to happen. We never meant to hurt you."

And just like that, the feeling is gone. "On what fucking planet do you think the *two of you* belong together in the same sentence?"

She looks as if I've slapped her, as tears begin to slide down her cheeks. She reaches for me again, but I take a step back, leaving her hand outstretched.

"Don't . . . don't touch me." I reach into my bag to snag my sunglasses and slide them into place.

And then I realize something.

"Oh my God. The other day when you needed me to take you to the doctor because you weren't 'feeling well,' but didn't want your mom to know because she'd freak out over nothing." She only nods, but her lips stay sealed. "Jesus, Mick—I skipped school to take you. I missed my calculus exam. And then you lied and told me it was only some stupid stomach bug. God, you *used* me."

"No, Mack—that's not it at all. I needed your help. I *still* need your help. Please don't do this."

I can't help but laugh, even though it feels so out of place. So wrong in this moment. Rubbing my forehead, I try to make sense of anything I've just heard, but it's all one giant and twisted mess that has no answer. "I can't believe this is happening. . . . I can't believe you'd do this to me." I start walking backward. "Just stay away from me. Just leave me the fuck alone."

I turn and leave her standing there and don't look back. Thank God I'm leaving for Hawaii in the morning. Because, suddenly, I can't wait to get the hell out of here.

My hands shake as I grip the steering wheel, and I force myself to calm down and release pressure off the gas. The last thing I need right before I leave is a speeding ticket, or worse.

I have the strong desire to hit something really hard, but using my car is not the solution. Then I near my house and see Tyler's car parked in the driveway.

I used to get so excited when I saw his car. It was the same feeling I'd get right before a huge swim meet, my nerves a swirling chaos of excitement. But somehow with Tyler it was always ten thousand times better than even that. And I'd actually find myself *looking* for his vintage gray Mustang wherever I went—school, football games, swim meets.

It was even better when I'd spot his car somewhere I wasn't expecting him to be. Then my stomach would practically turn itself inside out.

But now I have to fight back an entirely different feeling brewing deep down inside. It doesn't help that Tyler is leaning against his passenger door, arms crossed over his chest, waiting for me.

I slide my car into the space in the driveway next to his, as he reaches forward to open my door. I resist the urge to climb out the passenger side instead. He can't see my eyes because of the sunglasses I'm wearing, but I know he doesn't need to.

"You have no idea how sorry I am. Please . . . I can—"

"After everything. *Everything*. I can't believe you'd do this. And with my best friend!" An almost laugh escapes from my lips as I hear exactly what I just said. "You know what? Forget it. I have absolutely *nothing* to say to you." Chin lifted, I walk toward my house, hoping he doesn't see my bottom lip quiver. He's an easy foot taller than me, having breached the six-foot mark his sophomore year, but he lags behind as if afraid to keep up.

"Sloane, wait—I know you're pissed, but you have to let me explain." Oh, he's going for the full first name right off the bat. Not "Mack" like everyone else here calls me. Not "Slo" like he normally does. But Sloane.

"Oh, I don't have to let you do anything. Besides, I'm pretty sure you've done enough." I'm up the three steps and on the path that leads to the front door when he grabs my arm, forcing me to turn around and face him. I'm almost as tall as him now as I stand on the top step, and he's below, on my driveway.

"Could you please take off your sunglasses?" He holds my elbow, his fingers softly pressing into my skin like he's trying to keep me from slipping away. I cross my arms tight over my chest. "Come on, Slo."

He reaches up and grips the back of his neck, then slides his fingers up and tugs at his hair. His hair distracts me. It always has. It's this tangled mess of blond that has the unique ability to tweak in a variety of directions, but still appear amazingly soft. What stops me from wanting to run my own fingers through it like I've done countless times before is thinking of Mick doing the very same thing only a month ago.

"I don't know what I can do to prove how sorry I am. And I'm sure there's nothing I can say—but you need to know, I never, ever, meant to hurt you." He holds a steady hand near his brow to shield him from the glare of the sun as his gray-blue eyes lock on to mine. He almost seems convincing. *Almost.* "She doesn't even matter to me, and you know how much I love you. Shit, I've pretty much been in love with you since kindergarten." He waits a second for me to respond. "Sloane, please—I'll do anything. Anything you say. Please just forgive me."

My insides churn, and my hands start to shake as I ball them tightly into fists. I open my mouth to tell him exactly what I think, but that's the very same moment the garage door opens and my dad pushes the lawn mower out. He sees us, smiles, and raises a hand in a wave, then slowly lowers it when neither of us turns his way. He takes the mower and quickly retreats to the side yard.

"Come on, Slo, would you just say something?"

I wait to respond because I want my dad to be out of earshot before I unleash the real fury. As he disappears out of sight and before I can open my mouth, stupid falls out of Tyler's.

"Sloane, it was only those two times, I swear."

My lips part slightly, and I scoff in utter disbelief. Tyler's face falls, and I know he now realizes his mistake. That I didn't know they'd done it twice.

I feel the immediate crunch of something breaking, as my fist makes contact with his face, and my hand explodes in pain.

"Holy shit that hurts!" I yell, shaking my hand at the same time Tyler cries out, "Jesus Christ!" He's clutching his nose between his fingers, as blood oozes down the length of his arms and sprinkles the driveway.

Red is everywhere. My own hand. Tyler's face. His T-shirt. The ground around us. I stare at it all, then back up at Tyler, stunned.

Oh my God, what did I just do?

My dad reappears, whistling, from around the corner. But then the whistling stops.

"What the hell's going on here?" My dad races over and rests a hand on Tyler's shoulder to stop him from swaying. I don't know what to say. I don't know how to justify what I've just done . . . let alone to my father.

"I . . . I'm sorry." I say this more to my dad than to Tyler as I cradle my hand to my chest.

"Son, I think it's time for you to leave." He goes to the garage and grabs a roll of industrial blue paper towels, then returns and shoves them against Tyler's chest. "You're in no shape to drive, so I can either take you home myself or call your mom."

Tyler brushes him off, holding a wad of paper towels to his nose. "I've got it, Mr. M." He looks at me one last time, at first with narrowed eyes, but then they soften. He's pissed at what I've done, but he knows what he did was worse and doesn't want to leave it like this. Sometimes it sucks how well I know him. "Sloane . . . ?"

"Let's go, Tyler," my father says quietly.

Without waiting to watch him leave, I turn and walk away.

And for the second time today, I don't look back.

Two

I have no idea what just happened. I don't even know where to start. And I can't decide if I want to cry or scream or break something . . . or all of it combined. But I feel like I want to tear my own skin off, because what I'm wearing is suddenly too small.

My hand hurts like a mother and for good reason. There's a nasty rip across the skin of my first two knuckles, and the swelling is so bad, I now have my very own foam finger for a hand. It throbs like it contains its own heartbeat.

If I broke my damn hand on that asshole's nose, I'm really gonna be pissed.

I somehow make my way upstairs to my bathroom and run cool water across the surface of my skin. I can no longer see the bumps of my knuckles, as it's all one giant mass now. And it hurts to flex my fingers.

Crap, crap, and crap.

My dad is waiting for me out in the hall, holding an ice pack. He looks seriously worried and I don't blame him—but I don't know what to say.

"I can't, Dad, not right now, okay?" I bite my lip, hoping beyond hope it doesn't betray me.

"You should at least put some ice on it—and when the swelling comes down a little, I'd like to take a look." He hands me the ice pack, leans down, and kisses me on the forehead, then lets me pass without another word.

Clutching my hand to my stomach, I sit on the edge of my bed.

My best friend. My boyfriend. It dawns on me that within a matter of minutes I no longer have either.

And now the two of them are going to have a baby. What the hell are they gonna do with a baby? We're only seventeen. We just finished our junior year of high school. Mick's an amazing dancer who without a doubt will be headed to Juilliard after our senior year. There's no room in any of that for a baby.

I realize I have no idea what Mick will even do. Is she considering abortion? Will she give it up for adoption? Hell . . . will she keep it?

Keep it. Oh my God. Mick and Tyler are going to be *parents*.

The thought of either of them attempting to change a diaper makes me laugh. I'm literally laughing out loud, when I stop suddenly, unsure if that's an appropriate way to be handling everything—or if that's a clear sign I'm not handling it at all.

Around me, my bedroom mirrors the chaos of everything that's happening. Clothes and shoes are strewn everywhere, since I was trying to pack when Mick called and asked if I could swing by to pick her up. Of course I'd dropped everything. Literally.

Because what kind of friend would I be if I'd said no? When she'd called, I could hear it in her voice that she needed to see me. I didn't even think twice. It's how it's always been with Mick. And I've never once second-guessed that.

Then again, I also had no idea the destruction she was about to unleash.

Which makes me feel like such an idiot. What was Mick even thinking? Is she in love with Tyler? And have I just been too blind to see what was happening right in front of my own face? I can't help but wonder what would've happened had I not gotten sick the night of Jansen's party.

I reach for the inhaler sitting on my nightstand, just in case. I want so desperately to get out of my own head, but the only real place I can do that is the swimming pool. Swimming has always been my go-to stress reliever, and God knows I could definitely use the distraction. There's something about putting on a suit and cranking out lap after lap that helps everything else slip away into nothing. And I so could use nothing right about now. But with my hand in the shape it's in, I have a feeling the pool may not be an option for a very long time. And, with everything going on, that terrifies me.

I stare at the several pairs of suits and goggles that now sit in the bottom of my unpacked suitcase and contemplate my options. My running shoes are sitting right next to them. And if I'm going to be honest, running away seems far more like the answer.

A rap of knuckles sweeps quickly across my door, and I hear my dad shuffle on the other side.

"I hope you're decent, because I'm coming in." The door flies open, and my room is suddenly filled with my brother. "Tell me the rumors I just heard aren't true? Tyler and Mick? Are you kidding me? I'd kill him myself, but holy shit, Dad said you busted his nose?" He pauses for a second but only to take in a breath, when he spots my hand. "Oh my God, did you break it?"

Penn is supposed to be playing a game of hoops with the boys. Funny how fast bad news travels. Especially when you're a twin and you share the same group of friends.

"No, I didn't break it. It's just . . . really puffy." I hide my hand behind my back and look up at a face that mirrors my own. Because Penn is a boy and I am not, there's obviously no way we could've been identical, but you'd never know by looking at the two of us.

We have almost the exact same shade of blond hair—mine long and sometimes stringy, his super short and oftentimes fluffy. In fact, Penn hates how fluffy his hair gets, why he practically shaves it all off. But it's been a few weeks since his last cut, and right now, it's this matted sweaty mess that clings to his head in various clumps.

I stare into a pair of pale green eyes identical to mine and it's then I notice his face is flushed. I'm not sure if that's from being in the middle of a basketball game when the news broke or because he's pissed at what he's heard.

I try to pick up a few folded T-shirts with the wrong hand and wince. It's even bigger than it was five minutes ago.

"Holy shit, you didn't tuck your thumb inside your fist when you hit him, did you?" Penn grabs for my wrist, and I grit my teeth.

I have no idea what he's talking about. "How the hell would I even know where my thumb was? It's not like I've ever decked my boyfriend before."

And then I remember. Tyler is so no longer my boyfriend.

Penn whistles loudly. "That must've been one helluva punch. I wish I could've been there to see it! And I hate to break it to you—no pun intended—but this is totally broken." He flips my hand over, and the purple hue of a deep bruise is evident well across the pad of my palm, making him whistle again.

"Oh, no it's not." I pull away from him, grimace in pain, and pick up a pair of shorts. And then I start to pack. Because if I keep myself busy, I won't have time to register everything that's so evidently broken about my life, pun intended. And I won't have time to cry.

"Sloane, you gotta go to the ER. If you don't get that in

a cast, it's gonna stay like that, you know. And it'd be awfully hard to swim and surf this summer with a club for a hand." He waits, but I have nothing to say, so I continue to pack—turning away when a jolt of pain shoots up my arm. He pokes my foot with the tip of his shoe, and I know it's coming. "Hey, I'm really sorry about what happened."

I don't look up at him, because I know if I do, the floodgates will open. "I don't really feel like talking about it, okay?"

I'm not even paying attention to what I'm throwing in my suitcase. For all I know, it could be my winter down jacket, which won't be of much use in the hot summer sun of Hawaii. I bump my hand again and cringe. Penn snags the flip-flops I'm holding and chucks them into my bag.

"Stubborn isn't going to win you any points." He places his hands on my shoulders and steers me from the room.

"Penn, what the hell?"

"Did you not understand me when I said your hand would turn into a club? A club, Sloane, a club. And we can't be having any of that." Before I can respond, he sweeps down and tucks an arm under my knees, while the other circles around my back. Five seconds later, he's carrying me downstairs.

"Dammit, Penn—if you don't let me down this second, I'll . . . I'll break your nose, too!"

"Yeah you will." He rolls his eyes, snagging the car keys off the peg by the garage door. Which is the exact moment the door opens and my dad steps into the kitchen.

He looks from my brother to me, with one eyebrow raised.

"She busted her hand on that d bag's nose. We're going to the ER," Penn explains.

"Oh, Sloane, didn't I ever teach you not to tuck your thumb in when you throw a punch?" my dad says, shaking his head. I know he's only trying to lighten the mood, but it's not really working right now.

"Ohmygod, whatever. You're both being ridiculous; my hand is fine." I thrust it forward so he can see for himself, but even that movement makes the blood rush from my face.

We sit in the ER waiting room, Penn on my right and my father on my left. This is the hospital my mom used to work at, and we've known most of the staff for years. We're practically family here, which, lucky for me, means I won't have to wait long.

"It'll just be a few more minutes, Sloane—Dr. Craig will be with you shortly," Colleen, one of the evening ER shift nurses, says as she squats down in front of me. The rubber soles of her practical shoes squeak on the slick linoleum surface of the floor. "Wow, you really did a number on your hand, didn't you?" Her face shifts as if she's realized something. Like I said, we're practically family. "I don't suppose this is in any way connected to Tyler Hudson's broken nose?"

"Wait, what? He's here?"

"Oh, he's here all right—been in X-rays for the last

twenty minutes. But don't worry, we'll make sure to put you in one of the exam rooms on the other side." She clucks her tongue in mild disapproval, then gently pats my knee. "So how has your mom been?"

"Good, I guess. We're headed out in the morning to spend the summer with her." I try not to think about the fact that Tyler is somewhere within a fifty-foot radius of me right now. And then my name is called, and we're following another nurse through the huge set of double doors that automatically ease open.

And that's when I see him.

"Sloooo! You came!" Tyler is being pushed in a wheelchair by his dad, his mom walking next to his side.

"I hope you're happy with yourself, young lady—Tyler will need at least two surgeries to repair what you've done." His mother glares back and forth between me and my father, and I wonder if I'm going to be in some serious trouble.

"I'm so sorry, Mrs. Hudson, I guess I just reacted and I—"

"Reacted? Is that what you're calling it? You practically took my son's head off!"

Before I can say anything else, my father steps forward and says something to Tyler's parents that I can't hear.

"Moooommmm, stop," Tyler croons, waving a hand in her general direction.

His once gorgeous face is now almost unrecognizable. He wears a large transparent splint that covers almost everything from his forehead to just below his nose, giving him the appearance of Hannibal Lecter. Both eyes are black-and-blue, and glassy, as if he's heavily medicated. I can't believe that I'm the one who did this to him.

"Man, you're the best girlfriend ef-fer," he slurs, wiping at his mouth with fumbling fingers.

My body stiffens at the mention of the word "girlfriend," and I feel Penn grip my left arm as my father takes my right.

"Oh, no you don't," my dad says in a low voice. "I think you've already done enough." They force me to walk forward, making a wide berth around Tyler, just in case.

"Sloane, whereya goin'? Man, I love youuuu."

Everything inside me deflates. How can I suddenly feel so sad when I'm still so angry? Everything is such a mess, and I can't stop the constant static noise of all these feelings—betrayal, frustration, and one hundred percent complete confusion. I wish I knew how to turn them off.

My dad releases my arm and motions for Penn to keep following the nurse. I turn to see him trailing the Hudsons out into the waiting room as Tyler becomes fascinated with his own fingers mere inches from his face. He's still repeating "I love youuuu, I love youuuu . . ." as he turns the corner and disappears out of sight.

"Jackass," my brother whispers as he guides me into one of the rooms. I know he's only saying that because of what happened. After all, Tyler and Penn have always been pretty tight.

Penn is unsure of where to put his hands to help me onto the bed in the middle of the room, so he gives up and takes a seat in one of the hard, straight-back chairs. I somehow manage to climb up myself just as Dr. Craig comes in. He and my mom were good friends, and even though she is no longer a doctor here, they still keep in touch.

"Well, well, well, would you look at what the cat dragged in?" His smile stretches wide across his face as he comes to stand in front of me. "And what, may I ask, have you gone and done to your hand? You didn't tuck your thumb in when you threw the punch, did you?"

I scowl back and forth between him and my brother, daring Penn to say one word. "Why does *everyone* keep asking me that?"

With a knowing smile—proving that this has to be a guy rule I didn't know about—Dr. Craig lifts my hand, his fingertips a little on the cold side, as he gently flutters them from my wrist to the tip of my thumb. And I'm not gonna lie, even that slight contact hurts.

He immediately orders a set of X-rays and walks me back to the lab where they take them. He makes small talk about my mom, asking how she is and sharing old memories from when they worked together to help pass the time.

As soon as we're finished, he walks me back to my room, but excuses himself to check in on another patient. Penn and my father are talking in hushed voices when I enter, but then all goes quiet when they see me.

"Really? Please, don't stop talking on account of me." I'm suddenly feeling light-headed, so I clamber back up on the plastic mattress and lie down.

My dad hesitates for a moment before launching in. "The Hudsons say Tyler got McKinley pregnant. Is that true, Sloane?"

I look away, and both of them let out a string of expletives that would make even a trucker blush. So it seems Penn didn't know the whole story. And that's probably a good thing, since he would've broken more than Tyler's nose, and I would've spent my summer alone in Hawaii, while he spent his in juvie.

My cell phone buzzes with an incoming text, then buzzes quickly again.

"It's been doing that a lot," Penn says. He nods toward my bag sitting on the chair next to him, but I shake my head no. It buzzes again before Penn reaches in and turns it off.

And I know word has gotten out.

With the rate gossip flies around the halls at my school, I can only imagine how everyone is chomping at the bit to hear the juicy details of what happened . . . but I also know very few actually care if I'm okay. Those that do will leave a message, and at some point, I'll talk to them. Just not now.

I wonder if any one of those incoming texts might be from Mick, with an answer to my "why." With a real reason for doing what she did. Something, anything, that will help me understand how I came to be sitting here right now.

My dad grips my foot in my flip-flop and gives it a shake. "I think heading out to Hawaii might be exactly what you need right now."

I can't help but think that maybe he's right.

Two hairline fractures, one black waterproof cast, and an enormous bottle of heavy-duty painkillers later, we're finally back at home. Dinner is quiet; no questions, no idle small talk, no nothing. And it's exactly what I need.

I pop a painkiller and head upstairs to finish packing. I realize how difficult it's going to be to swim with this giant mass of a right hand, especially if it's expected to stay in a cast for the next four weeks. I'm going to have to come up with something. Anything to keep my mind off everything else. Everything that's trying to creep forward in my mind, as if I've forgotten.

Like I could forget.

I can't decide what's worse . . . Mick's betrayal or Tyler's. It's a constant battle between my brain and my heart, flipping back and forth.

That same sinking feeling I felt earlier in the park is back with a vengeance. I want so badly to wake up and find out that none of this is real, but my mind won't let me get out of it that easily. And I realize so much of what's been important to me my whole life is no longer there.

I finally check the texts and voice mails on my phone. I can't believe there are over forty different messages, some of them from people I barely even know. I respond only to three of them—close friends of mine on the swim team—letting them know the exact same thing: Yes, it's true what they've heard. No, I'm not okay. And thanks, when I feel like talking, I will.

There's also a text from Mick:

So sorry about your hand. Please talk to me. Please.

I ignore her and attempt to tackle brushing my teeth with my left hand—although I'm not sure how good a job I do—and change into my pj's. That's when the room starts to spin and I feel like I've downed an entire fifth of vodka, all on my own. But at least my hand doesn't hurt.

I start shoving who knows what into my luggage, and everything else gets kicked under my bed or thrown in my closet. I'll deal with it when I get home at the end of summer, along with everything else I know I'll need to face sooner or later.

But then I see the framed picture of Tyler and me on my nightstand. Our photo from prom last month, the night we had sex for the first time. Two weeks after he slept with Mick.

And that's when the tears begin to fall.

I swipe at my face, trying to make it stop, angry that my own eyes are betraying me. Because I don't want to feel this way.

Before I can stop myself, I pick up the picture and hurl it against the wall with a deafening scream. It shatters, then litters the floor in a million tiny pieces. I sag against my bed and slide down to the carpet, joining all the broken shards. They look exactly how I feel.

Penn is in my room a moment later. He sits down next to me, knees pulled up in front of him, and leans his shoulder up against mine. Hiding my face in my hands, I mumble, "Why? Why did he do this?"

"I don't know why," he says. He doesn't make up any crap, and he doesn't say things just to make me feel better.

"And . . . and what makes it worse? I slept with him after prom!" I stutter.

Penn stiffens next to me.

"I'm s-sorry, P., I know you don't wanna hear that."

I turn away from him, and the black cast on my arm that outweighs the rest of me sinks against the side of my leg. I kick at the edge of my bulging suitcase with the tip of my slipper. What the hell did I pack?

Penn rakes his fingers down his face and takes a deep breath. "You've been with the guy forever. I figured it had to happen sooner or later." He holds up his hands as if to cut me off from sharing any details and shakes his head. "It only makes it worse, 'cause now I really wanna kick his ass."

The damn tears start all over again as I cover my face. "One year. One year I'm with that asshat. And now I feel like I didn't matter to him at all. Like what we had didn't matter at all."

"Sloane, you know that's not true. Tyler may have fucked up . . . big-time—but that doesn't mean he didn't care."

I doubt my brother even realizes that what he's said is in the past tense. *Didn't* care. As in Tyler cared in the past, but doesn't anymore. Maybe that's why he did what he did. Maybe he stopped caring and I never even noticed.

It takes a while for me to calm down and finally fall asleep. But then I dream I walk in on Mick and Tyler and I see certain body parts that, while I've seen separately, I definitely shouldn't see together. I wake up over and over during the night, sweaty and panicked, hoping it's my crazy imagination that's creating these stupid dreams. But then I see the cast on my hand and I know it's real.

I know it really happened.

Three

Our flight is early in the morning, and the hustle of getting to the airport and getting through security has kept my mind occupied. By the time I sit down in my seat and shut off my phone, all I want to do is close my eyes and fall back asleep.

Penn grabs his earphones and plugs them into his phone, but doesn't turn it on. "Are you looking forward to seeing Mia? I talked to Shep yesterday, and he says they'll have the bonfire ready."

Shep and Mia are two of our friends that live in Honolulu. We met them our first summer there and have been friends ever since, for more than seven years.

"Yeah, I know. She's been texting nonstop about our welcome home party tonight. Fat chance I'll be getting out of that one." I muffle a yawn with my fist and pull out my phone, ready to hit play as soon as we reach the appropriate altitude.

My hand is throbbing, so I pop a pain pill and turn on a

random playlist. Hours later, I wake up as our wheels touch down and bump across the runway. My head aches from lack of water and six hours of stale air, and I just want off this damn plane. I take my phone out of airplane mode as we taxi toward our gate. And everything I thought I'd left 2,678 miles away all comes crashing back. Because a text message is waiting from Mick:

> Hope u had a safe flight. Maybe we can talk later?

And several from Tyler.

> I'm so sorry.

> I feel like shit. Man, that was a def right hook. :)

> But I forgive u.

> I need to talk to u. Please let me fix this. Please.

> Crap, forgot u were flying. Please call or text when u land.

> Love u.

One text after another, after another. My phone continuously beeps as it catches up with every message I missed while in the air . . . and that's all I hear—nonstop beeping. Like my phone doesn't know how to do anything else. I scramble to try to turn it off, but can't seem to press the right buttons thanks to my fumbling fingers and stupid cast, as my screen flashes with the next incoming text.

Oh my god, oh my God, make it stop!

After everything I've done for the both of them, after all the times I've been there for them, they go and do what they did, and expect me to *still* be here now. Like they want me to soothe them after the rough day they both had yesterday. Like I'll forgive them so quickly now that thousands of miles are between us.

I can feel my lungs shutting out what little air is left. Penn grabs my phone and replaces it with my inhaler. Somehow he's able to make the beeping stop, but it still echoes in my ears, reminding me that nothing is ever too far away.

I take a deep pull on my inhaler and close my eyes while Penn grabs our bags and shuffles me off the plane.

Immediately I'm hit with the welcoming scent of tropical flowers mixed with suntan lotion. A familiar smell that somehow makes everything better. And one that always reminds me of my mom.

"Okay?" Penn asks as we walk farther and farther away from the plane.

"Okay." I nod. In fact, I'm more than okay. It's like the tropical air is magic, as the breeze that passes through the open walkways floats over me and flutters my hair around my face. And just like that I realize I want absolutely nothing to do with Mick and Tyler. Nothing to do with what's happening back at home. Screw them both. They don't deserve any of my time, and they sure as hell don't deserve *me*.

Penn has both of our carry-on bags slung over one shoulder, leaving me with only my handbag to hold as we wait for the Wiki-Wiki shuttle that will take us to the baggage claim terminal. We're surrounded by hundreds of hot and sweaty passengers from our flight and others that landed at the same time, from all different corners of the world. Most of those around us are tourists. Entire families itching with excitement to be here, already wearing matching floral-print Aloha shirts and dresses, preordered from Hilo Hattie's before their trip. Everywhere I look, there are way too many exposed legs that are far too pale to be seen in public. Several people even rock white knee-high socks, their heat-swollen feet crammed into dingy running shoes that have probably never been running.

I look down at my own pale feet, already sporting a pair of flip-flops I bought here last summer, waiting for their chance to have a go with the sun.

My mom and stepdad, Bob, are down at baggage claim, both looking completely unaffected by the high temperatures and humidity, with beautiful plumeria leis in hand. Mom raises an eyebrow at my cast as she slips the garland of flowers over my head and pulls me in for a hug. I hadn't wanted to at the time, but my dad made me call her last night to tell her what happened.

"Oh, baby, I've missed you so, so much. And your hand! Does it hurt?" She squeezes me tight, and I realize how much I've really missed her, too.

"That's a pretty fierce-looking cast you got there, kiddo," Bob comments, arm around my shoulders. But if he says one word about where I should've put my thumb, I'm gonna scream.

"If you think that's impressive, you should've seen Tyler's nose," Penn tells them as he watches for our bags to circle around. "I don't think any amount of surgery is going to make it go back to what it was like before. Although it's gotta be an improvement for his looks."

"Penn, would you shut it?" I glare at him, and he pretend glares right back. I know he's trying to make me laugh but I'm not in the mood, so I make myself busy trying to rub off a scuff mark on the ground with the edge of my flip-flop.

My mom steps in and whispers so only I can hear, "You deserve so much more, Sloane. The right one is waiting out there for you somewhere, I promise. But maybe next time, you save your hand and don't break his nose, okay?"

Penn is still going on and on about my trophy-worthy right hook, pretend air jabs included, as he pulls my bag from the carousel with a grunt and sits it on the floor next to his feet. "You do know we're only here for the summer, right?"

I'm about to really lay into him when my mom steers me out the exit and across the street to where the car is parked. But instead of the SUV she had last summer, she's replaced it with a shiny new convertible, top down, glistening in the sun. There's an identical car parked right next to it, but silver instead of red.

"Surprise!" Mom says to Penn and me as Bob pops the trunk on the silver one and starts loading in our luggage. "I thought you guys could use your own transportation this summer." I gape at my mom, then back to the car. "Oh, don't give me that look, Sloane—it was practically buy one, get one free!"

Leave it to my mom to buy us a car that will only be used for a couple of months. Not that I don't love the idea of having a set of wheels while I'm here, it's just that she tries *so* hard. She's always sending stuff in the mail—new clothes, new shoes, expensive handbags. There's not a month that goes by when I don't come home from school to find a package on the doorstep, often containing something crazy like a formal ball gown—as well as the shoes, accessories, and clutch to match—even when I have no place to wear it.

I hate to think it, but it feels like she's trying to buy my love. Maybe it's because we live so far apart from each other or maybe it has to do with her feeling like she left us when she moved away. But I guess we left her, too. Penn and I had a choice, and we both chose to stay in Seattle. I just wish she'd realize she doesn't have to prove anything to me.

Penn kisses my mom on top of her head, then grabs for the keys in Bob's outstretched hand. "Sweet, Mom—thanks! I'll race you home!"

"Actually . . . you hungry?" My mom looks at me as she says this. "I thought we'd grab some lunch, perhaps enjoy a little therapeutic shopping, and then I made appointments for us to get our hair done. Figured you could use some girl time." She pokes me on the tip of my nose as she says this. "Cool?"

She reaches up and ruffles the hair on my brother's head. "Don't worry, Bob has made plans for the two of you . . . although it looks like you could've used a haircut, too." Penn gives her a look as he tries to flatten his hair back down. And I wonder if she knows exactly how long it took him to get it just so. "But maybe keep the racing to a minimum, okay?"

"Thanks, Mom." I hug her tight around the waist, and she hugs me back.

Honestly, I'll take a little quality time with my mom over a new car any day.

After lunch and some serious shopping, I contemplate how short I want to cut my hair. Right now, it falls in limp waves below my shoulder blades, and I tend to never do anything too drastic. But one look down at my cast and I decide today's the day that all changes. I don't know when I forgot, but it's about time I started to live.

Besides, if it's shorter, it will be so much easier to handle with my hand in this stupid cast.

I emerge from the salon with varying light blond

highlights streaked throughout my hair. It's been cut to below my chin in a shag style, my bangs sweeping across my forehead.

And I love it.

We get our toes done next, sitting in massage chairs, surrounded by ginormous piles of shopping bags. To be honest, I'm not even really sure what's in some of them. But what I do know is that the last time I had a pedicure, I was sitting next to Mick instead of my mom, and we were contemplating what crazy shade of polish to paint our toes. When I look down at my feet now, I realize I picked the exact same color Mick had chosen that day, because she'd insisted, *Desert Poppy will be perfect with tanned toes!*

I'm still a long way from the tanned part, but even so, Mick's choice of colors makes the corners of my mouth turn up, at least just a little. I go to twist on a strand of hair and realize it's no longer there.

"That will take some getting used to," my mom says, watching me from her own chair. "But I'll bet it feels a million times lighter, huh?"

"You can say that again." I shake my head from side to side.

"I promise, Sloane—there's no better cure for a crappy breakup than spending your summer here. Enjoy the time away from all the drama, relax—hell—sleep in until noon, because I promise, it will all still be there when it's time to go home. At least maybe then you'll have had enough time to figure things out for yourself. And that's what's most important. But right now, the next few months are all about you, all about the fun you're going to have . . . it's all about the summer of Sloane!"

"The summer of Sloane . . ."

I like the sound of that.

Screw what's happening back in Seattle. Let them deal with all that crap. I'm here and they're not. This is *my* summer, not theirs, and it's going to be epic.

My mom reaches over and squeezes the fingers on my uninjured hand. "I'm going to make sure we spend some mother-daughter time together while you're here. I know that hasn't always been the case in the past, especially with how slammed my office gets over the summer months, but I'm really going to try—starting with dinner tonight." Honestly, the four hours we've already spent together is more uninterrupted time than we've had since she left Seattle. And it feels good to hear her say she wants to hang out even more. I only hope it actually happens. Because she's right. For some reason, all the broken ankles and arms, all the random injuries, they always seem to get worse over summer break, and my mom ends up practically sleeping at her office.

But for now, I'll take what I can get.

My phone buzzes with an incoming text and I'm hesitant to look at it, but then it buzzes again. I go to shut it off and see that the message is actually from Mia:

Hey, chica! I so cannot wait to see u. Don't forget, bonfire tonight @ 6pm, you know the place! You and your bro better be there!

I shoot off a quick reply about how excited I am to see her, too. "So, um, about dinner tonight?" I look over at my mom, while holding my phone, and she starts to laugh.

"Okay, maybe dinner *tomorrow* night . . . that is if you can find some time on your calendar," she replies with a smile and a wink.

My mom and I have majorly windswept hair and flushed cheeks by the time we step out of the car back at the house. The neighborhood we're in is south of Waikiki and the infamous Diamond Head, and my mom and Bob's house sits right on the beach.

As soon as I walk through the double front doors, the first thing I see is the entire back wall—or lack thereof. It's made of movable wood and glass panels that slide open, allowing every possible sense to tune in to the surroundings. The sound of waves crashing on the shore, the smell of sea salt that drifts along the warm current of air, and, finally, the uninterrupted views of the beautiful ocean beyond.

Even my room has the same movable panels, which are already open when I walk in. I close my eyes as I listen to the rolling of the ocean mere feet from where I stand.

In the center of the room is the most magnificent

four-poster bed with sheer white drapes that hang down to the floor and flutter gently in the breeze. And on top of the bed is a pile of wrapped packages, complete with bows. My mom really outdid herself this time.

My entire room looks like it came straight from the pages of one of those dream home magazines, because knowing my mom, it probably did.

I settle in to unpack and shoot Mia another text to let her know I can't wait to see her tonight. Her response is immediate:

> OMG, can't wait to c u too! xoxo.

When I've finished unpacking, I realize not only did I bring a heavy cashmere sweater along with my spring formal dress, but also a hat, one leather glove, and two and a half pairs of wool knee-high socks. But I've forgotten my tooth-brush, flat iron, and cell phone charger.

Why, thank you oh so much, Mr. Pain Meds—looks like I'll be going shopping again tomorrow.

Making my way over to the bed, I pick up my phone and see I've received more text messages: a couple from Mick, but most of them from Tyler—the latest just ten minutes ago:

> Please talk to me. Can I call u?

All I want is to see my friends and hang out, like nothing's wrong. Like my life didn't fall apart twenty-four hours ago. So no, you can't call me right now.

Mick's texts aren't any better:

> Hope you're enjoying all the sun . . . I'm so jealous, it's sprinkling here right now. :/

Ignoring both, I do a quick pass through in the bathroom, running my fingers through my new short hair. I can't believe I cut it all off. I'll probably freak out about that later. My phone rings, and the screen flashes with Tyler's name and the picture I took of him after football practice last fall. Sweaty and still wearing his pads, he had just run in from a scrimmage on the field. It was one of my favorites.

I stare at his picture as my phone continues to buzz with the incoming call. But I can't talk to him. Or maybe I actually don't want to. I slide my finger over the screen, sending him straight to voice mail, and throw the phone in my bag.

Taking a deep breath, and heeding my mom's advice, I promise myself tonight is going to be the start of what is sure to be one wild and crazy summer. Which means there will be no wallowing. There will be no letting others control how I feel. And there will definitely be no drama. None of that.

Because this time, it's all about me. It's all about the summer of Sloane.

Four

Mom has supplied us with kalbi ribs and chicken teriyaki skewers, mac salad, and all the makings for s'mores. There's even a half rack of beer that came with the cursory "please call me if you need me to come pick you up" speech.

We don't have far to go. In fact, it's only a little over a mile to the beach where we're headed. I text my dad on the drive there to let him know we made it okay and all is well, then send him a quick shot of Penn and me driving in our swank new ride. He responds immediately:

> Nice haircut. The car isn't too bad either! Although you're missing a great M's/Yankees game! Bottom of the eighth, NYY up by two.

Then a moment later:

> And, Sloane, regardless of everything else, please try to enjoy your summer. Love you.

I text back that I can't believe he went to the baseball game without me. It's always our thing. Even though we're both fans of the Mariners, my dad grew up watching the Yankees, and for years, we've been going to their games whenever we can.

I don't miss his comment about what's happening back at home, and I know he's worried—but I also think he's trying to give me the space I need, which I'm grateful for.

When I close out from his text, I see there's a new one from Mick:

> Was craving those awesome cheesy chicken burritos from the Pollo Loco food truck we found near the mall! I decided to go down and get one, and can't tell you how bummed I was when it tasted bleh. Ugh, I think I might become a vegetarian. God, we used to eat those things by the truckload . . . of course we'd always pay for it later, huh? :)

I don't want to, but I laugh, remembering all those late nights we hit that food truck thinking it was the best idea ever, only to find ourselves moments later practically splitting an entire bottle of Tums. If she's trying to make me miss her, it's working.

Penn pulls the car into an open space, and I'm immediately hit with wafting curls of salty sea air infused with the rich scent of burning wood, and I inhale deeply. So many great memories come flooding back from all the bonfires we've had on this very beach—memories that have absolutely nothing to do with what's going on back at home. And without even thinking, I delete Mick's text . . . because I don't want it to somehow taint what I know is waiting for me, just a few sandy steps away.

I see Mia's cute red convertible VW Bug. Not one of the new ones, but an old-school Bug from the '70s, the white top folded down and resting behind the rear seat. I smile, remembering the two of us losing both of our hats when we got on the H-1 highway last summer. First hers—I laughed as she swerved slightly when the wind tore her floppy sun hat from her head, and then mine only seconds later, as Mia gave me a mischievous grin and tossed it to the wind herself. God, I love spending the summer here.

"You ready?" Penn is already out of the car with the bags of food in hand.

"You have no idea."

We walk along the beach access path until it opens up onto pristine golden sand and nothing but thousands of miles of turquoise unfolds in front of us. It's hard to tell where the blue of the ocean stops and the same brilliant hue of the sky begins. My flip-flops are off in seconds, and my toes flex into the warmth as tiny granules of sand slide over my feet. But the best part is the heat of the Hawaiian sun that drenches every square inch of exposed skin. I can already feel my cheeks welcome it. Heaven.

I hear laughter down the beach and turn to see a bunch of kids, many I know and a few I don't. Some are out in the water playing chicken, the boys carrying the girls high on their shoulders as they try to make the others crash to their watery demise. A few toss a football along the beach, while something grilled and delicious-smelling sizzles on one of the many hibachi barbecues that have been set up around the bonfire. Music blasts from speakers I can't see. And it all feels like exactly what I need.

"SLO!"

I hear the high-pitched squeal before I see Mia. She's running down the length of beach with Shep alongside her, elbowing her playfully out of the way. We call him Shep because his last name is Shepherd, and for the life of me, I can't seem to remember his first name. Kyle? Ken? Kai? Something with a K, I think, but no one ever uses it. They continue to jostle each other along as they run our way, and I realize something seems different between the two of them. Then Mia flings her arms around my neck, and Shep and Penn give each other one of those weird back-slapping man hugs.

Mia's taller than I am, of course, because most people over the age of ten usually are. Her skin has a beautiful dark bronze glow to it, which isn't only because of her access to the sun on a daily basis; it's just the way she is. Her golden-brown hair cascades in spiral curls down past her shoulders, and everything about her reminds me of sunshine and summers past.

"Holy cow, you cut off your hair! I LOVE IT!" She tugs on the ends as her eyes travel down to my cast. "And what the hell did you do to your arm?"

"Hey, you gonna hog her or can I say hello?" Shep says, nudging Mia out of the way. He picks me up and spins me around. "Hey, sucka, how you been? Sweet cast."

Shep is native Hawaiian—well, mostly, and more than the quarter I am. His skin tone is similar to Mia's, but his hair is a dark brown, almost black, and his eyes are a close match. He's all limbs and outlandishly tall, with a surfer's body full of muscles. He towers even higher above me than he did the summer before.

Shep sets me down on the sand with one last squeeze and turns to pick up Mia's hand. And that's when I realize what's different. They're together. As in *together* together!

"Whoa, what's that all about?" Penn points at their joined hands as a flush heats up Mia's cheeks.

Her gaze drifts away for the briefest of seconds, but she recovers quickly and smiles, bumping her hip against Shep's. "Yeah, we're trying something different."

"So how's the boyfriend?" Shep says. We trudge along the beach, making our way to the bonfire. "You two about ready to tie the knot?"

Penn gives me a look.

"So, um . . . this kind of happened," I manage. Not knowing what else to say, I simply hold up my cast. "Evidently you're not supposed to tuck your thumb in when you throw a punch. Who knew?"

"No *shit*," both Mia and Shep say in unison. They look from the cast to me, then to Penn, then back to me.

"Yeah, Rocky Balboa here broke his nose in three places with a solid right hook," Penn adds. And if I'm not mistaken, he actually sounds proud. "Assclown has to have surgery next week."

I fill Mia in on everything as Shep and Penn jog ahead. She hangs on to my elbow and taps her head to mine.

"I can't believe it. I can't believe they'd both do that to you, after all this time. And is she gonna keep it? I mean, what's she going to do with a baby?"

"I really don't know."

I realize I have no idea what to say to any of that. I don't even know what I would do if it were me in her situation. The only thing I know without a doubt is it would've been Mick I ran to if things had been reversed. And I can only imagine how Mick is feeling right now, how lost she is with probably no one to talk to.

I have the sudden urge to call her, but before I even have a chance to go through with that stupid idea, Mia turns me to face her. Both of her hands are on my shoulders, and her forehead is pressed up against mine, her eyes going cross-eyed.

"You know what? Let's forget about all that. We're gonna

have one helluva summer. And I know just how to start it off!"

She grabs two brown longneck bottles from an ice chest near the fire, and with a flick of her fingers, the caps are flying off both.

"Cheers, Sloane!"

She clinks her beer against mine, and I love her for calling me Sloane instead of Mack. Thinking back, she never called me that. I guess it was just something my friends in Seattle did, and in some small way, I'm glad it stayed there.

Mia holds her bottle to the air, and everyone around the fire raises their own.

"Welcome home. And welcome to the start of our kick-ass summer before senior year, *bitches*!"

We all cheer, bottles raised, then drink.

And I fight the urge to spit mine out.

It tastes like feet. Or pee. Or someone peed on their feet and I'm drinking it. Bleh. I force down another swallow and cringe. I've had beer before. Okay, maybe only once. But that's only because it tastes so awful.

Mia and I stand near the bonfire and watch the boys as they toss the football around. "So when were you gonna tell me about you and Shep?"

She shrugs and takes a sip of her beer. "It's really not that big a deal."

I give her a look that clearly says I don't believe what she's saying. *"Really?"*

She shoves me lightly and tries not to laugh. "I swear!

We kinda hooked up at a party a couple weeks ago, and now we're just seeing where things go. Besides, when have you known me to get all caught up in a relationship?" She clinks her bottle again with mine, and it occurs to me that Mia has never really been serious with a guy, at least not one I've known about. Then again, it's not like I'm ever here long enough to find out all the details.

I see a few girls that I recognize and make my way over to say hello. After hugs and a quick fib about why my arm is in a cast—I don't feel like sharing those details with *everyone* just yet—I sink to the sand next to Mia. I'm sitting next to two girls I don't remember from last summer. They both seem younger than us, I'd guess between twelve or thirteen, so maybe that's why we haven't met.

"Hey, I'm Sloane." I smile and wave a cast at the both of them.

Mia points between the two girls, "Slo, this is Luce and Ashley. Luce and her family moved here from LA a few days after you left last summer, and Ash is one of her friends."

Ashley doesn't hide the fact she's staring at my cast. "What's up with your hand?" She's this little wisp of a thing with shiny, long black hair and alabaster-pale skin. Not that much of her skin is showing, because she's clothed from head to toe, as if afraid of the sun.

"Catfight," I say nonchalantly, and Luce's eyes go wide.

"Really? *No way!*"

She's super cute, wearing a baseball hat on backward

with dark brown hair winging out from under the edges. Her mouth is full of metal, and the afternoon sun glimmers off her braces as she smiles. But it's her eyes that capture my attention. They're this intense pale blue in the center that blooms out to a deeper navy.

"Luce, she's just pulling your leg," Ashley says, rolling her eyes. Oh, if she only knew.

Luce raises her eyebrows, clearly hoping for more, and I can't just leave her hanging.

"Nah, I broke it swimming the other day. Guess I miscalculated my turn."

Mia gives me a look. I've been swimming since the age of two. I don't miscalculate my turns. But these two don't know that.

"Wish I could swim better," Luce mumbles low under her breath.

"Yeah, you'd think that was a prerequisite in order to move here." It's another snide comment from Ashley. "I'm surprised they let you in."

I fight the urge to flick her. Really hard. "You know, Luce, I give swim lessons. If you want, I'd be more than happy to teach you."

Her eyes go wide again. "Really?"

"Really. Just shoot me a text, and we can figure out a good time." We exchange numbers, and honestly, just the thought of being back in the pool has me in a much better mood.

Turning back to Mia, I fall into conversation with her

about the last school year. We cover easy topics like how she and the entire girls' volleyball team—along with the entire boys' varsity baseball team—were almost suspended for a little Saturday night party involving an out-of-town neighbor's pool.

I'm somehow on to my second beer, having no idea how I managed to choke down the first, but notice this one's taking much less effort. The boys have started a game of football as the girls who were out playing chicken in the water come over to the fire. I know all three of them and stand to give hugs.

It feels good to be here. Like I somehow managed to escape all that happened at home in Seattle, while Mick and Tyler are stuck in that hell. Although that could also be the alcohol talking. But I hope it's not.

From the corner of my eye, I see someone jogging down the beach. The football is launched in his direction and easily finds its way into his hands. He twirls the ball between his fingers with the ease of someone who's done it a thousand times before. Whoever he is, he seems to already know everyone here, as he smiles and confidently shakes his head at the boys rushing toward him. Without hesitation, he expertly plants his foot, then bullets the football back in a perfect Hail Mary spiral, just before the boys tackle him to the sand.

And then it's a messy pile of limbs everywhere, as one by one, they peel off to get up. He stands and dusts the sand out from his hair as Shep pretend jabs him in the stomach, which he quickly blocks. Slapping a few of them with high fives, he tugs his shirt off over his head and shakes it out. I stare, then look away, then stare again at the ripples of muscles that ease their way down the front of his stomach and disappear somewhere below the waistband of his swim trunks. Then I look away. Then back again. Because while I may be heartbroken, I'm definitely not dead.

"Who's the Arm?" I ask Mia. "He's new."

The ball is thrown his way again, and I watch him catch it one-handed, then launch another perfect spiral some forty yards down the beach with ease.

"Oh, that's Finn, Luce's older brother. And if he'd finally say yes, he'd also be Punahou's starting QB." She whispers this as she watches me watch him. "Like that, do ya?"

Well, what's not to like? As he shakes hands with my brother, I see he's several inches taller than Penn. His hair is the identical dark brown that peeks out from under the baseball cap Luce wears, and I wonder if he has the same mesmerizing ice-blue eyes. His skin is a golden brown from plenty of days like today out in the sun, and a wicked tattoo races up one well-muscled bicep and over his shoulder. Normally I'm not a huge fan of ink, but there's something about this one, wild and reckless.

Note to self: look into getting a tattoo this summer.

"Slo?" Mia is snapping her fingers in front of my face, and I turn back in her direction. "Yummy, huh?"

"Yeah, you could say that."

This one screams trouble from a mile away, and I can't help but grin. Perhaps that's exactly what my summer needs.

After the boys finish their game, they come over to where we sit by the fire. Shep flops down in the sand behind Mia and wraps his long legs around the sides of hers. She leans against his chest as he threads a marshmallow onto one of the skewers and whispers something in her ear that makes her laugh. They're great together, something I've seen over the years we've all been friends. I'm just glad they finally figured it out.

"Hey, Luce, think fast!" Luce giggles as she catches the football, then squeals as the Arm noogies the top of her head. She places both hands on top of his and gives them a squeeze. "What's up, Mia? How's it going, Ash?" He pokes her with his toe, and she instantly giggles and looks down at the sand. "And who's this?" Turning away from Ashley, his gaze slides onto me. "Sweet cast, but I'd hate to see the guy on the receiving end of that."

"Funny, so would I." It's the first thing that falls out of my mouth. Of course he has no idea how true that really is.

Mia grips my hand between us and gives it an encouraging squeeze. "Finn, this is Sloane, Slo, this is Finn. She's the other half of—"

"Let me guess, of Penn?" he interjects. "I can spot a twin when I see one. Slo, was it?" He stretches a hand out, and I raise my cast awkwardly, not knowing what to do with it. He tugs gently on my pinky finger in a mock handshake. "Nice to meet you."

51

"Nice to meet you, too—is it Finn or Phineas?"

For a second, one of his eyebrows arches in surprise, but then just as quickly, a cocky glint finds its way to his eyes. And his eyes. They are indeed a match to his sister's. He gives a small, quick nod, confirming I guessed his real name correctly, then turns and pokes Shep in the side before stealing away the marshmallow skewer from his hand without another word. Gee, I seemed to have angered him, perhaps?

"Only our dad calls him Phineas," Luce quietly tells me, "and since we both can't stand him, Finn doesn't like it much. He always goes by Finn, or back in LA, his friends used to call him Mick." She mistakes my sharp intake of air and explains. "Mick as in McAllister, our last name?"

Oh, you've *got* to be kidding me. I travel almost three thousand miles to get away from one Mick, only to find another one right in front of me? Awesome.

I chug down the rest of my beer and find a new one in my hand. It's when I've finished with it and try to stand that I realize maybe mixing three beers with narcotics wasn't such a good idea. Then again, I kind of don't care at all, and I love that feeling.

"Come on, Mia—we're up for chicken! You ready to lose?" I yell far too loudly, pulling her away from the fire.

"Oh, you're so going down, Slo." She tugs her T-shirt up over her head and unfastens the button on her jean shorts, letting them drop to the sand at her feet. Someone whistles.

She's wearing an orangey-red bikini and, man, does it not only make her boobs look tan, but huge. I so wish I had boobs like that.

I attempt to take off my own T-shirt with as much finesse, but struggle with getting it over my cast—cursing as I stretch it to fit over my arm—then slide out from my shorts. And a few more whistles sound at the two of us. My bikini is similar to Mia's, only in all black. But I am in no way tan or have the boob-a-licious thing going on.

I point at Finn. "Not sure if you've heard, but I just happen to be the queen of all things chicken. Think you're up for it?"

He actually snorts. Out loud. "Now this I've got to see. Although I somehow feel you're only using me for my height."

"Using you? Pshaw . . . not even close. It's called a tactical advantage, *please*."

I leave him standing there as Mia and I run out into the water. Holy shit, it's cold! I cross my arms over my chest to hide the evidence of just *how* cold, and bounce up and down trying to acclimate. The waves crash into my legs, and the world spins around me. Suddenly I realize two things: one, there's a slight chance I may puke, and two, I pretty much just told the hottest guy on the beach to get his ass out into the water to be my partner, in not so many words.

Mia is already hoisted on top of Shep's shoulders as I wade farther out, and they tower high above me. I turn and cup my hands over my mouth to yell for Finn, just as a brown cap of hair breaks the surface of the water next to me. Brilliant blue eyes follow, and a tattooed shoulder rises slowly after that.

"Cold much?" He eyes my chest with that one damned raised eyebrow of his and a dangerous smile. I contemplate my chances of success at pulling his eyebrow back down with my own fingers. Before I can say anything in return, he's already ducked back under the waves. I feel him swim between my legs, and a moment later, I squeal louder than I've ever squealed in my entire life as he rockets me up high out of the water. My stomach stays somewhere down near the sand, but it's not anything I can even think about with my face on fire like it is.

His hands firmly grasp both of my knees. As he wades out to deeper water, a wave crashes into us, and he wobbles slightly. Instinctively I grab at his hair and hang on tight.

"Hey, think maybe you can let me keep some of that up there?" He squeezes both my knees and continues out farther into the water.

"Sorry, not like I have much else to hang on to up here."

I pat him gently on the head as we turn to face our opponents. Shep and Finn are almost the same height; Mia and I are not, so they've got us there. But I've got muscles from years of swimming, which I'll put to good use. Then again, I also have this obnoxious cast, which isn't going to help me at all, unless there's even the slightest chance I can use it as a club to knock her off-balance. Which of course I'd only do as a last resort. Maybe.

"Whatcha got for us, McAllister?" Shep taunts. The boys come closer together and circle each other, until Mia and I are arm's length apart. Well, her arm's length, that is. She picks the perfect moment to strike and sends me crashing to the water below. I come up dizzy, spitting mouthfuls of ocean as I watch her pump her fists high in the air.

"Oh my God, that was almost too easy!" she shouts my way. "Please tell me you've got more than that?"

Shep slaps at her knee. "Hey, go easy on the cripple, wouldya?"

Oh, that's it. Game. On.

Ignoring my faint queasiness, I yank on Finn's arm and tug down on his shoulders. But he doesn't even budge. He looks down at me as he realizes what I'm trying to do and a lazy grin widens across his face as water drips from his chin. "Oh, I'm sorry, you want up again?"

"Well, I can't exactly climb up there myself!" I cross my arms tight over my chest in my stubborn stance, my cast pressing against my wet skin. Um, duh.

He shakes his head, then ducks under the water again, sending me skyward as he stands up.

"Queen of all things chicken, huh? So maybe you'd like to stay up there longer than five seconds this time? You know, actually play the game?"

I attempt to swat the top of his head, missing by a mile

as he continues forward. "Or maybe you can be quicker? You know, and move out of their way?" I try my best to mock him, but it only makes him laugh.

He hangs on tighter to my knees as Mia and Shep head toward us. But this time I'm ready for her. She's flailing off Shep's shoulders in five seconds flat. We do this several more times and the score is tied 3–3, when I taste the sting of something nasty in the back of my throat.

"Hey, guys, I don't feel so hot, I think I need to head in." I cover my mouth and pat Finn gently on the head. "Can you let me down?"

"Ah, come on, Slo, one more! Just one more!" Mia yells as Shep holds up one finger with a puppy-dog face. "You can't leave this in a tie!"

I press my fingers firmly against my stomach and wonder if I'm imagining things. Nope. I've gotta go in. I can feel the bile rising in my throat.

"Come on, Sloane, I know you've got this!" Finn moves toward the tower of the other two, and the sway of his movement is what seals the deal. I turn my head and chuck up my entire dinner.

"Oh, shit," Finn mumbles, lowering me down into the water and tucking out behind me. Thank God for the waves that quickly erase any trace of my puke from around us, although we all swim a few cautious feet away.

"Looks like the fish will be eating good tonight," Shep

jokes. "I think I actually saw a whole marshmallow come out."

"Hey, not cool," Finn says, shaking his head. I feel his hands around my waist as I bob in front of him. "You okay?"

My face burns with an intense heat I can only pray he doesn't see. I sink under the water with all intentions of drowning myself.

So much for the summer of Sloane.

Five

Date: Sun, 9 June 23:17:49
Subject: I'm sorry . . .
From: T_Hudson69@copemail.com
To: SKMcIntyre@copemail.com

Slo—

I didn't get to say good-bye. Fuck, this isn't how I wanted to leave things between the two of us. I made a mistake, Slo, a huge mistake. And I don't even know why I did it, why it even happened. But I need for you to give me another chance. I'm sorry. So very, very, sorry. Please tell me what I can do to make this better? I'll do anything, I swear. Anything.

I love you . . .

—T.

The e-mail came in late last night, followed by a string

of text messages—he even called and left a voice mail. But I couldn't get myself to open the e-mail until now.

It's early morning, a light breeze is drifting in through the open doors to my lanai and I can hear the ocean beyond that in the distance. The lull of the waves is what gave me the courage to click on his name in my in-box. But after reading his e-mail, I so badly want to go back to before. To before everything. To before I got it. I'd at least settle for going back to before reading it, so I could delete it and not have to hear his words replaying over and over in my head. But who am I kidding? There's no way I'd have the courage to do that. At least not yet.

Tyler has been a part of my life for as long as I can remember, just like Mick. I met him on the first day of kindergarten when, instead of going to sit at the table with the other boys, he had nodded their way with a cocky grin—well, as cocky as a kindergartner could have—then came over and sat in the seat right next to mine. Little did he know that once he'd picked his seat, he was stuck there the entire year. Stuck at a table with both Mick and me, while all his friends sat together without him. But instead of letting it bother him, he spent the year making sure I knew he was there. And he did that every year thereafter, too.

But if he's so sorry, then why can't he tell me why he did this? Why can't he explain why it happened not once, but twice, instead of constantly stumbling over his own words without a clear explanation?

Not that I'd forgive either of them any easier, but if they'd only done it once, I'd maybe understand it was a mistake. That maybe they were so drunk, they had no idea what was happening, until it was . . . happening. But twice?

I don't even know when they did it the second time or where they were—where I was. But I can't help thinking there's something more going on here. That maybe there's something between the two of them I failed to notice.

Staring down at my cast, I try to clear my head of all things Tyler. Because it hurts to keep spending so much time thinking about it. About him. And about her.

One part of my brain wants to rationalize why they did what they did. How Mick could so blatantly step over that line and destroy a friendship fifteen years in the making. How Tyler could throw away everything we had. Not just the last year, but the last decade and then some. It makes me wonder if there's something wrong with *me*, if both my best friend and my boyfriend decided I wasn't worth it, after all the times I've been there for the both of them. And now I realize how little I mean to her. How little I mean to them both.

Especially for them to do it twice.

God, if only I'd stayed at that party. Maybe things would've turned out differently. I know Mick has never had it easy growing up with her controlling mother, the pressure insane to never settle for anything less than the starring roles in ballet, not to mention maintain perfect grades. Freshman year, when Mick had landed a perfectly good B-plus in

English, her mom had grounded her for a month to make her focus on getting it back up to an A.

It's because of her mom that Mick is the way she is. She doesn't stop until everything she wants is compartmentalized into perfect little spots in her life. Which now includes Tyler.

But why did it have to be *my* boyfriend?

I guess what bothers me the most is that I didn't even know Mick had a thing for Tyler—or the other way around.

It hurts to my very core, and it makes it hard to breathe. It feels like I could lose control at any moment and the air will stop being there like it is for everyone else. And I absolutely hate that feeling of being out of control.

My phone vibrates across my desk, and I look at the screen to see who the text is from. So many lately have been from Tyler, so I'm surprised when I see a different name come up on the screen.

> Hey, it's Luce. Still open on those swim lessons? Let me know . . .

> Sure am. You free today? Say around eleven? You can come over here.

> U bet! Address?

I send her my address and offer to pick her up, but she tells me she can get a ride no problem.

And then I suddenly panic. Because what if she's getting a ride from her brother?

I still can't believe I threw up on him. I mean I've had some pretty impressive moments in my life, like that time Mick and I were walking down the sidewalk in front of DaVinci's—one of the popular hangouts for all the kids at school—and I walked straight into the pole of a stop sign. You'd think that wasn't as mortifying as it sounds, but DaVinci's has an open counter that faces the sidewalk, so when the weather gets nice, you can eat your pizza and people-watch. It's the place to see and be seen. So of course pretty much the entire junior class witnessed my head-on collision with metal. I can still hear the pinging sound echoing in my ears and see Mick rushing to my side to see if I was okay. I was so grateful when she waited to laugh until I did.

But throwing up on Finn? Yeah. That might possibly go down as one of my most embarrassing moments. Ever.

I haven't seen him in two days. Mia invited me to another party on the beach last night, but I couldn't bring myself to go, knowing he'd most likely be there. What do you say to somebody after you puke on them? Besides, I promised my mom we'd have dinner together and it was nice to finally sit down with her, Bob, and my brother for the first time since last summer.

I change into my suit, take my morning cup of coffee out to the pool, and stare at the ocean. The water, my home away from home. The monotony of it is completely not to mention therapeutic, the waves coming in, then pulling back out, again and again. I think being here in Hawaii is screwing with my head, because even though my heart reminds me it's only been days, my brain wants me to believe it could've been months ago when everything fell apart. It's amazing what a few thousand miles and a change of scenery can do.

"Hey, you have a visitor," Penn says, breaking into my thoughts. I turn to see him standing in the door to the living room, Luce tucked in behind him.

"Oh, crap! Is it eleven already?" I have no idea where the hour went. "I'm so sorry! Come on out." I grab my cap and goggles and the extra pair I snagged for Luce, just in case, and motion toward the pool. "So, how comfortable are you in the water?"

She twirls a strand of hair around her finger and stares past the pool at the ocean, like at any moment a wave might jump up and sweep her away.

"I . . . I used to be okay."

"Used to be?"

Luce looks down at her feet and slowly shakes her head. "I'm just not very strong," she whispers.

It's obvious something has her freaked-out, but it doesn't sound like I'm going to get much more out of her than that. I decide to leave it for now and hope I can work around whatever this fear is.

"Well then, we'll start at the beginning. I promise I'll

have you spinning laps in no time." I rest my hand on her shoulder until she looks up at me. "We'll be working in the pool for a while, so no worries, okay?"

She stares at me with those blue eyes of hers and nods.

"So before we start, I want to lay a few ground rules." I hate to sound like a control freak, but when it comes to the water, I kinda am. "First, it's really important you never swim alone. As you're learning, you should always swim with someone else, preferably someone that's a stronger swimmer than you. You also need to understand there's a huge difference between swimming in a pool and swimming out in the ocean."

I tick off a number of reasons, from currents and riptides to ocean predators that swim faster than we do, especially here in the Islands. When she nods her head feverishly in agreement, I know she's hanging on to every one of my words.

"Have you ever worn a cap and goggles?" I ask, handing her the extra set.

"Nope."

"Okay, that's where we'll start."

We ease into the shallow end of the pool, and I show her how to get her cap on correctly. Now that my hair is shorter, it's much easier to tuck it all up under the stretchy silicone material, but it takes a bit of work with Luce's thick mane. We both laugh when her cap goes flinging across the pool and I have to swim to retrieve it. I decide to hold off on the goggles for now, because I get a sense she's not going to be too keen on putting her head underwater just yet.

"So first we're going to start with floating." I walk over to the edge of the pool near the steps and grab on to the side, then let my feet slowly rise out behind me. She watches my every move as I bob in the water for a few seconds, kicking my feet ever so slightly. "Okay, now your turn, but I'll help you, okay?"

She looks relieved when I hold a hand out to her and guide her over to where I'm standing. Slowly, she reaches for the edge of the pool, and I hold on to her waist.

"Hang tight to the edge, but let your legs go. . . . Don't worry, I've got you." She's hesitant at first, but she lets her feet eventually float out from under her, and I place one arm under her stomach and one under her thighs. She grips the edge of the pool with brute strength, her knuckles actually turning white, but when she realizes I've got her and I'm not letting go, she lessens her hold a bit.

"So last spring when I was lifeguarding, there was this boy, probably around eleven or twelve years old. I'd seen him a couple of times at the pool, but couldn't recall if he was a strong swimmer or not. Anyway, this kid walks out to the pool deck like he owns it, and all his friends are laughing and cheering him on. He looks over at me, then goes right to the deep end and jumps in. And after several seconds of flailing arms and water splashing everywhere, I realize he has no idea how to swim."

Luce stares at me as she kicks softly in the water, her grip on the edge of the pool not quite as viselike. "So what did you do?"

"Well, he was taking in mouthfuls of water like he was determined to drink the entire pool." I can feel the heat in my cheeks, and I know my face is getting red. "So I blew my whistle to alert the other guards and dove in after him."

"And then what?" she asks.

"He was unresponsive when I got to him, but I managed to haul him out of the pool. With all his friends and everyone else crowded around me, I started CPR. But when I leaned in to give him mouth-to-mouth, the little punk stuck his tongue in my mouth, and I screamed." I smile at Luce, who is now floating on her own and doesn't even realize I've let go. "Turns out the entire thing was a dare from his friends, to see if he could kiss me."

"Oh my God, what a jerk! That's not even funny!" She squeals, but her smile tells me differently, and I know she's finally, truly, relaxed.

Her confidence grows a little bit more with each story I tell. Eventually she's even okay with me floating right next to her. And while there are a few moments where she panics and drops her feet back down, I can tell she's really trying to make this work.

From there, I show her how to float on her back as I hold her in place. "All you're doing is letting your body get comfortable in the water. At any time, if you start to get scared, remember you can always stand up."

I slowly walk around the shallow end as she floats out in front of me, and that's when I see Finn. I'm not sure how long he's been standing there, but something tells me he didn't just get here. Propped up against the frame of the large open doors to our living room, his ankles crossed and his arms folded over his chest, he watches Luce float. There's a pained expression that wrinkles up the space above his nose, but when his eyes connect with mine, any trace of emotion vanishes.

"Okay, Luce, I think that's our lesson for today, but tomorrow we're going to learn how to submerge your face underwater." She brings her legs down, until she's standing on her own. We discuss times that will work for us to meet on a consistent basis as we make our way over to the steps of the pool. When she spots Finn, her face falls ever so slightly.

"I asked where you were going today and you lied." He doesn't speak loudly, and I can tell he's trying not to embarrass her. He holds out a towel for her to take. "I'm not sure why you felt like you needed to, but don't ever do that again, okay?"

"Geez, who are you, her father?" I smile as I reach past him for my own towel, but the dark look that crosses his face tells me it was so the wrong thing to say. "Whoa, lighten up, it was just a joke."

Luce tugs the towel from his outstretched hand with a heavy sigh. "I didn't tell you because I knew you wouldn't like it. And obviously since you're here, I'm right." She looks from Finn to me, clearly asking for some help.

"I'm the one that offered to teach her, so please don't be

mad at Luce." I put my hand on her shoulder and motion toward the open doors to my bedroom. "Go ahead and use my bathroom to change."

"Thanks for the lesson, Sloane." She grabs her bag and makes her way to my room.

When she's safely out of earshot, I turn back to Finn. He studies me a moment. His eyes are so intense it makes me shiver, and I pull my towel tighter around myself.

"Did Luce tell you why she's afraid of the water?" he asks.

"No. I asked, but she didn't go into any detail." I pause, hoping maybe he'll fill me in, but he doesn't say anything more. "I do know she wants to be a stronger swimmer, and I can definitely help her there. You okay with that or do I need to have you sign a permission slip?"

The corners of his mouth slowly hitch up. "Yeah, I'm okay with that. But please be careful with her, Sloane. And please don't push her if she's not ready."

I hold up my hand. "Scout's honor, or however that goes. Whatever. You have my word." I wait until he gives me a full-blown smile before moving on. "So if we're past that . . . there's something . . . So about the other night."

He pretends to itch at his nose to cover his mouth, and I can tell he's trying not to laugh. "Yeah, talk about first impressions. But *that* was impressive."

"Hey! I'm pretty sure I asked you to put me down, in case you forgot." I poke his foot with my own.

"Yeah, you asked, but not even five seconds later, you

hurled all over me. Maybe give me a little more warning next time?" Before I can respond—not that I'd even know what to say to that—Luce makes her way back over to us. "You ready to blow this joint, Lemon?"

"Lemon?" I smile as I walk them out to the front.

"Yeah, can't remember when that started, but it just sort of stuck, huh?" He ruffles Luce's hair, making her giggle.

I'm surprised to see a black SUV with heavily tinted windows waiting in the driveway. A driver stands near the back door and opens it as soon as he sees us. Huh, a personal chauffeur? That must be rough.

"Go ahead and hop on in, I'll be right there," Finn says to Luce.

I don't miss the eye roll she gives her brother before she turns to me. "Thanks again, Sloane. I'll see you tomorrow afternoon?" She shades her eyes and looks at me as if I might change my mind.

I reach out and hug her close. "Luce, you're going to be a fantastic swimmer when we're done here, I promise. And yes, I'll see you tomorrow." She squeezes me back, then heads toward the car.

Finn watches as she climbs up in the backseat, then turns back to me. "Thanks for helping her, really."

"Honestly, it's no problem. Anything to do with the water, I'm in."

"Well, if that's the case, I know some great spots here on the island—maybe we could go check them out sometime?"

It suddenly feels about fifteen degrees warmer outside. "Yeah, I think I'd like that."

"Good, 'cause I'd like that, too." He holds my gaze for just a second longer than necessary, then strides toward the car and in one swift movement swings up into the back of the SUV. And then he's gone.

I shut the door and lean up against it. There's a slight chance I may have just said yes to going out with Finn.

And of all things, I actually can't stop smiling.

Six

I've been in Hawaii for almost a week, and like clockwork, a text message has my phone all riled up. I don't even need to look at the screen to know who it's from at this hour in the morning.

Tyler. But of course.

If you added up all the texts, e-mails, and voice mails he sends, I'd have more than ten forms of communication from him every day since I got here. But the messages are always the same. *I'm so sorry. I love you. I never meant to hurt you. Will you please talk to me.* Yada, yada, yada. This one's only slightly different:

I know I screwed up. I miss you. Please talk to me.

I have a funny feeling Tyler's sleeping about as little as I am, if he's texting me at eight thirty in the morning, his time. During summer vacation.

There are also several texts from Mick:

> Remember spring break in the fifth grade when we walked to the store to buy candy? We'd scraped together as much money as we could. You even searched in the cracks of your couch!

> Then, afterward, we stopped at McDonald's on the way home to get French fries, only to realize we didn't have enough money left as we stood at the counter.

> I was so embarrassed, but you calmly dumped out your entire purse and counted out the exact change we needed, most of it in pennies and lint.

> Those were the best French fries. Ever.

> If you'd let me, I'd buy us a million orders of fries and we could sit and talk like we used to.

> Because I could really use someone to talk to. I miss you.

I know what she's doing. Trying to get me to think back to all the good times we've shared. Like I don't remember them. Like I could forget.

But it wasn't me that threw our friendship away. It wasn't me that decided fifteen years of being best friends was worth destroying. So even without her reminding me of happier times, I'm stuck with it all. I get to remember everything, the good and the bad. And I have absolutely no idea what to do with any of it.

Every text, every e-mail, every voice mail makes me feel something different. It all depends on when I read them and what they say. Today I feel nothing but sad. Sad because of everything that's happened. Sad because I actually miss Tyler and Mick. Sad because I know Mick is probably dealing with all of this by herself. And sad because I don't know if I should talk to them or just leave it alone for the summer.

I so desperately want to type a reply as my fingers hover over the keyboard. It takes everything for me to exit out from the screen and throw my phone on the bed, then head out to the kitchen for breakfast. Because I made a promise to myself that this was *my* summer and neither Mick nor Tyler would suck me back into their crap. And responding to either one of them would be doing exactly that.

Not today.

It's early and no one's up yet, but at least it's a more respectable hour this time. Okay, maybe five thirty in the morning isn't really respectable, but still, it's better than the day before.

I still haven't slept much since I got here, but not for lack of trying. The three-hour time difference from Seattle hasn't exactly helped, either.

I put a pot of coffee on and rummage through the fridge, but nothing looks good. It seems when sleep decided to run away, it took my appetite with it—and all I'm left with are these chaotic thoughts and a very creative imagination that likes to reenact whatever it wants, regardless of my opinion.

"Hey, kiddo, can't sleep?" My mom stifles a yawn with a tightly closed fist as she pads her way into the kitchen.

"Guess you could say that." I grab two mugs from the cabinet, pour the coffee, then dress them with cream.

"It will eventually get better, Sloane, I promise. Maybe it doesn't seem that way now, but it will." She tucks a strand of hair behind my ear and takes one of the mugs from my outstretched hand. "So, what's on the docket today?"

I shrug. "Not much. Hanging out with Mia at the beach. Oh, I might take up a few hours lifeguarding at the pool, you know, maybe teach a few lessons and make some extra cash." The coffee is good this morning. Only took me three tries to finally get it right.

"I hope you know you don't need to do that. You're supposed to be on summer break." She eyes me over the rim of her coffee mug. This is her "I'm being your mother right now" look. It's a look that's been a little out of practice since she moved away from Seattle. Not that I took it seriously when she was there.

"It's only a few hours a week, Mom. No big deal. And besides, everyone else is working this summer—including you. I'm so bored by myself." I have her there, and she knows it.

"I'm sorry, Sloane, I promised we'd spend more time together, and I haven't exactly stuck to that."

"It's okay, Mom, I know how slammed you've been, really. And at least this job will give me something to do, something to keep me busy."

She takes another sip of coffee then nods her understanding. "Well, I guess a couple hours a week might be a good thing, but please remember this is your summer, okay?" She brushes a kiss across my forehead and leaves to get ready for work, and I head back to my own room, gripping my coffee cup in my one good hand.

My other hand doesn't look nearly as bad as it did last week. Most of the swelling has gone down—at least what I can see from my fingers that poke out from the cast. But the skin is still this lovely shade of a purple swirl, mixed with a tinge of green. What's worse is undoubtedly what will be found underneath the cast when it finally comes off. I was already a pasty shade of white, but after several weeks in the Hawaiian sun, it will take forever for my arm to catch up to the rest of me.

"Mornin'." Penn is sleepy-eyed with hair all askew as he emerges from his room. Seems I'm not the only one having issues with the time difference.

Wearing a pair of loose-fitting basketball shorts, he leans up against the doorjamb and crosses his arms over a chest that's already a much darker shade than it was a few days before. He yawns, takes my mug of coffee, and settles it under his nose.

"Get any sleep?" he asks.

"Dude, get your own coffee." I snag the mug back right as he's about to take a sip.

"I guess I'll take that as a no?" He rubs at his face, then takes a deep breath. "He called again last night."

By "him," I know he means Tyler. "Yeah, well, he called me, too. And e-mailed. And texted. Join the club."

"All I'm saying is, you know at some point I'm gonna have to talk to him."

I wave a hand nonchalantly in his direction, like I don't care. I think I'm the only one that's fooled. "Feel free to talk to him, Penn, whatever. But you know the rules. I have zero intentions of hearing one word from that asshole. Not one."

"And I have no intentions of playing counselor or messenger to the unhappy couple . . . I mean, the two of you." He frowns. Clearly he's not quite used to Tyler and me no longer being a couple. He's not the only one.

But who am I kidding? Of course I want Penn to tell me all about their conversation when it actually happens and Penn knows that, too. How much Tyler misses me, how big a mistake he made, how much he loves me and wants me back, how he could've done this to me. Because having Penn hear it in person might seem more real than the voice mails, e-mails, and text messages Tyler's been leaving for me. Because Penn would be able to tell if his best friend were lying. And my brother wouldn't stand for that.

"So in other news . . . I'm headed down to that new hotel

in Waikiki in a few hours to interview for a guard position—you know, the one next to the Hilton? Care to join me?" I know he'll say yes, but I also know he'll make me work for it. "They're looking for more than one guard if you're interested."

My brother has been around a pool as long as I have. He practically breathes through gills. So it's a good thing I already sent over both of our résumés yesterday and almost immediately got a call from their HR department that they wanted to meet the two of us this morning.

"Are you kidding me? A job? Did someone not tell you we're on summer vacation?"

"Oh, come on, Penn. Think of all those hot girls in bikinis, fresh ones rotating in every week. And all of them will be at the mercy of you, your fine muscles, and your aquatic supremacy." I really hope my innocent look is working. Penn only rolls his eyes.

"We haven't even been here a week and you're already bored?" By the way I blow out my breath, he knows he's on the right track. "Sure, I'll go with you. But I'm only doing it for the hot girls and their right to experience a proper breaststroke."

I spit out my coffee as Penn flicks at pretend dust on his flexed bicep without missing a beat.

Taking a cue from him, I roll my eyes and leave him standing there, saunter into my room, and grab a gossip mag off my coffee table. Think I'll sit out on the lanai until the world wakes up.

My phone beeps with another incoming text and I'm relieved to see that it's Mia:

> Have to work in an hour, off @ 2. We still on to meet up at the beach?

> U bet! I've got a swim lesson with Luce until 2:30. I'll head over right after. Cool?

> C U then!

A few hours later, Penn and I swing our shiny new convertible around the loop to the front entrance of the hotel. Two guys dressed in all white open both of our doors.

"Welcome to the Echelon," the valet that's holding my door says with a polite nod. "Checking in?"

"Oh, no, just visiting, thanks."

My brother hands the keys over, then heads around the front of the car to join me. The lobby is impressive. Small rivers with koi fish are recessed into the floor and weave various paths toward the front desk, concierge, and elevators, and on to the shops and pool beyond. The expansive wall behind the check-in counter is embedded with thousands of rocks. Water cascades over them, with a tranquil hum that's mesmerizing. And the smell. It's lavender with a hint of vanilla, and with one sniff, I feel like I've entered a spa.

It smells expensive but relaxing all at the same time. And it's exactly what I need.

After two hours, two interviews, and more paperwork than I would have guessed was needed for a summer job, both Penn and I are newly employed at the Echelon Hotel. Ms. Evans, head of HR, motions toward a lifeguard on duty as we walk out to the pool area.

"This is Logan Wolfe, our head lifeguard here at the Echelon. Logan, this is Penn and Sloane McIntyre."

Logan is a few years older than us, but I'm instantly on alert. Because not only is he a little too California surfer boy for my tastes—with the dark tan and bleach-blond hair—but he looks very much like Tyler.

"Hey, it's really nice to meet you." He stretches out a hand to shake mine, sees the cast, fumbles, then shakes Penn's hand instead. "It's gonna be great to have the two of you on board." He's all dimples and a goofy grin and immediately my hackles go down.

"Penn will be with you on deck here at the pool, but I've set Sloane up over at the activities counter until her cast comes off," Ms. Evans confirms. She points to a tiki hut out near the beach, not far from the pool. "Logan can arrange your scheduling needs and will also get you set up with uniforms. Unless you have anything else, it was a pleasure to meet you both. Welcome to the Echelon." She hands us each a business card, then clicks away in her heels.

"Wow, I'm so glad I wore my nice swim trunks. That

must've been what sealed the deal." With a look that's all boy, Penn watches the retreating form of Ms. Evans as she disappears back into the lobby. Fighting the urge to shove him into the pool, I follow Logan into the back office.

Armed with our new attire, Logan gives us a tour, including the shack where I'll be working, and introduces us to a few of our fellow coworkers back out by the pool.

And that's when I see him.

Stretched out on a lounge chair a few feet away, Finn is reading a magazine, occasionally smiling at the many girls at the pool who are trying to get his attention. But then he zeros in on me, like he somehow felt me looking his way. He's sitting next to a bottle blonde with a barely-there bikini and miles and miles of tanned, gorgeous skin, slick with suntan oil. She tilts her head down a bit, and I can tell by the way she narrows her eyes that she's staring at me over the rim of her sunglasses.

Yeah, you should so be worried about all this, I think as I stare down at the bulbous monstrosity of a cast on my arm.

Logan looks in the direction I was staring. "You two know each other?"

"Yeah, I guess you could say that." Before I can explain, Finn is already up and on his way over. I can't stop staring at his tattoo . . . or his bare chest. Hell, it's like my eyes are magnetically connected to the well-defined hip bone just above his swim trunks.

"Hey, you. I texted you this morning. Thanks for the reply." He places one hand over his heart in mock heartache and shades his eyes with the other.

"You did?" I pull out my phone and see I missed two texts from him, another few from Tyler, and one from Mick. "Oops, *sorry*. Guess it's been a little bit of a busy morning."

"I guess so." The corner of his mouth twitches ever so slightly. "How's it goin', Penn?" He slaps hands with my brother like they've been friends forever. I've always been amazed how guys can do that. "So what time are your swim lessons with Luce today? Maybe I'll bring her over."

"We're on for one this afternoon. You in need of a lesson, too?" He laughs, and it makes my stomach shift in a way it hasn't done in years.

"I think I'm good, but I'll let you know if that changes." He eyes the uniforms tucked under my arm, then those under my brother's. "Hold up, don't tell me the two of you are working here?"

For a second, I think he's giving us a hard time for getting a job, and it makes my face flush. "Why, what's wrong with working here?"

"Nothing. Nothing at all. But I think this summer just got a lot more interesting. *A lot* more." He starts walking backward, that devilish grin now more present than ever. "I'll see you this afternoon. Oh, and, Sloane, you still owe me a chicken rematch. Don't think I've forgotten." He taps the side of his head before he turns and walks back to his chair.

And I feel my heart actually skip a beat. Like I've never talked to a cute boy or something.

We weave in between hotel guests as Logan leads us back out to the lobby. "Any idea what that was all about?" I ask.

He laughs and I get the feeling I'm not going to like what I'm about to hear. "Oh, you don't know? Finn's dad is the owner of the Echelon. He lives here."

"Huh, no shit." I glance over my shoulder one last time at Finn, who's lying back on his chaise lounge. He doesn't even try to hide the fact he's watching me from over the top of the magazine he's picked back up. I can even see his smile from here.

Of all the hotels in all of Waikiki, I pick the one where Finn is a permanent resident.

And now I work for his father.

Seven

I stare at Mick's name in my in-box, but can't get myself to open up the e-mail, let alone read it. I hover over the delete key, then press enter. Thirty seconds later, I go to my trash and retrieve it, filing it away in Mick's folder. I've been at my mom's for a little over ten days now, and I can't believe it's already been that long since Mick and I were standing in the park and she was unleashing her monsoon of crap.

I've read a few of her texts, but for some reason, I can't get myself to open up and read any of her e-mails, or letters for that matter. She's already sent me three of those in the mail. They're sitting, fat and unopened, in the top drawer of my desk.

I'm not sure what it is that makes her e-mails or letters seem that much more intimate, more personal, than a stupid text. Nor can I explain why I can read the ones from Tyler, but not the ones from Mick. Maybe deep down inside, the betrayal hurts more coming from her, because she knows me better than anyone else. She knows every last detail of what makes me tick and somehow it feels like she took advantage of that. Advantage of me. Whatever it is, all I know is that whenever I see her name in my in-box or her handwriting on the outside of an envelope, it literally makes me want to fold myself into tiny confetti-sized pieces and hope a giant gust of wind will blow me away.

I glance at the clock. Three A.M. It's moved only two minutes since the last time I checked, even though it seems like it's been well over an hour.

I hate McKinley. I hate everything she's done and how she's changed my life. But I also hate Tyler. From his many messages, I know he's trying to pin this on her, like he had nothing to do with it. And based on what I've heard from Penn, our friends have all but abandoned her, like she's carrying some form of the Ebola virus and not a child. How cruel and quick the unfriend button can be.

What's worse is knowing what that's going to do to Mick. As if it weren't bad enough already that she's pregnant, seventeen years old, and about to start her senior year of high school. If everyone's bailing on her, leaving her to deal with it all by herself, I can only imagine what this is doing to her. She must be *freaking out*. But then part of me thinks she deserves everything she's got coming her way and I shouldn't feel sorry for her at all.

But I do.

Because Mick and I have been through so much together, and I've always been there for her, no matter what.

Like the time she asked me to help her with the Justin Donovan "situation." For months, Justin wouldn't leave her alone, and she'd begged me to get him away from her. Begged. So I did what was needed. Granted it all didn't quite go according to plan thanks to a little too much liquid courage on my part. But when Mick ended up slapping Justin for trying to stick his hand up my shirt while I was passed out, it had all been worth it. Because Justin never bothered her again. Or me, for that matter. Later that night, she even held my hair back as I puked something nasty into the hedges.

And it would be impossible to count how many of her dance recitals I've sat through over the years, even though Mick didn't always make it to my swim meets.

But after everything, she still betrayed me in the end. I mean, if she'd wanted a boyfriend, fine—but why did she have to go after mine? Why would she do the one thing she knew I'd never forgive her for? Whywhywhywhy?

I don't know how I'm going to go back to Seattle at the end of summer and show up for my senior year as if nothing's changed. How I'm going to walk the halls, sit through class, and act as if a few months in Hawaii cured me of everything. Because I know how everyone is going to stare, that pathetic look in their eyes, the tilt of their heads. Like they're sorry for me, but really, they're all just hoping I'll blow up at Tyler or Mick and cause some epic drama in the hallways.

And what do I do if Tyler or Mick tries to talk to me? Do I ignore them? Do I talk to them indifferently? Do I pretend like I'm fine? I don't think I have enough courage to do that. I'm not even sure if I can handle seeing her pregnant, like that will be the defining moment that makes it all real.

All of it makes me want to stay here, in Hawaii, far away from them and everything else back at home.

I realize my dad is probably in the middle of his morning commute. It's been a couple of days since I've talked to him, so I pick up my phone and shoot him a text:

Good morning . . .

A second later, my phone rings. "Hey, Dad. You on your way in to work?"

"Hey, kiddo, I'm headed in to the office now. So . . . do you want to tell me why you're up at, what is it there, three thirty in the morning?"

"Oh, you know, hard to sleep in paradise."

"Yeah, I'll bet that's really tough. Hey, while I have you on the phone, I should probably tell you that both McKinley and Tyler came over yesterday—not together. Although their reasoning was the same. They both wanted to apologize. And to ask if I'd talk to you for them."

I squeeze my eyes shut tight. Because it pains me that they would have the nerve to go and talk to my dad. I'm pretty sure I've made it clear I want absolutely nothing to do with either of them, so I don't understand why they think wrangling my dad into all of this is an obvious choice.

I'm trying to move on, and so should they.

"I'm sorry, Dad. What did you say to them?"

"Well, I told them both it's not me they need to apologize to; I'm not the one they hurt. But I did also tell them that they need to give you some space, let you figure everything out . . . even if the result isn't in their favor. But can I give you some advice, Sloane?"

Honestly, I really hope he has the answer to all of this, so of course I'm all ears. "Sure."

"Even if you can't bring yourself to let them back into your life, you do need to try to find a way to forgive them for what they've done. *Everyone* makes mistakes, Sloane, some worse than others." He pauses for a second and maybe I'm just imagining it, but it sounds like he might be talking about more than just Mick and Tyler. "Just know they'll have to live with the guilt of what they've done for the rest of their lives."

I hear him, but I'm not quite sure how to respond. I think it's the words "the rest of their lives" that hits me the hardest. Because unless Mick decides not to carry out this pregnancy, in less than nine months, there's going to be an entirely new person added in to all of this that will be a constant reminder of what happened.

"I'll try," I manage.

We chat for a few more minutes about how Hawaii is and how Mom is doing. I know he misses her, and I can almost guarantee there's a hidden meaning behind what he said. I can't believe I never put it together before, never really asked why they got divorced. I only cared how much it had impacted me. I guess as a nine-year-old, I only noticed that my mom and dad weren't both there, together, in the same house. And then as the years went on, it was something I grew used to, never giving it any further thought. Until now.

A few hours later, I drag myself to work for my first day. I can't stop thinking about what my dad said, and deep down, I know he's right. But then the beach is there in front of me and the sun is slowly beginning its rise for the day, and somehow that makes it easier to ignore everything else that's taken an ugly turn in my life lately. Not to mention, just pulling into the hotel parking lot now makes me think of Finn . . . and I wonder if maybe I'll see him today.

Then I realize I'm *hoping* I'll see him today. And it feels good to be thinking about someone who's not Tyler—to be excited about someone who's not Tyler.

I can't believe how busy the activities counter is, especially at seven in the morning. There are actually people milling around, waiting for it to open. But I guess when you work in a city that caters to people from time zones all around the world, there's no such thing as closed.

Whoever else I'm supposed to be on shift with isn't here yet, and I don't have a key to unlock the door, so I smile and explain this to a few of the guests. I'm not sure if they all understand me, as some of them don't appear to speak English very well.

A local girl around my age, with tattoos on both arms and wearing the same uniform I am, scrambles my way with less than five minutes before we're slated to open. I recognize her from the bonfire party the other night, but we never actually met. Her dark hair is still wet, but tied up in a messy ponytail, and she has toothpaste on her cheek. She fumbles with a set of keys to unlock the door.

"Folks, it will be a few minutes while we get everything ready." She repeats the same thing in Japanese for the customers I feared hadn't a clue what I said earlier. Everyone nods her way as she turns back to me. "Hey, I'm Maile. And no, even though it sounds the same, I'm not like the singer. And you are?" She unlocks the slatted door and shoves gently against it with her shoulder to pop it open, then motions me inside.

"Sloane McIntyre. Nice to meet you, not-like-the-singer Maile."

She shoots a grin in my direction, then flings her bag in a closet behind the cash register, exposing another tattoo on the small of her back when her shirt hitches up slightly. She sets about getting everything ready before opening the doors for the customers. I gesture at her cheek.

"You've got a little toothpaste there."

She slaps a hand to her face, yanks open the door to the closet where her bag is stored, and checks out her reflection in a small mirror that's mounted to the inside.

"Damn. I just can't get myself out of bed on time!" She scrubs at her face until the toothpaste disappears. "If I'm late one more time, Rick's gonna fire me for sure."

I can sense the urgency in her voice as she flings the closet door shut and hurries around the small shack. It's definitely meant to look like a tiki hut, with a fake coconut tree up against one wall and thatched grass tacked up on the ceiling and counter. Even the floor is covered in a thin dusting of sand.

I feel like I should dash around with her, to get whatever needs to be done, done. "What can I do to help?"

"Turn on the open sign behind you, the printer over there, oh, and you'll need a name tag." She points toward the closet where her bag is. I dump my own bag with hers and pull a couple of the name tags off one of the shelves. Yeah, I think I can pull off being Kela Kekai from Hilo, Hawaii, today. I clip the tag to the front of my polo, then scramble to get the other things done as Maile powers up the computer for the cash registers. She motions toward the rolling door over the counter that opens to the outside. "If you can open that window, I'll get the front door. And would you look at that, we still have twenty-two seconds to spare!"

Fifteen minutes later, we've successfully handled the five people waiting to book a scuba tour and a sunset dinner cruise. Well, I should say Maile handled the five people as I stood there and listened to what she offered them and booked them into the system. And I must say I was super impressed when she checked the Japanese couple in for their dinner cruise all while speaking to them in their native tongue.

A guy a few years older than us with a buzz cut and starched khakis strides by. He gives Maile a two-fingered salute, taps his watch, then gives her a thumbs-up. She shoots him a fake smile and returns the thumbs-up, but as soon as he's out of sight, she replaces her thumb with her middle finger.

"Asshole." She blows out a breath, then cracks a real smile for me. "That's Rick the Dick. He supervises the activities counter and dive shop and is always waiting for me to screw up. Oh, and he's bipolar but severely undermedicated, so do your best to keep up with his many moods." She flips off the space where he was again, just for good measure. "Man, he's such a jerk. But thanks for your help in opening on time. I'm pretty sure you just saved my ass from getting canned."

"Hey, no worries." And I mean it, too. We only just met, but Maile has somehow managed to make me feel like we've known each other much longer than that. Something I didn't think was possible without having years of history together. She's so different from Mick, and I almost feel like I'm cheating on my best friend, but maybe this is exactly what I need right now.

At one point during my shift, I think I catch a glimpse of Finn out by the pool. Then again, the pool is crowded with a million bodies, so I'm not sure if it's really him or some creative part of my brain hoping it is. Maile takes her time getting me trained on the system in between helping guests. Within an hour, I'm actually pretty proficient at getting guests set up with booze cruises and those cheesy luaus. The ones where the staff is *so* not Hawaiian and they're wearing plastic grass skirts and fake coconuts over their boobs, all while training the guests to say "a-looooooooo-HA!"

And even Rick the Dick stops by to introduce himself, but funny, he leaves that last part off his name. He disgustingly flirts with Maile as he subconsciously picks at a scaly patch of dry skin near his elbow, laying it on thick even with all the signs she gives that he doesn't stand a chance. He leaves when his walkie-talkie squawks, and Maile instantly pulls out a bottle of spray bleach and a cleaning rag, dousing the counter area where he was leaning. My guess is she's totally done that before.

"So disgusting. Gawd, and to think I actually kissed him once." She tentatively looks at the damp cleaning rag in her hand as if she might use it to disinfect her lips, but thinks otherwise.

"Oh, you've gotta give me more than that. Come on." I cross my arms and wait, letting her know I'll stand like that forever until she spills.

"It's not that big a deal, really. Just a stupid drunk moment a few months ago, but believe me, nothing else happened." I give her another look. "Seriously, nothing else happened, because . . . well, I kinda threw up on him while we were kissing."

She cringes, and I burst out laughing.

"Oh, shut it, I already feel bad enough as it is!" But she laughs along with me, so I know she's only joking.

"I'm sorry, Maile, it's just that something really similar happened to me. And I can't tell you how relieved I am to know I'm not the only one who's ever puked on a guy!"

Shaking her head, she leans over with her fist extended, and we bump them together. Yep, Maile and I are gonna get along just fine.

She prints out the report for our sales that morning, as another girl around our age walks in, laughing. A guy with shaggy blond hair and dimples that make me want to dip my pinky fingers in and twirl ducks in behind her. They're both wearing the same uniforms as Maile and me.

"Looks like our replacement crew is here!" Maile chimes as she knocks the register drawer shut with her hip.

"What's up, ladies! You're both officially done for the day! And if I were you, I'd run . . . run as fast and far away as you can!" The girl takes Maile's bag from the closet and replaces it with her own. I notice that she's grabbed mine as well. But before handing the bag over to Maile, she leans in and kisses her, then tucks a loose strand of hair behind Maile's ear.

"That is *so* hot." This from the guy with the dimples. He's staring with that dumb look only guys ever get, leaving no doubt which head he's thinking with.

"Oh, shut up, Drew." Maile rolls her eyes and takes her bag from her friend. "Stace, this is Sloane McIntyre. Sloane, this is my girlfriend, Stacey Silver."

"Nice to meet you, Sloane. And this is Drew, but he also goes by Horndog." Stacey walks over and hands me my backpack with her left hand extended. Clearly, she saw my cast. She's a cute little thing, no taller than me. Her blond hair is slicked in a perfect ponytail, and she flicks her bangs from her eyes as if they've reached that point where they're just a tad too long.

I shake her hand and take my bag. "It's nice to meet you. And nice to meet you as well, Horndog, was it?" I offer up my hand to shake his, but instead, he flips it over and brings it up to his lips.

"Baby, you can call me whatever you want." His mouth pauses against my knuckles, before both Maile and Stacey groan out loud. Drew ducks as paper clips and wadded-up balls of paper fly his way. "What, you know I'm only teasing!"

"Yeah, *we* know that, but Sloane doesn't!"

After saying good-bye—and reassuring Maile I'll be back again in two days—I cut through the pool area on my way to the parking garage. I casually glance around for a particular tattoo and am a little bummed when I don't find what I'm looking for.

With thirty minutes to get home, I have just enough time to swap the car with Penn so he can get back here for his shift this afternoon. Pulling out my phone, I shoot him a quick text to let him know I'm on my way and see I've got four new messages along with an e-mail, all from Tyler. Ignoring them, I click open a new text from Mia.

As I'm busy reading about the drama that ensued at the floral shop where she works—something to do with a crate of tropical flowers that came in today, complete with rare spiders not native to the Islands—I maneuver my way around guests and the occasional deck chair with ease. I can only imagine how badly Mia freaked out. She hates anything with more legs than her, and the visual of all five feet ten inches of her needing to be scraped from the ceiling makes me laugh out loud.

Of course being glued to my phone like I am means I don't see the rowdy bunch of tweens that just so happen to pick that moment to swarm around me and dive into the pool. Taking me with them.

Eight

Breaking the surface, I sputter out half the pool and swipe dripping hair from my eyes. Limbs and water fly everywhere as kids whoop and holler, and my cell phone is now sitting at the bottom of the pool, my half-zipped backpack and some of its contents floating all around me. Of course that's also when I hear him laugh.

I turn to see Finn standing on the deck in a pair of swim trunks, a towel slung over one bare shoulder, his tattoo peeking out here and there from underneath. He laughs even harder when I take a lesson from Maile and flip him the bird.

Setting his stuff down, he dives in and glides smoothly under the water, breaking the surface in front of me. Slicking back his hair, his steel-blue gaze lands on mine.

"You do know I have the power to have those kids removed from the hotel, but only if you ask nicely." He smirks, like he actually wants me to test this theory out, then turns and gathers my bag and a few of my things, shoving them inside. I take a deep breath and dive down to retrieve my phone. The screen has gone black with an eerie purplish liquid that squishes around behind the glass. It's definitely a goner.

Finn plunks my bag by the edge of the pool, then hauls himself up, and the view I get of the muscles in his arms, stretching the tattoo in all directions, is insane.

"Here, let me help you," he says.

I swim to the edge and his extended hand, but give him a skeptical look, like he's got ulterior motives in mind.

"Seriously? You're already wet, what more could I do?" His grin is back, along with my urge to flip him off yet again, but I take his hand anyway. It's a little bit awkward since it's my left hand, but Finn lifts me from the pool as if I weigh nothing more than my wet backpack.

"You okay?" He grabs a towel and places it around my shoulders, then picks up my bag and now ruined phone.

"I think so," I say, shaking out the water from my ears.

"Good. Come on, let's get you dried off." He presses a hand between my shoulder blades and leads me away from the pool.

"I'm pretty sure I'm fine. . . . Um, where exactly are we going?" I look back at the pool over my shoulder one last time—so of course it's at that moment my wet shoes take the opportunity to slide on the slick tiles. I'm like Bambi on ice. I try to regain my balance as Finn grabs my arm to steady me.

He gives me a look as if asking if I'm capable of keeping my feet underneath me. Like any of what's happened has actually been my fault. *Please.*

And then he turns and keeps walking, prodding me along. "You're soaking wet and your shin is bleeding. You can come upstairs to my suite to dry off and change, and I can take a look at your leg. Plus, I've got a first-aid kit in case, ya know, you need stitches, or—worst case—I need to take it off below the knee." He actually does a great job in keeping his poker face intact, but by now, I know this guy enjoys trying to rile me up.

I glance down at my leg and notice the wet trickle of blood that's now staining the top of my sock a pink hue.

"Yeah, I'm pretty sure I'll live, not that I don't trust your mad doctoring skills." I can't believe I'm actually trying to get out of seeing his suite, so I quickly change tactics. "But if you have anything dry I can borrow to change into, that would be great."

We pass a few female employees from the hotel, and they all smile and say hi to Finn in singsong unison.

"Ladies." He nods in their direction, then, instead of heading toward the main bank of elevators out near the lobby, veers off down a side hallway and stops in front of a lone elevator. Once the doors open, he presses in a code on the panel that has replaced all the floor buttons, and we ascend.

When the doors ease open, there's an impressive living

space in front of us, which is anything but typical of the hotel rooms I've been in before. I realize with one glance out the span of windows in front of me that we're on the top floor. And from the looks of my surroundings, it's the *entire* top floor. Finn sets my bag down on a table that's covered by a ginormous tropical floral arrangement, then crouches near my leg, placing one hand behind my calf. Immediately I'm covered in goose bumps.

"Sorry to say I think it needs to come off after all." This earns him a light swat to the head that he laughs off. Standing, he motions to a door off to his right as he pats down his hair like I've messed it up. "You can use the bathroom in there. I'll get you something dry you can change into."

I start toward the bathroom, then spin back around. "Oh crap, Penn!" I check my watch. "Damn, five minutes! Phone?"

He raises one eyebrow, taps his ear, then taps his forearm with two fingers. "Sounds like, two syllables. Go!"

He laughs when I place both hands on my hips and tap my toe. "Are you done?" I ask.

"Hey, I'm good, but I'm not *that* good. Afraid I'm gonna need a few more words than 'Oh crap, Penn!'"

I take a deep breath and let it out slowly. "Sorry, I have the car, and Penn's shift at the pool starts in five . . . scratch that, four minutes." I grab my cell, hoping maybe it might still work, but I get nothing but the black screen.

Finn calmly takes my hand and slips his cell phone in it.

"Hey, don't worry, I'll send a car to pick him up, and I'll let Logan down at the pool know he's on his way." He's already on the phone in the hallway as he covers the mouthpiece and says, "Call Penn."

I dial Penn's cell and close my eyes. He picks up before the first ring has ended.

"P., I'm so sorry! I got pushed in the pool after my shift." I hear Finn laughing behind me and whip around with my best glare.

"Damn, Sloane, I'm gonna be late for my first day. And what do you mean you got pushed in the pool? Wait . . . never mind. Don't answer that." I can actually hear him rolling his eyes at me. "How much longer will you be? I need to call Logan."

"Actually, Finn's sending a car out to pick you up, it should be there any minute. He's on the phone with Logan now." Penn whistles between his teeth, but I cut him off before he can say anything more. "Don't even go there, Penn. And by the way, my cell phone is toast—it went in the pool with me—so you guys won't be able to get a hold of me for a while."

Hanging up, I thank Finn, then excuse my still dripping-wet self to the bathroom. I stop abruptly when I see I'm actually walking into Finn's bedroom to get to it.

The room is all glass and white and light-colored wood, and one wall is made entirely of solid windows, overlooking the ocean and beach below. I walk along the opposite wall, which is covered in frame after frame of somebody ripping apart a gnarly wave on a surfboard. There are several pictures, each shot taken in rapid-fire succession, and as I scan the images from top to bottom, I see that it's Finn. Confirming this, a rather used and abused surfboard that mirrors the one in the pictures hangs on the wall above the bed. A large king-sized bed.

I make my way to the bathroom, grab a wad of toilet paper, and wipe up my shin. It's nothing but a small scratch, so it doesn't take much. I must have hit the edge of the pool when I went in. Plucking a fluffy towel from the rack, I attempt to dry off my hair, but my clothes are literally dripping water all over the floor, so I peel them off and wring them out over the tub. Standing in my wet underwear, I jump when someone knocks on the door.

"Hey, I left some clothes out here on the bed. I wasn't sure what would fit, so you've got some options."

I mumble my thanks and wait for the click of the outside door to shut before opening the one from the bathroom. A variety of outfits are lying on his bed, a mixture of items belonging to both him and his sister. There are three pairs of shorts: a pair of khakis I'm afraid are going to be a tad too small, a pair of girls' black athletic shorts that look exactly like the ones I wear after swim practice, and a pair of guys' basketball shorts. Which I'm sure will look more like pants on me. I opt for the black athletic shorts, a rather large LA Dodgers T-shirt I cringe to wear—but only because it's not an M's or Yankees shirt—and since I'm slightly cold from being wet, an oversized gray hoodie that definitely belongs to Finn. It smells of sunshine and salt water.

Which is so opposite from Tyler's faint hint of cologne and fabric softener. And I can't believe I'm even thinking of Tyler right now.

I jam my feet into a pair of Luce's flip-flops that are a little too big, but they'll work. I wring out my wet clothes one last time, fold them into a small stack, and decide there's not much that can be done with my hair. It's too short to put up in a ponytail, so it will just have to do. Cleaning up behind me, I head back out to the living room and find Finn parked on the sofa, one ankle propped up on the opposite knee, flipping through the sports channels on the large flat screen in front of him.

I clear my throat. "Hey, thanks for letting me borrow some clothes." A small smile tugs at the corner of his mouth as he takes in the getup I've got on. His sweatshirt is almost long enough to be a dress, so you can barely see the shorts I'm wearing underneath.

"Yeah, no problem." Turning off the TV, he springs up from the couch and heads toward the table in the hall. Everything from my backpack is strewn out across the surface, and I can tell he's tried his best to dry it all off. My wallet's a little fatter than normal—I'm sure because the few receipts and money I had in there have expanded from being wet—but other than that, most of it looks fine.

"You already know your phone's toast, but everything else looks okay."

"Yeah, guess I'll be making a trip to the mall." I shrug and begin to throw everything into my backpack. "Thanks again, I appreciate everything—and I'll get these clothes back to you on Thursday, when I come in to work." I turn for the elevator, but he grabs my wrist before I can make it that far.

"Hold up, I'll give you a lift."

"Wait, what? I don't need to go there right now."

"Why, because you've got so many other exciting plans? Come on, admit it, you'd really rather spend more time with me anyway." I know he's only joking, but I still blush. Damn cheeks, they're always giving me away.

"*Oh please*, it sounds to me like the other way around." I say this to his back as he disappears into his room, and I hear him laugh. He comes back out with a motorcycle helmet, then grabs another from the entryway closet, which he hands to me.

"I'll drive."

We head out through the front lobby and there, already waiting for us, is a sleek motorcycle—all carbon and white, with small hints of yellow. It looks fast and slightly dangerous and I have to admit, it makes me feel kinda like a badass. Well, in a might-pee-my-pants badass kind of way.

Putting on his helmet, Finn swings a leg over the bike and straightens it out. Key in the ignition, he pulls back on the throttle, and the engine revs with a throaty hum that echoes under the covered roundabout of the hotel as everyone around us turns to stare. He looks over his shoulder and nods his chin in my direction, letting me know it's my turn.

I wonder if he has *any* idea how he looks on this thing. My guess is he does, but for some reason, I don't really care. Because right about now my body tingles like I've touched something electric. And I haven't even gotten on the bike yet.

Slipping on what I'm sure is Luce's helmet, I realize that actually getting on the bike may require a skill I'm not quite sure I possess. After all, the seat I'm supposed to sit on is up higher than where Finn is sitting and I do have this oh-so-sexy cast on. As I attempt to hike my leg up to the foot peg, Finn swipes his hand under my ass. I let out a yelp of surprise as he swings me up on the seat behind him. He makes note of tapping a button on the underside of his chin, and I feel along my own helmet for the same one.

"Damn, you've got to weigh less than a buck," he mumbles in my ear. "Can you hear me?"

"Loud and clear. And what I weigh is none of your concern," I respond tartly as I tighten the chin strap, then wonder what exactly I'm supposed to do with my hands. I settle for grasping handfuls of his T-shirt as best I can.

"You're gonna need to hang on tighter than that." He pulls my cast and my one good hand farther around his waist, clasping one over the other, which causes me to press my chest up tightly against his back. I hear a hitch in his breathing as his hands hesitate on mine for a few seconds longer. I can't believe I'm actually doing this, but oh, how I wish Tyler could see me right now.

Finn clicks the bike into gear, revs the engine once more, and releases the brake.

And then the bike shoots forward with such power, it's almost as if we're flying.

Nine

It's a gorgeous day in Honolulu, and we're at the outdoor mall in Ala Moana, the sun tickling my cheeks with finger-like rays. Even so, I'm not exactly sure how I feel about being here, at the mall, with Finn—especially since shopping was something I always did with Mick.

As I check out the stores and the gazillion people with shopping bags that bustle around me, I realize this is something Mick and I won't ever do again. Something as trivial as shopping with my best friend is now a thing of the past, and I wonder if she ever stopped to think about that. To think about how much life would suck without each other. And if she now believes it was all worth it.

"Earth to Sloane, come in, Sloane." Finn snaps his fingers mere inches from my nose and I zero in on his face. "Oh, there you are—nice to see you again."

"Ha-ha, very funny." I laugh, shaking off my negative

thoughts. "Just trying to remember what all I need to get while I'm here. How about you, you need anything? Perhaps a year's supply of chocolate-covered macadamia nuts is calling your name?" I fan my arm out toward a gigantic display of the candies as we pass by an ABC store.

"No, wait, don't tell me. It's that sexy Hawaiian outfit you can't live without." I point at a matching Aloha shirt-and-short set as we walk by a store selling tropical-printed clothes. Not cool in a retro kind of way cool, but the ones that are identical so husband, wife, kids, *and* pets can all be wearing the same thing.

"Only if you promise to get the matching muumuu?" He starts flipping through the front sales rack, but I grab his arm. "What? I think the green set would be perfect for us, don't you? Although you might be a tad too short." He holds up the dress, but instantly scrunches up his nose. There's literally about three extra feet of polyester green goodness. "Wow, not even close." He grabs the matching one made for a little girl and holds that one up to me instead. "Ding, ding, ding—I think we have a winner!"

"Yeah, if I were a *stripper.*" I snag the hanger from his hand and put it back, then pull him away from the store as he continues to look over his shoulder. "Not gonna happen, Finn. So not gonna happen."

My new phone is shiny and pretty and oh so empty. It was easy to transfer all my contacts over, but my text message history died with the old phone, so there's not a single one.

And I wonder if maybe that's a sign for me to really move on from what happened. Maybe.

"So when does that sweet cast come off?" Finn asks as we walk along.

"Unfortunately, another couple of weeks." I eye the tips of my fingers and cringe at what may be farther up underneath the layers of plaster. At least it doesn't throb like it did the first few days. "But I can't wait."

"I'll bet. But I hate to tell you what it's like when that sucker starts to itch. It's the worst."

I start to ask what bones he's broken, but I don't get very far, because a hot pair of shorts wearing some wannabe blonde has picked that exact moment to call out Finn's name. As she gets closer, I realize it's the same girl that was sitting with him at the pool the day I interviewed at the Echelon.

I'm surprised when he doesn't bother to look in her direction. Instead, his eyes are focused on me, like he's waiting for me to finish what I was saying. I'm torn between continuing and acknowledging our new friend. But then I'm distracted by her sugary voice as she once again calls out his name. She calls him "Finny" instead of Finn, like she's trying to be cute.

"Hey, Gianna," Finn finally says.

Gianna has an accent I can't place. Italian or maybe Spanish. She's also a few years older than me, easily in her early twenties. I'm not sure how the two of them know each other, but there's no getting around the fact that they do. Or the fact she'd like to know him a lot better than she does.

Aside from her nonexistent shorts, she wears these outrageously tall espadrille sandals that would make most girls stumble just looking at them, but she walks—scratch that—*sways* our way in them with ease, like she was born with them strapped to her feet. She flings one arm around Finn's shoulders and plants a loud kiss on each of his cheeks. With those shoes, she's almost as tall as he is. Which means I find myself eye level with the biggest and most fake pair of boobs I've ever seen.

And *that's* awesome.

I look down at my own barely B cup and sigh—and by "barely," I mean only on a good day, when I'm wearing my super bra. Which is so *not* what I'm wearing under Finn's hoodie right now. I glance back at Finn and notice his eyes are still on mine, and I hope he didn't just see me size myself up against Miss Espadrilles. But I have a feeling he did by the way the corner of his mouth tweaks ever so slightly upward. Guess I'll add that to my growing list of fine moments with Finn.

"Where have you been?" she purrs in his ear. Even I know it's only been a couple of days since they last saw each other at the pool, but by the way she's acting, you'd think it's been years. She doesn't even notice me standing there. Must be the spectacular wardrobe I've got on. I mean, come on, the hoodie screams hottie.

Finn soaks up her smile with one of his own, without missing a beat. "Gianna, this is Sloane; Sloane, this is Gianna." Her eyes never leave his face.

I clear my throat, and she finally looks at me as if I'm some pesky mosquito that's buzzing around her. "Oh. Hello there. You are so *piccola*, or how you say . . . little." She motions with her hands as if I don't get what she's saying.

And I scoff. Out loud. Did she just call me little?

She stares at me as if she's waiting for me to respond, but then whispers something into Finn's ear with a giggle. He rolls his eyes at me, but for some reason, that isn't enough. Maybe in the past it would've been. But not anymore.

"*Yeah*, I think I'll leave the two of you alone. Thanks for the ride, Finn. See you around." I don't wait for him to say anything before I turn and walk away. The mall is only a few blocks from the hotel, so it's not like I have far to go. Besides, after that episode, I could use the walk.

I pick up my pace and make my way outside, but someone grabs my wrist and spins me around.

"Hey, please don't walk away. I'm really sorry about that back there, about Gianna. I don't think she realizes how blunt she is." Finn seems slightly out of breath, like he was running to catch up. And then he actually leans over and grabs both of his knees. "Damn, you can haul ass for being so small. Who knew?"

I have to bite my lower lip to contain my smile. And that irks me because I want to be mad. "It's no big deal, Finn, I can make it back on my own."

"I have absolutely no doubt you can. Hell, with those legs, you'd probably make it back before I did." He stands upright and motions toward the parking garage in the opposite direction. "Look, I'm sorry about Gianna. She's here on business from Italy for the year and staying at the Echelon. And honestly, I think I might be her only friend here." The way he says "friend" makes me want to laugh in a non-ha-ha kind of way, because it's evident in every way she wants to be more than just that. "Hey, let me make it up to you. Let me take you to dinner."

"Right now?" I look down at what I'm wearing and think maybe he might be joking.

"Yeah, right now. Unless you've got other plans?"

Wow. He actually wants to take all *this* out to dinner instead of Gianna? Huh, how can I possibly say no to that? "Dinner . . . now . . . sure."

"So is that a yes?"

"Yes. Dinner sounds great."

We ride to the north side of the island. It's almost a different climate over here, breezy even. Which makes me glad I'm wearing his hoodie. And while not my most attractive outfit—not to mention the chaos that is my damp hair under the helmet—I can either freak out about it now or brush it off.

I decide the latter is my best option, because I guess if he doesn't like me as is, then it's his loss.

"This place actually catches their fish fresh every day, and I haven't tasted anything like it." He eyes me skeptically as we sit at a small table outside, facing the beach. The waves on this side of the island are enormous and nothing like the small swells down in Waikiki. "Wait . . . you like seafood, right? I'm sorry, I should've asked."

"No, no, it's fine. I love seafood. Sushi even more, for that matter."

While I'm not sure what this place is that he's brought me to—after all, the outside looks like a dilapidated shack—I'm willing to give it a go. Besides, it's usually restaurants that look like this that serve the best food.

After we place our order, Finn sits forward in his chair and taps his fingers lightly against the top of the table.

"So, tell me something about you."

Immediately, my mind goes to some of my favorite stories about my best friend and boyfriend, and I start to open my mouth to share. But then I remember all the reasons why I can't go there. I fiddle with my straw and stare at the ocean.

"Well . . . my parents divorced when Penn and I were in the fourth grade. My mom moved back down here and remarried a year later and we've been coming down every summer since. I love to swim and I race competitively. And you already know that Penn and I are twins, and we're seventeen. Oh, and we live outside Seattle with my dad."

"Which one of you was born first?"

Our waitress sets a steaming pot of clams on our table with a platter of garlic bread. The air around us smells like butter and all kinds of goodness, and I realize I may have actually just drooled.

Using the tiny fork the waitress left behind, I snag a few clams and scrape them from their shells. "By luck of the C-section draw, Penn was, but only by thirty-six seconds."

"Only thirty-six seconds, huh? Bet he holds that one over your head all the time."

"You have no idea." I pop a couple of the clams in my mouth and chew slowly, savoring each one. Of course they taste even better than they look. "So what about you?"

"What about me?" He soaks a piece of garlic bread in the broth, then takes a bite. His eyes close for a few seconds as if he's eating the absolute best thing in the world. From what I've tasted so far, he might be right. "Well, I'll be eighteen at the end of September, and Luce is twelve. But if you ask her, she'll tell you the exact number of months it is—down to the day and maybe even the minute—until she turns thirteen. We moved here from LA last year when the company my asshole father owns bought the Echelon. But he's hardly ever here, since this hotel was a package deal with several others over in Asia that he's trying to get rebranded and opened. He bounces back and forth between Japan, Thailand, LA, and Honolulu, but he's here the least—only long enough to keep anyone from asking questions about his minor kids living by themselves. Guess that won't matter once I turn eighteen."

I'm trying to decide if Finn would rather have his father around or if he prefers that he's not. I have a sinking feeling it's the latter, even if that means he's practically raising Luce on his own. "And your mom?"

His eyes flick my way, then quickly turn out toward the water.

"I'll tell you what. You tell me how you really broke your hand, and I'll tell you about my mom."

I glance at the table and realize we've polished off the giant pot of clams, because it's no longer there. "Nah, you don't want to hear about that. Besides, it's not that exciting, I promise."

"Ah, come on, try me."

"Seriously. It's just a bunch of crappy drama. Besides, why would you even want to know?"

He sits back in his chair and goes back to drumming his fingers lightly on the table. "Because I've seen you in the pool with my sister, so I'm having a hard time believing that's where you broke it. Plus, I'd like to get to know you better. Drama or not."

"A few swim lessons in the pool does not a great swimmer make."

"Oh, come on, Yoda, you're being modest. Besides, Tawyna Evans has never hired anyone to work for my father after an interview that was shorter than an hour—no matter what the position. And your interview was less than thirty minutes. Answer the question. *Please.*"

I have no idea how he knows about my interview, but he says it so smoothly and all in one breath. And because he was being so direct, I decide I will be, too. I turn to face him straight on and look him square in the eye. "All right, if you really want to know—your very first guess when we met on the beach was correct."

It takes only a second before that eyebrow of his arches skyward. "Huh, I'll definitely have to remember that."

"You do that. But if you say one thing about my thumb being tucked in when I threw the punch, I'll be forced to try it again, left-handed. Now your turn. *Please*."

"Whoa, that's it? That's all you're gonna give me?" He sits back and crosses his arms over his chest.

"Hey, you only asked how I broke it. You didn't ask for the details."

"True that, smart-ass. Fine, I'll go." This time he doesn't hold back his smile, but it also doesn't take long for it to fade. "My mom walked away from our family when I was ten. Never said why and didn't bother saying good-bye. I haven't heard from her since, and I have no idea where she is. My dad was an asshole before, but her leaving made him an even bigger one. Now he's only around when he absolutely has to be. Which isn't often. So I take care of Luce." He takes a sip of water, then sets his glass on the table. "How's that for drama?"

"Finn, I . . . That's . . . I'm so sorry." It's all that comes out and I know it sounds lame, but I realize I have absolutely no idea how to respond—and I get the feeling this isn't something he's shared with too many others.

"Yeah, I know, it's a lot." He leans forward, resting his

elbows on the table. "But it is what it is and now you know my sob story, so spill."

I'm grateful he's letting me off the hook easy. "So . . . this guy." I motion toward my cast, in case it wasn't clear. "I guess you could say we go back a long way, all the way to kindergarten." I'm still unable to bring myself to say his name out loud, but I smile, remembering a five-year-old Tyler picking me in a game of Heads Up, Seven Up. "I guess in a way it was always him and me."

I take a breath and decide to just state the facts and hope no emotion comes out with it.

"We'd been dating almost a year when he decided our relationship—or maybe it was me—wasn't good enough, so he slept with my best friend . . . *twice*." I glance at my cast and sigh. "Oh, and he knocked her up, so I broke his nose in three places."

There. Just the facts. I'm shocked I was able to do it.

We look at each other for a brief second, and I have absolutely no idea what he's going to say. To any of it. Or if he thinks I'm crazy.

But then he starts to laugh.

And I wonder if maybe he's the crazy one. Because I can't believe that's his reaction. I've basically just shared my darkest moments and he's laughing.

But then I think about everything we just told each other and how ridiculous it all sounds. Honestly, I don't think we could've made up better sob stories if we'd tried. And I realize he's not laughing at me . . . he's laughing at *us*. And before I know it, I'm laughing, too.

"Wow, we're pretty pathetic, aren't we?" I say.

"Maybe, but at least we're good-looking pathetic people, so there's that." Ignoring my offer to split the bill, he drops some money on top of the check and stands up. Holding a hand out for mine, he nods toward the beach. "Want to go for a walk?"

The sun is starting to bid its farewell for the day, casting the sky in the most gorgeous shades of purples and reds. Finn silently takes my hand, and it makes me smile. He doesn't seem nervous in the least and that makes me feel at ease, too—even after I remember that the last boy I held hands with was Tyler.

We walk down to the beach. His fingers feel nice around my own, warm. Comforting even. We walk but don't speak. And I actually kind of enjoy the silence. We sit and watch the sun set, his eyes catching every curl and dip of each wave, like the ocean is a long-lost friend he misses. And then I remember the photos of him surfing.

"When was the last time you were out?"

His eyes slide carefully over me, then back out to the water. "Well over a year."

I feel the moment he closes back up. This isn't a topic he wants to talk about. At least right now. So of course why wouldn't my phone take this opportunity to beep with an incoming text from Tyler?

Jeez, Sloane. I made a mistake. Would you please talk to me?

Seeing Tyler's name on my new phone while sitting next to Finn seems, I don't know . . . wrong. Like Tyler somehow knows exactly what I'm doing right at this moment and wants to make sure I don't forget what's going on back at home. I hit the delete key, wiping my new phone clean once again.

I try to be nonchalant and hide this from Finn, but I can see from the corner of my eye that he knows.

"I should probably get you home," he says, but he doesn't move.

I don't really feel like going home, either. This is the first moment in days I've had such a good time. And I don't know why, but I wasn't expecting to feel this great, so soon after everything else that's happened—and that makes it that much better.

Maybe he feels it, too, because he takes his time getting us back to the south side of the island. For reasons beyond what I'm prepared to acknowledge, I find it much easier for my arms to curl around his waist as I settle in close to his back on the motorcycle.

When we arrive at my house, I hop off the bike, then strip off my helmet. Finn surprises me when he cuts the engine and prods the kickstand in place. Taking his own helmet off, he walks me to my door.

"I'll bring the helmet to work on Thursday with your

clothes. And thanks again for dinner. You were right, one of the best meals I've had in a very long time." My phone beeps again, and I cringe because I know who it's from.

"You're more than welcome. I'd really like to do it again sometime." He smiles, ignoring my phone, which beeps a second time almost immediately. "Besides, if you thought that was good, I know several other restaurants that are even better."

"Better than what we just ate? Oh, I'm *so* in." I reach for the handle on the front door. "Would you like to come in?"

"Not that I wouldn't love to, but I've got a hot date with my little sister and some romcom I promised I would watch with her." With his hands in the air, he shakes his head. "But definitely some other time?" He tucks a strand of hair behind my ear, and I fight the urge to close my eyes and lean into his hand. "Good night, Sloane."

"Good night."

I watch him walk back to his bike and start it up. He gives me a quick wave before he speeds away.

I look down at what I'm wearing, and the massive sweatshirt that still smells like him.

And realize there's a solid chance I'll end up sleeping in it tonight.

Ten

Mick is on my mind this morning, probably because I accidentally read a text from her, thinking it was from Mia. And boy was that a mistake.

> God, Sloane. You're being so immature about everything.

> I know I made a huge mistake, but you could at least respond to any one of my texts or e-mails or letters.

> Are you really never gonna talk to me again?

Ha. I'm the one being immature because I've decided to take time for me. Because I'm not responding according to *her* timeline. Because she thinks I should forgive her so easily.

I can't believe her. And I can't believe she has the nerve to be mad at me.

But I'm over it as soon as I hear the doorbell ring because my day is about to get a thousand times better.

"Hey, guys—good morning." I hold the door open for Luce and Finn to come in, but Finn only grunts as he passes by and I think it's because he hasn't quite woken up yet. Which I completely understand. It's barely seven in the morning and all our other lessons have been later in the day.

I've been teaching Luce to swim for almost two weeks now, and Finn has been with her ever since that first day. And I have to admit, I'm kind of glad he's decided to tag along.

"Good morning, Slo! What's my lesson today?" She's all static energy this early in the morning, and she seems to get more excited the more comfortable she gets in the water. We've already mastered the float, both on her stomach and her back. Teaching her to submerge her head underwater was a bit trickier and took over two lessons, but by the end of the second one, she was definitely getting the hang of it. I taught her how to kick using a kickboard during another lesson, and within an hour, she was motoring around the shallow end of the pool. We then moved on to the doggie paddle and the crawl, and earlier this week, she'd done a stellar job at treading water.

"Today we'll be putting everything you've learned together. And maybe your brother and Penn will get in the water with us?" I eye Finn as he leans against the wall with his arms crossed over his chest, dark sunglasses in place. He actually could be asleep for all I know. At least I hope that's what it is. "Yeah . . . maybe he needs some coffee first. I brewed a fresh pot in the kitchen. Help yourself," I say to Finn. "Cream is in the fridge."

With another grunt, he makes his way toward the kitchen.

"My brother's not much of a morning person, sorry." Luce actually does look sorry as we both watch Finn pour a large mug of coffee. I'm honestly a little relieved to know it's not me and that the guy just needs some caffeine to wake up. "I tried to tell him he could stay home today, but he wasn't having it. Don't tell him I told you, but I think he likes being around you."

Her eyes go wide, and she sucks in both of her lips trying to hide her grin, then walks out toward the pool before I get the chance to make her spill more details.

I feel someone staring at me and turn to find Finn standing a few feet away. Instantly, my cheeks jump up on the redness scale as I wonder if he heard what his sister just told me. In hopes he doesn't see my face, I hurry out to the pool, where Luce is waiting.

Finn follows me out from the living room, kicks off his flip-flops, and casually tugs his T-shirt over his head. I try not to stare as he lies down on one of the teak loungers next to the pool, but I can't help it. Even half-asleep, the guy still looks like a magazine ad for suntan lotion.

Slipping into the water with Luce, I go over everything she's learned, then show her how to put it all together. She falters a little at first and occasionally has to stand up and take a deep breath, but soon enough, she's swimming from one side of the shallow end to the other. Finn watches us the entire time, and like before, I constantly find myself sneaking glances his way. He catches me every time, and by the third glance, that eyebrow of his arches up like a cat that wants its back scratched. I have to fight the urge to slap a spray of water in his direction.

I haven't gone over turns yet with Luce, so when she reaches the wall, she stops and grabs the edge, then turns around and swims back to the other side. My brother comes out and shades his eyes with one hand, then gives a thumbs-up when Luce finally swims from one side to the other without standing up.

"Wow, she's doing great!" Penn says. "Hey, Finn, what's up?" He and Finn fist-bump as my brother takes the chair next to his.

"How about you swim out to me now?" I say, treading water in the middle of the pool. She's done most of her work in the shallow end and hasn't really ventured out to the deeper part, but I know she can do it.

She takes a deep breath and kicks off from the end of the pool, swimming toward me. She takes another breath, alternating each side with every third stroke, like I taught her. As she gets closer to me, I back up, until she finally comes to a stop on the far side of the pool. She grabs the edge, snapping off her goggles as she looks around and realizes how far she just swam.

"No *way* . . ."

"Yes way!" I cheer, smiling like an idiot.

"Way to go, Lemon!" Finn shouts, and pumps his fists, and something inside me melts just a little. He and Penn come to the edge of the pool, and Finn holds a hand out for her to give him a high five, then she turns and gives me one, too, and then slaps my brother's outstretched hand.

Since we're all high-fiving, I turn to Finn and hold up my hand—but when he goes to slap it, I grab it instead and yank him into the water. I can't believe he fell for that old trick. Luce squeals loudly as water splashes her way, and when her brother breaks the surface, he spits water in my direction.

"Oh, you did *not* just do that. I really hope you can swim."

Luce squeals again and cheers for me as I take a deep breath and shove off for the other side of the pool, Finn hot on my tail.

He's fast.

But I'm faster.

I reach the shallow end and dart up the stairs and out of the pool, running toward the beach and the open ocean beyond. If I can just get there, he won't have a chance.

"You should've stayed in the water; that's definitely more your element," he says, his voice low and way too close to my ear. An arm curls around my waist as my feet splash into the water, but then I'm lifted up and he's launching me high into the air and toward the oncoming waves.

I curl into a ball and take another deep breath as I plummet down, down, down. When I break the surface, he's right there, his brilliant blue eyes flashing with mischief, daring me to even try to get past him. Like he said, this is my element— he does realize that, right? But then a softness touches his face.

"I can't thank you enough for getting her back in the water." His hands find their way to my waist, supporting me so I no longer need to tread. "You know, you really are good at the whole teaching thing. Guess you're not too bad at the swimming part, either."

Beads of water slide down his nose and drop off as he looks out at the ocean. But even from the side, I can see the smile he thinks he's hiding.

"So, whatever. I'm *amazing* at the swimming part—I beat you back there in the pool, didn't I? And that was *with* this dumb cast, that's all I'm saying." This time there's no hiding the grin that takes over his entire face, and it's a good thing I'm floating out in the ocean because I'm pretty sure my own legs wouldn't be able to hold me up if we were on land. "Hey, we're having some people over tonight if you guys wanna come back later? My mom and stepdad went to Maui for the weekend to celebrate their anniversary, so we've got the house to ourselves. Nothing big, just barbecuing, maybe watch a movie."

"Yeah, sure, I'll be here. But Luce has a slumber party tonight with some friends. The invite still open if I come alone?" He waits, like he actually thinks I'll say no. And then his smile totally catches me off guard, and I can't help but return it with one of my own. "What can I bring?"

Later that afternoon, Penn and I head to the grocery store to pick up enough food to feed half of Waikiki. That's in addition to the mass amounts my mom made sure to pack the fridge and cupboards with before she left, giving us the okay to throw a party.

By the time everyone starts to arrive, we already have the barbecue going with marinated steak and chicken. Shep and my brother carry in a keg and set it out on the patio, where tiki torches are lit and paper lanterns and white twinkle lights zigzag over the pool.

I'm talking to Mia when the doorbell rings. Everyone else simply walked right in, so I have a feeling I know who it is. I open the door to find Finn standing there with a platter of fresh fruit. It was the only thing I could think of for him to bring, even though it had sounded so lame. I can't believe he actually did.

"You made a fruit plate—that's awesome!" I laugh as I take it from his hands since his other arm is loaded full of bags. "Come on in."

"Actually, the kitchen at the hotel made it, I just carried it here." He heads straight to the freezer and unloads several bags of Popsicles and ice cream bars. "I wasn't sure what else to bring, so I went with dessert."

"Believe me, you brought more than enough. Thanks for doing that, by the way."

He follows me out onto the patio, and we stand in line for food as Penn—armed and ready with tongs—starts dishing out the goods from the grill. Once our plates are full, we make our way to find somewhere to sit, but unfortunately, all the chairs around the pool have been taken.

"We can sit out on the beach," I say, motioning toward the sand. His plastic fork is sticking out from his mouth, since his hands are occupied carrying his own plate, plus two cans of soda for the both of us, so he only nods. My own plate is dangerously sagging under the weight of all the food I've piled on, and Finn cautiously eyes how it teeters in my hand.

"Hold up," he says, but it comes out more like "Holeup" as he tries to talk around his fork. He sets his plate down and jabs his fork into the mac salad, then plunks both cans of soda down before turning to take my food. "Your table awaits, Miss McIntyre."

He sweeps his hand toward the beach with a brilliant smile, and for some reason, I stand there like a complete dork as I stare at his mouth.

"Th . . . thank you?"

He clears his throat and those lips of his turn into something more of a smirk. I realize I'm still staring, so I quickly flop down in the sand. He takes his place next to me and hands me my soda, which I trade for his napkin. I have to admit, he makes things easy, or, I guess I should really say, easier. And I think I like that.

When we've finished eating, I snag one of the nearby volleyballs from our yard and roll it toward Mia, then motion toward the net set up on the beach. Oh yeah, we're so playing some volleyball.

"Come on, Finn—let's see if you're at least better at volleyball than you are at swimming."

He kicks sand my way and shakes his head. "You sure talk big for someone your size. Besides, how good can you be with only one arm?"

He may have me there, but I'm not worried in the least. Because once we pick teams, I end up with both Shep and Mia, so not only do I have the height on this side of the net, but Mia also happens to be the captain on her school's volleyball team. I almost feel bad when Finn ends up being paired with my brother and Drew from the activities counter. I have a feeling I practically won't even have to play.

"This almost doesn't seem fair. I mean, you've got a one-armed dwarf on your team." Finn mockingly lays a hand over his heart. My brother scoffs and shakes his head for an entirely different reason.

"Oh, that was the wrong thing to say, Finn. So the wrong thing to say," Mia mutters.

I may be short, but my height has never stopped me before. Even with me down a limb, we win three games to two.

Afterward, Finn and I stroll along the beach, the last traces of the sun streaking across the sky as if it doesn't want to go down without a fight. We sit in the sand, and his knee brushes against mine. I fight to hold back the shiver that tries to break free with every small touch of his skin.

"You know, you're pretty crafty for a midget, right? And who knew you could play with only one arm. I mean you're not even left-handed!"

I stare at him in mock disbelief. "Whatever. It's not my fault you picked the wrong team."

"You aren't serious, right? Like I could've guessed that at your height you can actually spike the ball over the net? I mean, you can walk under the damn thing without ducking, how the hell was I supposed to know you could practically jump over it, too?"

"Guess we don't know a whole lot about each other then, do we?" We grin at one another. "Quick," I say. "Give me your most embarrassing moment, and don't leave out the good stuff. Go!" I shoot him a challenging look, wondering if he'll actually play along.

He surprises me when he does.

"Hmmm. Well, I don't really embarrass that easily, but if I had to pick something—or better yet, some*one* I'm most embarrassed by—I'd have to say my father owns that category completely."

Shit. I was expecting something silly. I quirk my mouth to

the side, which makes him laugh, like he knows he caught me off guard. But that's fine, because I'm not done with him yet.

"Okay, what's your most recent happy memory?"

"That's easy. I'd have to say my sister getting back in the water. Which you know you're responsible for, so thanks for that." The way he says it makes me feel proud. Not only because I had something to do with his most recent happy memory, but also because I know how important Luce is to him. I watch as he scoops up a handful of sand and lets it slide through his fingers, covering one of his feet. "Same two questions right back 'atcha. Go."

"Huh. Maybe I should've thought out these questions a little more." I trace a swirl in the sand that's covering his foot. "Well, aside from puking on you—which is seriously right up there at the top of my all-time list of most embarrassing moments *ever*—I'd probably have to go with these stupid anxiety-driven asthma attacks I sometimes have. And something that's made me happy lately? Well, maybe you should ask me that question again in a month or so."

"Oh, come on, that's a cop-out." He kicks the sand that's sitting on his foot over toward mine. "There's got to be something."

I *really* should've thought about these questions more thoroughly when I asked him to answer them first.

"I think it's kind of obvious I've had a crappy couple of weeks." I hold up my cast as if that's supposed to prove my point. "But if you're fine with me not choosing something super recent, I'd have to say placing second in the fifty free at nationals this past March was pretty awesome."

"Wow, only second in the country? Yeah, you better work on that." He stares back out at the water, a smart-ass smile taking a curve to his lips. "So what are you supposed to do?"

Confused, I stare at him.

"When one of these anxiety-driven asthma attacks strikes. Is it something an inhaler can fix? And how long have you had them?"

I draw small circles in the sand. "I've had them for almost four years. And sometimes my inhaler works; sometimes it doesn't. I've learned to deal with them in other ways."

"Other ways how?"

"Huh, my one thing I'm most embarrassed about and you're making me talk about it? Gee, thanks." I bump him with my shoulder. In all honesty, I can't believe I'm talking about this with him, but he actually sounds genuinely interested, so somehow that makes it okay. "I've learned to focus on something in my mind, an image that I have to build up from scratch. I layer in piece by piece until the picture is whole again, and usually by then, I've managed to get my breathing back under control—at least, it works most of the time. An inhaler is still a good thing to have on hand, so I don't usually travel too far without one."

"See? This is useful information to have and I feel like I know you better already. You puke on random strangers, you can spike a volleyball over a six-foot net, you swim like you have a 350-horsepower engine strapped to your ass, and . . . well, you're a little cuckoo. Awesome." I make a face, and he bursts out laughing, not hiding from me this time.

"Funny much? I'm so glad I can keep you entertained."

"More than you know, Sloane. More than you know." He laughs again, then nudges me with his shoulder. "Quick, without explaining why, if you had to choose, would you rather lose an arm or a leg? Go."

"Seriously? An arm or a leg? Crap, I don't know . . . I guess my left arm, but only because—"

"Uh-uh, I said without explaining why."

"Fine. Okay, hotshot, would you rather lose your sight or your hearing, without explanation. Go."

"Neither." He stares at my face for a second, then belts out in laughter. "You never said I had to choose."

Damn, he's good.

Eleven

Date: Tues, 25 June 14:31:02

Subject:

From:T_Hudson69@copemail.com

To: SKMcIntyre@copemail.com

So your brother posted some pictures of you and some guy on Instagram yesterday.

Sloane, you're killing me.

I know I'm the last person on the planet you want to talk to, you've made that clear. But I'm asking you to remember the past twelve years we've known each other and the last year we've been together. Please don't do this.

I don't know if there's anything I can ever do to tell you how sorry I am, but if you tell me what it is, I promise I'll do whatever it takes. But don't ask me to leave you alone.

I can't promise I'll stop texting. Or calling. Or e-mailing.

Because I can't. Even if all you do is delete every single one of them or never answer my calls.

I miss you so much, it hurts.

Please, just let me try again.

—T.

I stare at Tyler's words. Reread each one a hundred times. Then read them over again. Like that will change anything.

But it's Finn, not Tyler, that I've been thinking about lately. The one I *want* to think about. But then I get an e-mail like this and I can't help it. A small part of my brain keeps going back to Tyler. Because after more than ten years of knowing each other, we have a history together.

I close my eyes and remember him walking into my room the morning I was leaving for swim nationals. Flowers in one hand and a sweatshirt draped over his shoulder, he wore a silly grin as I fidgeted with the bag I was packing.

"I have no idea why you're nervous—you've got this," he'd said. When I bit my lip to stop it from trembling, he only pulled me into his arms, resting his chin on top of my head. "I'm not joking, Sloane, this is what you do. And I don't know anyone better. But just in case, I brought you my lucky sweatshirt."

It was the sweatshirt he'd worn both years the football team went to state. He'd never let anyone else touch that sweatshirt, and I don't think it had ever been washed. When he'd pulled it from his shoulder and wrapped it around both of mine, it smelled *just* like him, and I'd inhaled deeply. And just like that, I'd felt a calmness overwhelm me that hadn't been there before.

I can still smell him as I open my eyes and see that I'm back in my room in Hawaii. My hands are balled into fists, and I'm shaking. I don't want Tyler to have this kind of control over me, especially when something so great is happening with Finn.

As if to make it all worse, a new text comes in from Mick, like they've somehow agreed to tag-team me:

> Seriously, this you not talking to me crap is getting old.

Without even thinking, I hit reply:

> Maybe you should've thought about that before you screwed my boyfriend. Before you screwed our friendship.

But I don't hit send.

Because that's exactly what she wants.

God, I'm so sick of all this. I'm so sick of them. My focus should be on what's in front of me now, not what I left behind. Even though I have no idea what's going on between us, Finn has had a lot to do with my summer turning out better than expected. It's been an amazing couple of weeks. Not to mention, the idea of something new is exciting. And I haven't felt that way in a long time.

As if he's somehow heard my thoughts, I get a text from him—it's a funny GIF of someone getting shoved unexpectedly into a pool.

> Can't put my finger on why, but thought this looked familiar.

> Ha ha . . . good morning to u 2.

I send him a GIF of one of my favorite late-night entertainers giving the camera the bird. He replies:

> Aahhh, u shouldn't have.

My phone beeps again, but this time it's from Mia:

> Day off. Pick u up in 1hr. Good? And bonfire 2-night @ 6pm. But no marshmallows for u! :P

Her text makes me laugh. Out loud. And that's when I realize that these are the type of people I need in my life. Finn and Mia make me happy. They make me smile. When I first got here, I said I wouldn't waste any more time on Tyler or Mick or what happened in the past. Yet somehow I keep letting them creep back in.

But not anymore. Because now I know I really need to keep that promise to myself. No more texts, no more e-mails, no more letters. No more nothing. All they do is bring me down and make me think—about them, about us, about everything. And I'm sick of it.

Instead, I reply back to Mia that I'll be ready in forty minutes and head for the shower.

"I love the dress!" Mia takes my hand and spins me around. "Damn, woman, you look hot today! Keep dressing like that, and you won't be single for long."

She kisses my cheek, then grabs my hand and pulls me to her car.

"Speaking of single," she continues. "Or maybe not . . . Shep mentioned you and Finn have been hanging out? So spill it, sister."

"Not a lot to spill. I've been giving Luce swim lessons, so he's been coming over with her. And we may have grabbed dinner a few times. I swear, he knows all the great restaurants, from pizza to the most ono poke." I wiggle my eyebrows, but hold up my hands when her mouth drops open. "It's not that big a deal, just getting to know each other better, I promise."

"But you do want to get to *know* him better, right?" She pushes her tongue into the inside of her cheek, and I laugh.

"Yeah, I think I do. Guess we'll just have to wait and see what happens." I lay my head back against the headrest and close my eyes to the sun. I wish it could be like this always. "So where are we headed anyway?"

"Oh, I thought we could go to Waikiki and people-watch today. Sound good?"

It's one of our favorite pastimes. We bypass our local beach and instead go down to Waikiki to watch all the tourists. On any given day, you never know what you'll see.

"That, my friend, sounds like a plan. We can park at the Echelon and cut through to the beach." I take my employee badge out from my bag and wave it her way.

"Ooohh, free parking, sweet!" Mia nods her head in approval. "And isn't Penn working today? Maybe we can swing by and say hi."

When we get to the pool at the Echelon, Penn is standing in the shallow end, giving a pair of blondes a few pointers on how to swim. They look to be about nineteen, not that my brother cares. Nor do I believe either girl has any interest in learning how to swim.

"Hey, P.," I say, crouching down near the edge of the pool. A current of wind picks up, and I have to grab at my hat to keep it from flying away.

He smiles, but then he sees Mia, and a cocky grin takes over. "S'up, Mia?"

Rolling her eyes, she walks away toward Logan's guard stand. Penn's smile falters slightly, but a second later, any trace of that hesitation is gone. He makes his way to the edge in front of me.

"Mornin'. You look happy today. Could it be because of a certain someone?"

He tilts his head ever so slightly to something over my

shoulder, and somehow I know who I'm going to see when I glance behind me. Sure enough, Finn is stretched out on a deck chair, reading a book.

"Maybe. Maybe not," I say casually. At least I hope that's how it sounds. "Oh, there's a bonfire tonight at our beach, six P.M. I'll hitch a ride with Mia, but I'll see you there?"

He starts to drift backward and lifts both arms, placing them around the waiting necks of the girls behind him. "Wouldn't miss it for the world, sis," he says with a wink.

Shaking my head, I stand and turn toward Finn. Even though he's wearing dark sunglasses, I can feel him staring at me. I stroll over, still holding on to my hat as it wobbles in the breeze.

"*The Outsiders*, one of my favorites."

He doesn't even try to hide that he'd actually stopped reading to watch me.

"Mine too." The paperback is tattered and bent from probably years of rereads, so I don't doubt that at all.

"Hey, bonfire tonight at the usual spot. Think you can make it?"

"I'll be there." He nods a hello at Mia, who's made herself busy talking to Logan, but then his face falls. "Fuck. What the hell is he doing back so soon?"

He stands up next to me, and I see an older man in a perfectly tailored suit, walking our way. Aside from the fact it's eighty-five degrees outside, even if he wasn't wearing a suit, I still don't think he'd look like he belonged out here. And then I see his eyes. They're this intense shade of blue that leave no doubt who he is.

"Phineas." It's said curtly.

"Father," Finn says in return, shaking his hand. What kind of father shakes hands with his own son? At the pool? "I'd like for you to meet Sloane McIntyre. Sloane, this is my father, Kent McAllister."

I go to stick my hand out, but then retract it quickly. Damn cast.

"Sorry, swimming accident, shark got me." Oh my God, did I really just say that? "But it's nice to meet you, sir."

For some reason, "Mr. McAllister" doesn't sound formal enough, and there's absolutely no way I'd have the balls to call him Kent. And he makes me want to babble, obviously.

"Miss McIntyre." He nods in my direction, but says nothing more. "Phineas, I'd appreciate you answering your phone when I call so I don't have to come out here to find you. I've had dinner reservations made for the family tonight. Eight P.M., don't be late. And please," he says as he eyes Finn from head to toe as if the mere sight of his own son embarrasses him, "put on a real suit. It was nice to meet you, Miss McIntyre."

Before Finn can agree to dinner or even say anything, for that matter, his father turns and strides away.

"Asshole." He mutters it under his breath, and I find that I have to agree. "Sorry, Sloane, looks like I'll need to take a rain check on the bonfire."

"Hey, no worries. Some other time, okay?" I want to stay and talk to him, but I see Mia patiently waiting for me.

"Yeah, some other time for sure," he says.

I hesitate for a second too long.

"Are you sure you're okay?"

"I promise, I'm good." But he doesn't sound convincing. "Believe me, it's nothing new."

Mia and I make our way down to the sand, weaving in and out between sunburned arms and legs. The beach is packed, but somehow Mia has convinced Logan to let us use one of the private beachside cabanas for the hotel. He's even laid out our towels, securing them to the chairs so they won't blow away.

I feel bad that I didn't try to talk to Finn more. It sucks that this is something he's used to, and I can't imagine that being my family.

"What was that all about?" Mia shades her eyes with one hand and stares at me. "Who was the suit?" She takes a sip from some tropical-looking drink that came complete with a little fake umbrella.

"The suit was Mr. McAllister. Looks like Finn won't be able to make it tonight after all."

"Wow, meeting the parentals already?" Shaking my head, I throw my little umbrella at her. "Seriously, though. How're you doing? Really?"

I pick up my drink with a sigh. "Actually, I'm sick and tired of Mick and Tyler. All their e-mails and texts, telling me how *they're* feeling. So this morning I decided I'm not going to waste any more time on them—that's it, I'm done." I stab my straw into my glass as if to prove my point. "But the worst thing? I have no idea how I'm gonna go home at the end of the summer. I honestly don't think I could ever look at either of them again."

"Slo, you know you can always stay here. Transfer to Punahou with me. Other than your dad, there's really nothing for you to go back to."

It's definitely something I've thought about. But I'm not sure if I can leave my dad, or Penn for that matter.

"Slo, you leave your mom at the end of every summer, what's the difference?" It's like Mia can read my mind. "Tyler will forever be the high school sweetheart you think about, even thirty years from now. And for him, you'll always be the one that got away. But don't let what he and Mick did control any more of your future than that. You deserve to be happy, and none of what happened is your fault. None of it."

I lean back against my chair with a sigh. I wish it were that easy.

We spend the rest of the afternoon in the sunshine, watching all the tourists on the beach. By the time we head to the bonfire, the sun is already making its way to the other side of the world to start a new day. The party is in full swing, the fire raging.

"Slo! What's up, sucka!" Shep picks me up and swings me

around before planting a big kiss on Mia and slapping her ass. "Woman, where you been?"

I grab two bottles from the cooler and hand one to Mia, then make my way over to Maile and Stacey to say hello. Drew is also here, and I wave as he spirals the football long down the beach.

Sometime later, my brother shows up with the two girls from the pool. Oh my God, my brother. He's wearing the two of them draped over each of his arms like they're the latest fashion accessory. I shake my head, but laugh, because I'm really happy he's having a good time. I think the Hawaiian air is doing something to the both of us.

I do wish Finn were here, though. It seems silly, but something is missing without him.

Of course it's at that exact moment I get another text from Tyler:

Love you.

I wish there were a way my phone wouldn't show a preview of the text on my screen. At least if it only said who it was from, I could delete it without having to see any words. Words like "Love you."

"Hey, everything okay?" Mia asks as she rests a hand on my arm.

I shake my head and hold my phone out for her to see.

"I know you don't want to hear this, but that boy does love

you." She wraps one arm around my shoulder and squeezes. "And unfortunately that means I don't think he'll stop until you acknowledge him. Why don't you just tell him to quit texting you? Tell him you'll talk to him when you're ready?"

"I just . . . I just don't want to talk to him at all. But I can't find it in me to block his number, either."

I delete his message, then tuck my phone in my pocket, but it's completely ruined my mood. I hang out for a couple more hours, but the alcohol seems to be having a downer effect and I know I'm moping.

"Sorry, Mia, would you mind if I headed home?"

She hugs me again. "No prob. I'll go grab my keys."

"No, no, stay here. It's a short walk." She opens her mouth, but I raise my hand to stop her from arguing. "I promise, Mia, I'll be fine. There's no need for you to drive me home when I'm literally right down the beach. And besides, I think I could use the walk."

She looks at me carefully as if deciding whether or not she should let me go alone, then simply kisses my forehead.

"Text me when you get home, then, okay? I love you, Slo."

She squeezes me once more, then lets go.

The house is dark when I finally get there. Mom and Bob are still gone for the weekend and won't be home until tomorrow night. I shoot Mia a text to let her know I got home safely and walk around the house to turn on a few lights.

After pulling on my pj's, I throw the doors from my bedroom to the back patio wide open. A soft breeze finds its way in and ruffles the sheer drapes that hang from the posters of my canopy. The waves outside drum against the shore as I climb into bed, soothing me to sleep.

I wake up to the doorbell ringing and someone knocking loudly. My clock says it's almost midnight. I kick off my blankets and grab my robe, cursing Penn for locking himself out. I'm sure he's just too drunk to remember where he put his keys.

"Hey, Sloane, you there?"

It's not Penn . . . it's Finn.

"Hang on, I'm coming." I rub at my eyes as he knocks loudly again. "I'm coming!"

He's propped up against the door, but almost falls in when I open it. I can smell the alcohol on his breath as he tries to straighten himself back up. He's wearing a suit, the collar of his shirt unbuttoned; his tie hangs loosely around his neck. I can't believe I'm thinking this, but he looks really, really hot.

"Hey . . . you weren't sleeping, were you? Because I didn't mean to wake you if you were. Sleeping, that is."

"Finn, are you drunk?"

"Hmmm?" He wobbles slightly, then grabs the suspenders he's wearing, stretches them out, and lets them snap back against his chest. "Maybe just a little." Motioning with his thumb and pointer finger, he denotes a small amount of space between, as if this clearly signifies the little bit drunk he is. He eyes what I'm wearing. Or better yet, what little I'm wearing. Reaching out and tucking a strand of hair behind my ear, he looks away, then looks back. "Do you know how absolutely beautiful you are? The first moment I laid eyes on you, that's exactly what I thought, *God, she's hot.*" He taps my nose in time with what he's just said. "That, and the fact I was glad I wasn't the guy that put your hand in that cast."

Wait. Did he just call me hot? I wonder if he realizes exactly what it is he's saying. Or better yet, if he'll actually remember he said it in the morning. But then I remember he's drunk and somehow still made his way over here.

"Finn, how'd you get here if you've been drinking?" I scan the driveway behind him, and my eyes settle on his motorcycle. "What were you thinking? You could've killed someone . . . or yourself for that matter!"

"I dunno . . . dinner . . . my asshole dad. Guess it just happened." He mumbles something else about his father, and even though I don't hear it, I get the gist. It's evident the situation with his dad is much bigger than I thought.

"Get in here. You're not driving home now." I open the door further, but instead of coming inside, he actually leans down and tries to kiss me. Like full-on kiss me on the mouth.

For a second, I'm torn between wanting this moment to happen, and not wanting it like this. Then I catch the smell of alcohol, and it snaps me back into focus. I turn just in time, and he gets my cheek instead.

"Uh, I don't *think* so." I press my hands against his chest and motion to my bathroom. "Why don't you go get yourself cleaned up? I'll be right there."

He stumbles to the bathroom, and I head to the kitchen. Filling a glass with water, I drop in two Alka-Seltzer tablets and walk back to my room. I can't believe he actually tried to kiss me.

I find him slouched against the side of my bed, rubbing his head. I hold out the glass for him to take.

"Sloane, I'm sorry, don't be mad. I had to see you." He reaches out and takes the glass. "My dad was forty minutes late, then had the balls to tell me I needed to start being more responsible. That I need to take better care of Luce and stop thinking of only myself." He barks out a hard, bitter laugh. "Only myself, right." He downs the water and sets the glass on my nightstand.

"I know it was stupid for me to ride over here after drinking, but I had to see you," he repeats. "Besides, I can't go home yet with him there. I don't care if I ever see his fucking face ever again." He closes his eyes. "Honestly, Sloane, I hate him. More than anything in the world. And the sad thing is, he knows it, too." His laugh is harsh, clipped. "But he doesn't even care."

My heart aches for him. My family may have splintered apart years ago, but at least I knew they always loved me no matter what. Clearly that isn't the case for Finn.

He falls back on my bed, defeated, still holding his head.

"You can hang out here for a while, and then I'll drive you home." When he doesn't respond, I give his knee a shake. "Finn? Seriously, did you really just fall asleep?"

As if to confirm that's exactly what's happened, a soft snore escapes from his lips.

"Well, that's awesome."

I untie his shoes and slide them off, then swing his legs up onto my bed. And he doesn't even stir.

Grabbing an extra blanket, I curl up on my couch a few feet away. I can't imagine growing up with a father like his. One who acts as if his children are merely a second thought. Or worse, a nuisance.

And then I realize that while Finn has his crappy father, I have my crappy exes.

And somehow I don't think either of us deserves any of them.

Twelve

Sweaty clumps of hair are plastered to my forehead, and my feet are twisted up in a blanket. And for some reason, I'm sleeping on my couch.

But then I remember what happened and look over at my bed.

Where Finn is fast asleep. Without his shirt on.

I can't believe he tried to kiss me last night, although I'm pretty sure he won't remember that.

I make my way to the bathroom, then head out to the kitchen to put on some coffee—but find that a pot has already been made. Penn is sitting on a barstool, reading the paper. He barely looks up when he sees me come in.

"Uhn." It's all he manages before taking a sip from his mug.

"Well, good morning to you, too, sunshine. A little too much to drink last night?" I grab a mug and fill it up. It smells extra dark today. Which confirms Penn is nursing a hangover of epic proportions.

"Please, can you not talk so loud?" He cringes and takes another sip. "And, Slo, no judgment on what you're about to see in the next few minutes, okay?"

Oh, good God, my brother brought home those two girls from yesterday.

"I guess only if you promise not to judge, too?"

Penn wrinkles his forehead. "Huh?"

But before I can explain, Finn walks into the kitchen, still not wearing a shirt.

Penn looks between Finn and me. "No way."

"Uh-uh, no judging, right?" I stop him before he can say or ask anything and walk to the fridge to get cream for my coffee. It's what I see when I start to close the door that makes me drop it, splattering cream all over the floor.

Because it's not two girls standing there in my kitchen. It's Mia.

But that's not the problem.

The problem is she's wearing the work polo my brother was wearing yesterday, over her shorts. And her hair is sticking up at all angles, like it's trying to get her better cell phone reception.

"Morning, Slo. Hey, Finn," she says, biting on the edge of her thumb.

"Morning." Finn nods at both of them. "Nice one, dude,"

he says quietly to Penn, knocking fists with him as he passes. He takes an empty mug from the cupboard and fills it with coffee.

For some reason, I seem to be the only one fazed that Mia is even here. I stoop to clean up the mess on the floor as Mia drops down next to me with paper towels to help.

"I've got it," I snap, wiping up the last of it.

I have no idea what's going on, but I have a solid guess at what happened last night. My brother and Mia? When did that become a thing? And what about Shep?

I stare at Mia. She bites her lip but won't look me in the eye—and that's a look I know all too well. I turn and glare at my brother, but he already has one hand raised and is shaking his head. "I thought we agreed to no judging, right?"

I snort out loud. "Oh, I somehow think we're past that." I turn back to Mia. "Just tell me something: Does Shep know where you slept last night? Or better yet, who you slept with?" Her face falls. I know it was a low blow, but I can't help it. "Oh, that's right. Neither of you would have *any* idea how it feels to be on the other side of whatever this is." I motion back and forth between the two of them, and I don't miss the concerned look Finn gives me.

"God, you guys both make me sick." I leave them standing there and storm back to my room. I can't believe they'd do this, especially to Shep.

Standing in front of the open doors that lead out to the

patio, I watch the ocean do its thing. I take a deep breath of the salty air and close my eyes. I feel Finn standing next to me a moment later.

"You okay? You wanna talk about it?"

"Thanks, but not really."

"Then how about we get out of here? Come with me today." He doesn't elaborate, so I face him.

"Come with you where?"

"No questions. Just put on a swimsuit and running shoes. Oh, and you'll need a towel."

"You had me at swimsuit," I say. "I'm so in."

We take his bike back to the hotel, where he asks me to wait for him in the lobby, in case his father is still upstairs. He's on his phone as he walks toward the elevator, but then returns fifteen minutes later, dressed in swim trunks, a T-shirt, and running shoes of his own. A backpack is slung over his shoulder; a small cooler hangs from one hand.

I head toward his bike, but he steers me instead in the opposite direction to a monster of a Jeep that's been pulled to the front steps by the valet. Roof panels removed, the thing is all black and ready for mud, with thick treaded tires. And if I thought getting up on the back of his bike was hard, there's a solid chance I'll need a stepladder to get into this sucker.

I attempt to climb in on my own, but unless I can get a running start, I'm going to need some help. "You know, they make these things called running boards, right?"

"Running boards are for wusses," Finn says, laughing. He picks me up and awkwardly plunks me on the front seat, as I barely avoid hitting my head against one of the roof cross bars. Shoving our stuff in the back, he hops in next to me.

"Show-off," I mutter.

"Not even close." He puts the car into gear and we pull out from the hotel, but I have no idea where we're going.

Heading up the Pali Highway, there are so many left and right turns, I lose track of where we are. At some point, we're no longer on paved road, and he switches the Jeep into four-wheel drive. We bump along over rough terrain as low-hanging palms whip the top of the car.

The long drive gives me time to think, even if that's not what I wanted. I can't believe my brother and Mia. And I wonder if Shep has any idea what's going on, or if maybe I should let him know. Thinking back to that moment with Mick in the park, I wonder if I would've wanted a heads-up. If I would've wanted someone to tell me. And I realize the answer to that is no. Because that would've been too easy for both Mick and Tyler, and they didn't deserve easy. Neither do my brother or Mia.

Pulling into a clearing, Finn cuts the engine. He looks at me, then my door, with that raised eyebrow of his.

"*Please*, I've got this." I slide out from the seat and drop to the ground.

I grab my backpack and Finn grabs his—along with the cooler from the back—then he picks up my hand. I love how he does this so easily now. Almost like it's a given.

"So where are we headed anyway?"

"You'll see. It's not far, just a little up ahead."

We hike over hard, uneven ruts in the dried-up mud and through tangles of palm fronds that Finn holds out of my way. But then everything opens up, and the sun is shining down. And it's beautiful.

The forest is this lush green quilt I want to curl around my shoulders, and the rays of sunlight slice through the branches, casting everything in a golden haze. A million birds I can't see twitter in stereo all around us, and there are tropical flowers growing everywhere I look—the same kind people pay loads of money to buy, only to be unappreciated in a vase sitting on some dusty shelf in their homes. Here they look wild, free. The way they're supposed to be.

Pulling a blanket from his bag, Finn spreads it over the ground. Stepping on each heel, he slides out from his shoes, then strips off his shirt in one easy motion. His hard, muscled chest is like a magnet for my eyes, not to mention his abs, and down farther, where his hip bones dip in and disappear beneath his shorts. And of course, there's that damn tattoo.

"You let me know when you're done. No, no, take your time, I insist." He smirks at me with his hands on his hips.

I feel the immediate rush of heat to my face as I bite my lip, then look away. "Does it mean anything? Your tattoo?"

"No, but I designed it myself and thought it looked cool. Ever think of getting one?"

"Not until I saw yours. Now it's definitely something

I'm thinking about, just not sure what I'd get." Stepping out from my shoes, my shirt goes next, and my shorts follow. "Although I'm not exactly a huge fan of needles, so there's that. Probably a good chance I'd have to be drugged or dead to actually go through with it."

Laughing, he takes my hand in his. "It's not really *that* bad, I promise. If you decide it's something you want, let me know." He points out a dirt path that snakes away from where we're standing. "Do you trust me?" I stare at him sideways, unsure of why he's asking. But for some reason I feel okay saying yes. "Then close your eyes."

I hesitate, but only for a second, then do as he asks. He leads me forward and I stumble once, but he steadies me.

And then I hear it. The unmistakable sound of loud rushing water.

"Open your eyes."

I slowly open them. We're standing at the top of a cliff, where the water falls, plummeting over the edge some sixty feet below to a pool that's deep blue in color. My breath catches in my throat as I take it all in, from the roar of the water, to the rainbow that floats along the mist where the falls crash below. In all the years I've been coming to Hawaii, I've never seen anything more beautiful.

"How did you find this place? It's . . . it's gorgeous."

"I found it while hiking a few months ago. Sometimes I like to get lost, see what I stumble across . . . and, well, I found this."

I stare out at the water as it cascades over the lip and falls down to the lake below. And then I realize why he asked if I trusted him. It wasn't because he wanted me to close my eyes; it's because of what's in front of us. Or better yet, what's *not* in front of us.

"Oh, hell no. That's way too far!" I'm shaking my head and backing away from the edge, but he grabs my hand again and leans in close.

"Come on, Sloane—live a little," he breathes into my ear.

I don't know how he knows that's the right thing to say, but everything that's happened over the past month hits me hard. He's right. I so need to live a little.

I can tell the exact moment he understands I've changed my mind, because the biggest grin takes over his face. We step up to the edge.

"On three. Ready?"

Closing my eyes, I take a deep breath as he squeezes my hand in time to his counting. I open my eyes on the third and final squeeze.

And then we jump.

I scream the entire way down, but he never lets go of my hand. I cross my feet at the ankles just before we hit the water, and we're plunged deep, deep, deep into darkness. Bubbles and swirling water surround me, but the force of hitting the water has knocked our hands apart and Finn isn't there. I kick, following the bubbles to the surface. A second later, Finn rises up next to me, still smiling.

"Holy shit, I can't believe we jumped!" I've never done anything so crazy in my entire life.

My adrenaline is pumping something fierce, my heartbeat so frantic to keep up it stutters against the inside of my chest. And then Finn does something equally crazy. He leans in and kisses me as the spray from the falls kicks up around us. He pulls me close, and this kiss is nothing like the sloppy attempt last night. The moment is so big, from the waterfall to the jumping to my crazy heart that's beating a mile a minute.

He trails soft kisses along the edge of my mouth, then makes his way along my chin, and finds his way to just below my ear. A wicked shiver courses down my spine as he pulls me in closer.

"Let's do it again," he whispers, and I nod like an idiot.

We jump a couple more times, and I never stop screaming all the way down. I'm exhausted by the time we hike up the path after the third time and tumble toward the blanket in a heap. Finn collapses next to me, and we both start to laugh.

He makes me feel free. He makes me feel alive in a way I've never felt before.

The cooler contains a lunch of fresh fruit and cheeses and different types of salamis. I'm sure the kitchen at the hotel packed it for him, but still. I'm starving, and everything looks so good. When we're finished, we lie back and stare up at the sky, his arm behind my head.

"Seriously, one of the best days ever," I say, closing my eyes.

"I couldn't agree more."

I wake up to my cell phone singing out Penn's jingle. The sun has dramatically shifted in the sky, and my skin is a much darker color than it was that morning.

"What?" I snap.

Our connection is spotty, and he's hard to hear. Not like it matters, because I'm still pissed at him.

"Slo, I can barely hear you, where are you? I've been calling for the last hour." There's a tinge of concern in his voice.

"What's the big deal? We fell asleep. What do you want?" I know I'm being short, but I don't really care. Static crackles loudly in the background. "Hello? Can you hear me?"

"I think you need to come home," he says.

I cut him off to ask what it is, but he reassures me that everything's fine . . . I just need to come home.

"Sis, listen . . ." but I don't hear anything more, because the call disconnects.

"Penn? Are you there?" All I get in return is dead air and zero bars of service. I glare at my phone like it can somehow finish Penn's conversation for him and notice there's a missed text from Mick. Sticking to my earlier promise, I toss my phone in my bag without reading it.

"Everything okay?" Finn asks. I explain the cryptic

conversation with my brother. "Hey, no worries. If we have to go, then we have to go."

We pack up the Jeep and head out. I'm trying not to let the tone of Penn's voice put a damper on how fantastic this day turned out with Finn. So we crank up the music and sing along when we know the words. When a song comes on that I don't know, I show Finn the old trick of mouthing the word "watermelon," which just makes it *look* like I know all the words. I even throw in some rad dance moves, swaying my head and shoulders and snapping my fingers in tune to a song I've never even heard.

He laughs so hard he goes into silent laugh mode as he clutches his side. Tears of laughter streak down his cheeks, and he actually has to pull over to the side of the road, we're both laughing so hard. It doesn't stop even after we finally turn into my driveway, nor when I jump down from the Jeep, or as we make our way up the path to the front door.

But that's when I stop laughing.

Because Tyler is sitting on the front step.

Thirteen

I instantly go rigid as Finn squeezes my hand, but I'm grateful he doesn't let go. Tyler is sitting there in shorts and flip-flops, like he owns the place. Like nothing's happened between the two of us. Like he didn't cut out my heart with the dull end of a spoon and grind it into itsy, tiny, un-heart-shaped pieces.

When his eyes connect with mine, the bouquet of flowers he's holding sadly droops from one hand. But he still has the audacity to look at Finn like *he's* the one that shouldn't be here.

"*No.* You don't get to do that." It falls out of my mouth before I even realize I've opened it to say something. I almost don't recognize my own voice. And I can't believe what just the sight of him has done to me. "I have absolutely *nothing* to say to you. In fact, I'd like you to leave." I march past Tyler into the house, glaring at my brother. I can't believe him. I can't believe he didn't warn me. "What the hell, Penn?"

I don't wait for him to answer. I don't give him the chance.

Finn follows me into my bedroom and shuts the door behind us. I lean against the edge of my bed, my face in my hands.

I am not going to cry. That asshole doesn't deserve another damn tear to be dropped in his honor. And I realize what I really want to do is scream. Or hit something really hard. But I already know what good that did me the last time.

God, I thought I was doing so well. I thought I was in control—ignoring him and all his texts and e-mails and phone calls. But one look at him sitting there on the front step with those stupid flowers, and everything from three weeks ago comes rushing back. Like it never actually left.

I sag down the side of the bed and slump to the floor. Pulling my knees to my chest, I hug them close. And I do exactly what I didn't want to do, especially in front of Finn.

He's at my side in seconds, sitting next to me on the floor. He doesn't lie and tell me everything's going to be okay. He doesn't fill the space with useless words, words that I don't want to hear right now anyway. But what I love the most is that he doesn't ask if that's "the guy," because I'm pretty sure how I've reacted has made it clear who it is.

"Tell me what I can do. You want me to kick him out? Done. Want me to kick his ass? *Gladly.* Whatever you need, Sloane—just tell me."

A half laugh, half sob escapes from my lips. "I'm s-sorry," I stutter, trying to get my breathing under control. Oh God, please don't let me have one of my panic attacks right now. *Please.* "I think I just need a minute."

"Whatever you need, it's okay." He wraps an arm around my shoulder as I take in one, two, three more deep breaths.

We sit like that for a moment longer before I really feel like I have things under control.

"I'm pretty sure he's not leaving . . . at least not anytime soon." I rub my forehead, pressing my fingertips against my eyelids. "Dammit. If I'd only responded to *one* of his stupid texts, he wouldn't be here."

"You couldn't have possibly known he'd come all the way down here. I mean, who does that?" The muscles in Finn's jaw flex, a telltale sign he's not happy about any of this. But he's handling it better than I would've had the situation been reversed.

"Evidently he does." I wipe at my eyes with the neck of my T-shirt. "But the sooner I get this over with, the better for everyone."

Finn turns to look at me and nods, then stands and holds a hand out to help me up. "I know you gotta do what you gotta do. And the offer still stands to kick his ass—just say the word." He hugs me tight and kisses the top of my head. "But please call me later . . . let me know you're okay, okay?"

"I will." I hug him back before letting go. "Thanks for everything, really."

I walk out with Finn and see Tyler and my brother standing in the living room. Finn doesn't even look at Tyler as we head to the front door.

"That's right, douche bag, leave. You don't even belong here," Tyler mutters.

Finn stops, his hands flexing into fists at his side as he freezes in place. He slowly turns, and both Tyler and Penn unconsciously take a step back.

"Jesus, you're even stupider than you look." He clenches his fists again, and I'm surprised when Tyler actually takes another step back. "But I swear to God, if you do anything . . . and I mean *anything* to hurt her again, I promise you your nose won't be the only thing needing surgery."

And with that, he's gone.

I take one look at Tyler and point to the pool. "Outside. Now. Before I change my mind." I leave him standing there.

He follows me out to the lanai, but stands a few feet away with his hands up, like he's trying to coax a cornered animal.

"Slo, please, I know you're mad. But I had to see you."

An almost manic laugh escapes my lips. "Mad? You think *this* is mad? You don't even know the half of it!" I cross my arms over my chest and turn away from him. "What the hell are you even doing here? You had no right to come down."

"But you wouldn't answer any of my calls or my e-mails or my texts. I didn't know what else to do."

He comes and stands by my side, and I can feel him staring at me, but I don't look at him. I can't. Instead I watch the waves as they crash into the shore, then pull back out and ready themselves to do it all over again.

"I can't breathe without you, Sloane. It's so hard to breathe." He presses a hand against his chest, and I know *exactly* how he feels.

But that crazy laugh slips out again before I can stop it. "God, Tyler—this isn't about *you* anymore."

"Why? Is it because of him? Are you in love with him now?"

"Oh, hell no—you don't get to go there!" I shake my head in disgust. "You're the one who fucked my best friend. Twice. *And* got her pregnant!" I turn and take a step toward him. "Game over, Tyler. You lose." As if to make my point, I shove him in the chest with my bad hand.

I give him credit when he doesn't move. He doesn't even flinch. Instead he stares down at my cast and drops his head, like he's finally seeing the impact of what happened between us back at home. Only when he closes his eyes do I see the same thing. Traces of a greenish-purple bruise run along his nose. A bruise that I gave him. There's also a raw scar that's on the road to healing; it must be from the surgery.

At first, it feels so good to finally tell him exactly what I've been holding back. To say everything I've been wanting to say. But then he looks at me and his eyes are brimming with tears. And as soon as one falls, it alerts the rest of them it's time to go.

I've never seen Tyler cry. Not once. But somehow I know this emotion is real, that he's not faking it. He's not doing this just to win a sympathy vote from me. And even though

I try to fight it, try to stop them from coming, my own tears decide his shouldn't be alone.

He holds out his hand. But I can't take it. I can't touch him—not after he's touched her. I turn back to stare out at the ocean and swipe at my face. He's near enough I can hear him breathe, and for reasons I can't explain, my insides vibrate with how close he stands, like we're magnetically bound to each other. I can even smell his familiar scent I've known for so long, and this time, it's real—not just a memory—and it makes me shiver.

"Sloane, I'm so, so, sorry," he whispers.

God how I hate that I feel everything in this moment. Maybe if I'd had a few more weeks, more time away from him, away from everything, I'd be able to just turn it all off. But I can't help it. I can't help any of it and him being here is so fucking hard, because I know that the way I feel about him is not something I can just hit the delete key on to make go away. No matter how much I want to.

And even though I thought I'd said everything, thought I'd gotten it all out of my system, I wasn't even close. Not nearly even close. Because without warning, my entire being breaks apart at the seams, and there's nothing left inside to hold me up. To hold me together.

I suddenly can't breathe. My lungs are so tight, they hold on to the last little bit of air they took in and stay that way, as whatever is left slowly leaks out. I squeeze my eyes closed, picturing the empty pool in my head.

I can hear Tyler saying something into my ear, something about focusing. He knows what my little trick is—of course he does—but he can't help me. Because this time the image is all wrong. It's broken when it should be whole. And that's never happened before.

I'm gasping for air, and my head feels so light I know I'm close to passing out. I no longer have any idea where Tyler is, but then he's right next to me, pressing something into my hand. I feel the familiar plastic of my inhaler and without even thinking I pump two quick puffs in my mouth and breathe deeply for what feels like the first time in minutes. I close my eyes again and focus on each breath, and my pool returns just like it should.

But then I open my eyes. And I see Tyler right there, right in front of me.

I'm so overwhelmed that he had the power to do this to me—that he had me and he had a choice, and he chose wrong.

"Why did you do it?" I whisper. "Why did you choose her and not me?" Because I know that's what hurts the most. That's really what has made the biggest hole in my being.

He grabs fistfuls of his hair, pulling so hard, his hands shake. "God, Sloane, because I fucked up! Because I wasn't thinking. And because . . . because she said she was in love with me."

And there it is.

His words slap me in the face with the force of a wicked backhand.

"Oh my God . . . oh my God."

Seconds, minutes, hours—I have no idea how long it takes for those words to finally sink in. After all this time, I finally have the answer, but I have no idea what to do with it. I feel like I've been punched in the stomach and I grab at my knees. "This whole time? The two of you? *Oh my God.*"

"*No.* No, no, no. I swear to you, it's not what you're thinking. I was confused at first—I didn't know what I was feeling. But I do now. Because it's always been you, Sloane. Always."

I want so badly to believe him, I really do. But I know I can't tell him that, because deep down, I don't believe him at all.

"She was my best friend."

Pain creases his forehead as he looks away.

"I swear, Sloane, I feel nothing for her. *Nothing.* And I know how this looks. I know I should've told you all of this back in Seattle. But I can't change that . . . so I'm telling you now."

It's evident he's trying his best to put everything into words this time. But it's too late. All of it is just too late.

And even if I could find it in me to forgive him, there's no way I could possibly let it go. Maybe if they'd only been together once, I'd believe it was a mistake and he really was just confused. But the fact they'd done it twice is what makes me sick to my stomach. Because that tells me there's something more there than even Tyler wants to admit.

"I can't do this, Tyler. Especially not now. Not after hearing that."

He squeezes my hand like he's trying to keep me from slipping away. Like he already knows that I'm gone.

"Please don't say that. Please . . . just give me another chance."

I slowly shake my head and I know he knows this is real.

"Just stop . . . please stop."

There's nothing—not even that smile of his that always makes me melt, that always makes everything better—that will make me change my mind. And it hurts, God does it hurt. But deep down in my very core, I feel that it's the right thing to do. It's the right thing for me.

And I'm finally choosing me.

"I love you, Sloane. I'll always love you."

But I don't say it back; I don't even hint that it might still be there. Because I honestly can't say that I feel the same. Not anymore.

Fourteen

It's been two days since Tyler was here.

Finn and I have texted, but he knows I need a little space. A little time. And I'm grateful he's giving that to me.

My brother tried to talk to me once or twice, but I can't even look at him.

Exhausted, I've slept for hours more than I should have and probably would still be asleep if my mom hadn't knocked on the door. She comes in carrying a plate of food in one hand, her other arm laden with countless shopping bags practically from wrist to neck. She doesn't pry and doesn't ask questions. Instead, she puts everything down and lies next to me on my bed as I cry into her shoulder.

When I finally get a hold of myself, my mom points at all the bags on the floor. God, she must've bought the entire mall.

"I saw a few things I thought might make you feel better. Try everything on. Whatever doesn't fit, we can take back or exchange."

"Thanks . . . but you really didn't have to do that."

It's when she rubs her palms along the tops of her thighs I somehow know what she's about to say isn't going to involve her recent shopping spree.

"You know your brother told me what happened, and he feels really badly about it. He's worried about you."

I close my eyes and roll out my neck. "Whatever, Mom. He should feel bad."

"Sloane, you should at least let him explain."

"He told you? Everything?" I scoff, because somehow I highly doubt that. "So then he told you that he and Mia are cheating behind Shep's back? Or did that not make the cut? They're both cheaters, Mom, just like Tyler and Mick."

She holds up her hands, "Sloane, you don't have all the facts, that's all I'm saying. Talk to your brother. I promise, not everything is as black-and-white as you think."

"Yeah, okay, whatever."

She pulls her lips tight together forming a straight line. And even though she hasn't been around a lot, I still know that's not a look I want to challenge.

"Okay, okay, I'll talk to him later." She gives me another look just for good measure. "I promise, all right?"

"Good. That would make me happy." But then she tucks a strand of my hair behind my ear and takes a deep breath.

Seriously? There's still more? "So I spoke to your father yesterday and told him about Tyler's little visit."

God, I'm zero for two. Pulling my knees up to my chest, I thud my forehead against them and cover my head with both arms.

"Sloane, just listen to me, okay?"

She waits until I mumble my okay, but I don't bother to move.

"What we talked about is that we both agree maybe it's time you knew the details around our divorce. Why it happened."

That is not at all what I was expecting to hear, and it makes me sit up.

"But I need you to understand it's been a very long time, Sloane—and it's important you know your father and I love you and your brother no matter what happened with us." She waits for me to look at her before she continues.

"So there was this new lawyer that had started at your father's firm. I first met her at their annual summer picnic, then again at the holiday party. I didn't give her a second look . . . but I should have."

My mom turns away and stares at something off in the distance. It's evident that even after all these years, she still hasn't let it all go, and a familiar sick feeling twists at my stomach.

"She didn't care that your father was married, or that he had a family. In fact, I'd even wager she saw that as a challenge." Her cheeks flush a deep red, and even though I haven't seen that happen often, I know she's angry. "Eventually, too many late nights working together got the better of him."

I shake my head. "You've gotta be kidding me," I whisper.

But she only continues. "When he finally broke down and told me, there wasn't anything he could say that would make me forgive him. Even after he swore to me he wasn't in love with her, nor was she in love with him. She even left the firm shortly after things ended and moved to New York."

Her eyes glisten as she wipes at her nose, then stares at her hands. I grab for the box of tissues on my nightstand and put them between us.

In a soft voice she says, "Maybe, had it only been once . . . well, maybe then I could've forgiven him and taken him back. But the fact it was more than that made me realize I'd never be able to trust him again."

Those words hit me hardest. But I don't know what to say. She's my mom. He's my dad. How do you have that conversation?

"But I did forgive him, Sloane. It took years, but I finally realized the impact those mistakes had on him, too, and what he lost because of them. Most important, I knew I couldn't harbor all that hate and pain. It would never change what happened, and worst of all, it was making me into someone I didn't want to be."

I hear what she's saying, but I'm not sure how to translate it all to what I'm dealing with.

"It feels like forgiving Tyler right now will make him think that what he did was okay. And it's not okay. And I can't even imagine forgiving Mick. She's in love with him, Mom . . . and she didn't even have the nerve to tell me. I mean, would you forgive the chick that slept with Dad?"

My mom puffs out her cheeks, but says nothing. I already know her answer.

"I don't understand why people can't be honest and up-front. Or at least have the decency to tell you about it first. They're all cowards, Mom. All of them . . . including Dad."

"That may be true. And I felt all those same things, back when it happened to me. But I'm not telling you to forgive either of them right away—only to think about it all and what it's worth to you. How much energy do you want to spend hating them? How much time do you want to waste wondering if it's all your fault, if you could've changed any of it? Because I can assure you, sweetheart, none of what happened had anything to do with you. It was between the two of them.

"And while I know hearing all of this now about your father might be difficult, please don't let this make you feel differently toward him. We all make mistakes, but hating someone for one they've made can ruin your life if you let it. Believe me, I'd know."

She's talking about my dad, but I know she also means Tyler and Mick. I want so desperately to get to that place where I can let it all go, because I know my mom is right. I can never undo something that's already been done.

But I can't even imagine it.

And then, there's my dad. It's hard not to hate what he did, but then I realize . . . he's still my dad. And I don't actually hate *him*.

"You're not alone, Sloane." My mom squeezes my knee. "Just remember that."

But even though I know she's right, I still feel alone. Because Mick would've been the first person I ran to, had things been different. I miss her. I miss us. I miss my best friend.

But she's half the reason I'm sitting here.

The next morning, I make my way out to the kitchen. Bob and my mom have both left for work, even though it's a Saturday, but I can't be mad that she's working today, because last night she let me know my cast is ready to come off. I have an appointment with her in a couple of hours, and I can't wait.

There's a fresh pot of coffee on, and I pour myself a cup, then add the cream how I like it and sit at the table. Staring at my phone, I realize there are so many people I've neglected over the past few days.

Other than a couple of texts, I haven't really talked to

Finn. He stopped by yesterday with a bouquet of hand-picked tropical flowers, but when my mom invited him in, he declined and only asked that she make sure I got them. They're sitting on my coffee table, and they're beautiful. I think it's his way of letting me know he's not going anywhere.

Mick also texted me, followed by an e-mail, but I deleted them both without reading. I'd venture a guess she probably heard about Tyler's little trip down here. Although I know she'd never even contemplate doing the same thing. Not pregnant. And especially not with a mom like hers.

I haven't seen Mia, either. I know Penn told her that Tyler showed up, because I overheard them on the phone. She's texted a few times to let me know she's here if I need to talk. And that she loves me and misses me. But I still don't know what to think about her and my brother. And what they're doing to Shep.

Out of everyone, though, I'm having the weirdest time dealing with the fact that I haven't heard from Tyler. In a twisted way, I miss all his texts and e-mails and voice mails, even though I'm the one that told him to stop.

I just can't believe he listened.

You always hear people say that breakups are hard, but that eventually, time heals everything. I think they're full of shit, whoever "they" are. I think they lied. Because breakups aren't just hard—they fucking suck.

"Okay, Slo, I've stayed away as long as I could."

I turn to see Mia standing in the entry hall. She holds on

tight to a stuffed monkey and balloons, but as soon as she sees me, she throws the monkey on the counter and lets go of the balloons.

"I know you needed your space and I know you're still mad at me, but seriously, woman, you're only here for the summer. And I miss you." She comes and gives me a fierce hug, squeezing me extra tight.

"So before I ask what the hell happened with Tyler, I need to explain a few things." She holds up a hand to cut me off. "Uh-uh, please, just listen, okay?"

"Okay. You've got five minutes."

She rolls her eyes, but takes the seat next to me. "Sloane, I know I should've told you and I know it was wrong for you to find out the way you did."

"That's not what I'm mad about—"

"You said you'd give me five minutes. But maybe we should start at the beginning." She settles into her chair and takes a deep breath. "So last summer when you both were down here . . . well . . . Penn and I . . . Penn and I kinda hooked up," she blurts out. "He was my first, and I was his."

Oh my God. This has been going on for over a year?

She sees the zillion questions in my eyes and holds up her hands again to stop me from saying anything.

"I know, I know, Slo, I should've told you then. But how do you tell one of your best friends that you just slept with her brother? And because it was right before you guys left to go back to Seattle, we decided we wouldn't say anything.

Besides, we didn't even know what it meant or how we felt.

"But then we started texting and e-mailing back and forth over the school year and even talked on the phone. I think . . . I think I've always had a thing for your brother. I just didn't know how to tell you. I wanted to the other day when we went to Waikiki. Crap, there have been so many times I've wanted to tell you. But it never seemed like the right time."

"What about Shep?" I ask, breaking the rules.

"So that night at the bonfire, after you decided to walk home, I realized what my deal was. Penn was with those two girls, and I guess I was jealous." She pulls her hair band out from her hair, then regathers her curls and wraps them up in a messy bun. "Okay, I know I was . . . and I ended up getting wasted.

"Then Shep and I got into this huge fight and . . . I broke up with him."

"What?" I blurt.

"Yeah. In front of everyone. God, it was awful. It was the shittiest thing I've ever done, and one look at his face, I knew he was crushed. But that didn't stop me, because the next thing I knew, I was with Penn."

So she and Shep had broken up before she and Penn did . . . whatever they did.

She rubs at her face and sucks in a breath, then lets it out. "Don't get me wrong, I love Shep, I really do. But the longer you and Penn have been here, the more I've realized how much Shep is just a friend . . . and Penn . . . well, isn't. And I should've told you the other morning that I'd broken up with Shep, but you were *so* angry . . . I just couldn't find the words."

She grabs a napkin from the holder and starts to shred long thin strips from it.

"I really like your brother, Slo. In fact, I don't think I've ever felt this way about anyone before. And I know I should've handled things way better with Shep. I don't know, called things off when I wasn't so tanked? He deserved at least that. Anyway, what a mess, huh? I'm sorry I didn't tell you sooner."

I blow out an overwhelmed sigh. "Not as messy as it could've been, that's for sure."

"I know, but still. Slo, please don't be mad at me . . . please. And please don't be mad at your brother. I'm the one that told him you needed to hear it from me. I'm really sorry for everything. And I didn't mean for you to think I was throwing this in your face, not after everything you've been through." She rests a hand on mine.

"I'm glad you told me . . . even though you should've done it sooner." I stick out my tongue to let her know I'm giving her a bad time. "And I'm not mad anymore. If anything, I feel crappy for assuming you hadn't ended things with Shep. I should've known better. I shouldn't have lumped you guys in with Mick and Tyler. I'm sorry, too, Mia."

"Then we're all good." A tentative smile bends her mouth

as she leans across and hugs me tight. "So how are you doing, really? Penn said Tyler showed up without telling anyone he was coming. That took balls."

"Yeah, I can't believe he came all the way down here." I pull a knee up on my chair and rest my chin on top and hug it close. "And I guess I've been better."

"Slo, the guy may have royally screwed up, but he loves you. There's no denying that. I mean he flew all the way down here to try to get you back," she says. "Do you think there's any chance you can forgive him?"

I close my eyes. "I don't know. Seeing him here, in front of me, it was just so hard. But deep down, I really don't know if I can forgive him. Especially after he told me that Mick said . . . she told him that she loves him, Mia. And I think he might have feelings for her, too. Or had. I don't know."

"Wait a minute . . . are you kidding me? She's in love with him? When the hell did that happen?" Her mouth practically hits the floor in disbelief. "Oh my God, I so did *not* see that coming."

"You're telling me," I reply. "He says he doesn't love her back, but that's hard to believe, considering. I pretty much told him it's over, but I have no idea what the hell I'm doing."

"Well, I guess it's a good thing you've got the rest of the summer to figure all of it out. Not to mention, you also have a nice distraction." She jostles my hand, but doesn't look away. "Speaking of Finn, I'm sure whatever is going on there isn't making this any easier."

I shrug. "No, it's not. But I think I really like him . . . and he makes me happy."

"And happy is exactly what you need right now. So if you want my opinion? I'd give him a chance, see where it goes. You don't have to commit to anything or anyone. Just enjoy your summer. You deserve that."

We talk for a little while longer before she has to leave for work. As we make our way to the front door, she jumps up to grab the strings from the balloons that drifted up to the ceiling. Handing them to me, she pulls me in for another hug, then slips out the front door.

Instead of going back to my room, I make my way out to the pool and realize how much I miss it. Sure I've got lessons, but I mean true swimming. Without my arm in a cast.

T minus two hours until this sucker comes off. And I can't wait.

I sit on the edge of the pool and dangle my legs in the water. I'm not sure how long Penn stands there before he comes and sits down next to me.

He leans into my shoulder and stays there. "Are you ever gonna talk to me again? You know, the silent treatment may work on everyone else, but I'm not buying it. I know you miss me. Like something fierce."

My brother has this uncanny ability to always make me smile. He's been doing it my entire life, and it doesn't fail him now. I bump him back with my shoulder.

"Whatever, P. You're just lucky Mia already came over and told me everything."

I kick my feet slowly in the water, then look up at my brother.

"Slo, just for the record, I had no idea Tyler was coming down here, I swear. He didn't say anything to me. Probably because he knows I would've told you."

He's telling me the truth, even though it didn't feel that way when I was staring at Tyler sitting on our front step. But my brother is still my brother, and I should've known better.

"What do you think you're gonna do?"

There's someone else I need to see. Need to talk to. "I'm not exactly sure, but I know where I need to start."

Fifteen

After taking a shower, I text Finn:

> Care to join me in getting this cast off?
> And I have a favor to ask.

His reply is immediate.

> I'll be right there.

I hear the throaty hum of his bike pull into our drive ten minutes later.

"Hey." He smiles and taps on my cast. "Ready to introduce me to that arm of yours?"

"You have no idea."

He stares down at me for a second. "Everything okay? You wanna talk about it?"

"Nah, it's all good." Honestly, I'm kind of tired of talking about everything.

"And are we okay?" he asks.

"Yeah, we're okay." I can't help but smile. And I'm relieved he thinks there's a "we" here.

He hesitates, but only for a second, before leaning down to kiss me. "Good, I was hoping you'd say that."

We head to my mom's office and half an hour later, the cast is off. I can't believe I'm staring at my own limb, because it's this god-awful pasty white that's a solid six shades lighter than the rest of me. I flex my fingers for the first time in weeks, and everything about my right arm is stiff, uncomfortable, like it actually misses being in a cast.

"So what's this favor of yours?" Finn asks after we've left my mom and we're standing next to his bike.

I pause for only a second, because I'm that confident this is something I want to do, even though the idea scares the hell out of me. It's something I decided the other night, after Tyler left—and I haven't changed my mind yet.

"I'm hoping you might know a place that would do a tattoo without parental consent." Considering he's not eighteen yet, I'm pretty sure he does.

He studies me for a moment, then the biggest grin takes over his face. "Hell yeah I do. Are you sure?"

"I think I am. No, I am," I say firmly. "Okay, maybe sort of. Just get me out of here before I change my mind."

He puts on his helmet, gets on the bike, and waits for me

to take my seat behind him. Not once does he ask why, nor does he attempt to talk me out of it.

We pull into a small parking lot twenty minutes later. The building is old, and the paint is peeling in so many spots, it's hard to tell what color it used to be from what color it is now. Not to mention there seems to be some very important letters missing from their sign, because I'm really hoping this place is called Island Classic Tattoos and not "Is ass too."

I'm suddenly wondering if it's too late to ask Finn to turn around. If he brought me here to discourage me, it's almost working.

A bell chimes overhead as we walk through the door, and a man with piercings in places I didn't even know were possible—not to mention tattoos on every visible square inch of skin—greets us. "Back for more ink, are you?"

"Not me, Sloane here." They shake hands. "How's it goin', Chris?"

Chris studies me, and I get the feeling he's about to ask my age. So I do the only thing I can think of. I cross my arms, let out a heavy sigh like I'm bored, then hold up a wad of bills saved up from working at the activities counter. It's more than enough. In fact, if I had to guess, I'd say it was double what it should actually cost.

"So, you wanna go and get yourself a tattoo, eh?" Chris smirks and takes the cash. "By the looks of all that gorgeous blank canvas, I'm guessing you've never had one done before, so you should know I only do 'em big and loud. None of this dainty fairy shit, if that's what you're thinkin'."

If this guy's screwing with me, he's got the best damn poker face I've ever seen.

I take in all his tats, then glance at the one that's peeking out from under the sleeve of Finn's T-shirt. I already know how big that one is, and I have no intention of getting one that size.

"You're right, no tattoos here. But I'm not interested in the least in getting a fairy—nor one the size of my head—so if you can't help, I'll gladly take my business elsewhere."

I hold out my hand for my money, but he and Finn only bust out laughing.

"Fiery little one, aren't you? I like her." He looks at Finn, then puts an arm around my shoulder. "Why don't you come on over here and pick out what you want, unless you already have something in mind?"

He brings me over to a wall that's full of pictures of tats he's done in the past. A table stands in front of me, with several photo albums of hundreds more, but instead of flipping any of them open, I pull a slip of paper from my back pocket.

"This is what I want," I say, holding it out. "And I'd like it to go down my back, along the side of my rib cage. But not big." Both Chris and Finn look over my shoulder and down at the piece of paper in my hand. The font is a beautiful script based on the handwriting of Paul Cézanne, a famous nineteenth-century artist. And it's only two words in Latin: *Memento Vivere.*

"'Remember to live,'" Finn whispers.

The fact he knows what it means makes me smile, and I can see from his expression that he also knows this is the most perfect tattoo I could possibly get.

"Well, damn, I was really looking forward to a giant dragon racing from your shoulder down your back, but I guess this will work," Chris jokes. He leads us back to an almost empty room that only has a massage table, a rolling stool, and one plastic chair in a corner. There's also a small metal table with various instruments strewn about that have suddenly caused the hair on my arms to stand upright. "You'll need to take off your shirt and bra and lie down on your stomach. I'll give you a few minutes while I go wash my hands."

As soon as he walks out the door, I start to freak out, because not only am I about to be stabbed with a needle, but I have to do it all with no shirt on. Clearly, I didn't think this through. But I realize I'd rather hurry up and get undressed and down on the table before Chris comes back in to find me still standing there with a dumb look on my face.

Finn turns around before I can say anything and pretends to focus on the wall. On one hand, I want him to leave for a second, but on the other, I'm afraid if he does, I'll wuss out and crawl through the window. Because right now, that escape route is looking rather promising.

So instead, I yank my tank top up over my head and unhook my bra, tucking it into the folds of my shirt.

"I have a feeling if I leave you alone, you may find a way to scramble out that window over there." He nods in the direction of my plotted escape route without looking at me, then holds out a hand. "Here, I'll hang on to your stuff."

I almost kick myself for being so transparent, but I hand him my clothes, then quickly lie down on the table. He pulls the empty chair up next to me and takes one of my hands in his.

"Not gonna lie, Sloane, this can hurt like a bitch—especially the spot you've picked."

"Hey, you told me before it wasn't that bad!"

"I did? *Oops.*"

"Yeah, oops. Thanks."

He squeezes my shoulder. "Just remember, if you feel the need to break something, maybe give your hand a rest . . . and my nose is off-limits, too."

"Ha-ha. It's a giant needle, Finn. *Giant.* I can't be held accountable for what happens in the next half hour."

Chris walks in a moment later, sits down on the rolling stool opposite Finn, and fiddles with some of the equipment. He explains the entire process, of which I hear very little, because the machine that's now emitting a low hum next to me has captured my full attention. He touches a latexed glove to my skin, and I jump almost clear off the table, which in turn makes both Chris and Finn jump, too.

"Okay, so that's not gonna work, sweetheart," Chris says.

"Sorry," I mumble as I squeeze my eyes shut and focus on building my pool.

"I'm just gonna draw out the design on your skin, no needles yet, I promise." I feel his hands again, and this time, I manage not to squirm. He works on the outline for a few minutes, then holds a mirror up for me to see his work.

It's perfect.

"So I'm going to press the instrument I'll be using against your back, but without the needle yet. I only want you to get a feel for the vibration, okay?"

I nod my okay, then turn my head to look at Finn instead. The intensity of his eyes is reassuring, and I feel like I can do almost anything.

"You've got this, I know you do."

I can tell by the way his forehead scrunches up that he's anxious for me. I'm anxious for myself. In fact, there's a solid chance I may wet myself right here. And as soon as Chris touches me, I jump again.

Damn, damn, and damn.

"Sloane, you can't do that," Finn says with a smirk. "I'm pretty sure this is something you don't want him messing up, and with you jumping like that, 'Remember to live' is not what it will end up saying."

I have the strong urge to flip him off, and by the way he laughs, he knows it, too.

I take a few deep breaths and let myself adjust to the feel

of the vibration against my back. As soon as Chris removes it, that movement alone makes me flinch again, but it's not nearly as bad as the first two times.

"Sorry!" I blurt out, before either one of them can scold me. I take a few more deep breaths and close my eyes. "Okay, I'm ready." When nothing happens, I pry open one eye. "Seriously, I swear."

I feel something cold against my skin, as Chris cleans it with a disinfectant and then applies petroleum jelly. Finn squeezes my hand as Chris touches the needle to my back. My eyes shoot open and a string of curse words spill from my mouth, but I don't move an inch.

"Oh, you have *got* to be kidding me! Who willingly does this to themselves?"

I've got both of them laughing as I bite back the pain.

"Obviously, you do," Finn replies. "And, well, me, and Chris here, and countless others. Welcome to the club." He squeezes my hand again and looks me in the eye. "Just try to focus on me and not what he's doing, okay? Look at me, Sloane."

I hold his gaze, studying each one of his features, making my way up from his chin to his lips, then his nose, then his eyes—oh, his eyes—and then his eyebrows, and finally find myself staring at his hair. And then I do the same thing all in reverse. And while the pain of a million sharp knives being jammed into my skin is still there, I find that this is helping me to breathe. And I wonder if I've found a new focus technique, aside from building my pool.

It takes about thirty minutes in total, and I'm so happy with the finished design, I have to wipe away tears of both pain and joy.

And even though it hurt like a son of a bitch and I can't say I'd ever do it again, it was a different type of pain than what both Mick and Tyler did to me.

And *exactly* what I needed to move on.

Sixteen

Now that my cast is off, I've been given the choice to stay at the activities counter at the Echelon or move over to the pool. Honestly, while I love being around the water, I've had so much fun hanging out with Maile for a few hours a week, I decide to stay there for the rest of the summer.

"Plans today?" Maile asks as we print out our report for that morning.

"I'm headed up to grab Finn. Not sure what we're doing, though." After Finn kept stopping by to say hello, I ended up telling her the two of us have been hanging out lately. Not that it wasn't obvious by the way I reacted every time he came over. "You?"

"Stace and I are helping her cousin move . . . again. I know you're totally jealous."

After jokingly reassuring her that couldn't be further from the truth, I say good-bye and head up to Finn's. As I make my way over to the elevators, my phone beeps with an incoming text. It's been quiet lately, and I have to admit, it's been kind of nice.

It beeps again as I step into the elevator, and I see that the messages are from my dad. I spoke to him the other day and was surprised how calm I was after hearing everything I had from my mom. But I love my dad, and even though I'm disappointed in him, I don't think that's ever going to change.

I shoot him a text back, letting him know how awesome it's been to not have that dang cast anymore, but I leave out the small detail that I got myself a tattoo.

Closing out from his message, I half expect to see one waiting from Tyler. When there isn't one, I barely feel anything. Maybe these things really do get better with time.

But there is a new text from Mick, and I read it before I can stop myself:

> I heard things didn't go so well with Tyler. I tried to warn you he was coming down, but you never responded to my text.

I scroll back through the few messages of hers I haven't deleted, because I have no idea what she's talking about. Sure enough I find one from the morning Tyler showed up, while I was up at the waterfall with Finn. Thinking back, I even remember seeing something from her, but of course I'd ignored it.

"Whatever, Mick. How about a text telling me you're in

love with my ex-boyfriend, huh?" I whisper to myself as the elevator opens. Finn is standing there waiting for me.

"Is he still bothering you?" He nods at my phone.

"Nope. He actually listened. I haven't heard a thing from him since he left that day."

"Good. Can't say I'm disappointed to hear that," he says as he walks into his bathroom.

I'm sitting on the edge of Finn's bed, staring at all the pictures of him surfing, when he comes out from the bathroom tugging a shirt down over his head. He slides it over his chest, then starts to pull it farther down over his stomach, but stops.

"Want me to take it back off and start over?" he jokes.

"Sure, if you want."

He smirks and sits down next to me. "So what do you feel like doing today? We could sit down by the pool. Get lunch and bring it to the beach." He snaps his fingers with a thought. "Ever been Jet Skiing?"

"Actually, I'd love to spend the day out on the water, but I had something else in mind." I know the last time we talked about this it quickly became a closed-off conversation. I stare up at the wall of pictures and tilt my head in their direction. "Would you mind teaching me how to surf?"

He eyes the pictures, and I can see him start to shut down.

"Finn, I know it's been a long time since you've been out, but I also know you wouldn't look like that in those pictures without being really, really good. Just one lesson. If it ends up being too much, we can stop, okay?" I lean into him. "Besides, the last time I tried to surf, I gave Shep a mild concussion with my board." I cringe at the memory. "He swore he'd never go back out in the water with me again. So now I have no one good to teach me." I pretend to pout and hope it works. "Besides, you have no idea how embarrassing it is to be part Hawaiian and not know how to surf. I think that actually goes against my heritage."

Instead of grabbing the one above his bed, he takes a deep breath, gets up, and retrieves a surfboard from his closet. I follow him into the living room and watch as he sets his board on the couch, then disappears into Luce's room. A moment later, he's standing in front of me with another board under one arm, and something navy, yellow, and white under the other.

"You'll need to wear a rash guard." He hands it to me, and I see that it's a long-sleeved spandex T-shirt. "I think that one should fit. I'll be right back."

He comes out a minute later wearing a royal blue long-sleeved shirt of his own, the color doing crazy things with the blue of his eyes. It's taut across his chest—so snug, in fact, I can see the outline of every single one of his muscles. He tightens the drawstring on the waistband of his shorts, and I notice he's no longer wearing his flip-flops.

"You gonna just stand there? I thought you wanted to learn how to surf."

"Hell yeah! I'm just surprised you're saying yes, is all."

I yank my T-shirt off and pull the rash guard on over my bikini. It's tight, but from what I've seen of female surfers, this is how it's supposed to fit. I look up to find Finn staring.

"I can start over if you want," I joke.

Laughing, he picks up his board and heads for the elevator.

It takes some serious effort to not hit anything—including Finn—with the long board I now carry, but we make our way down to the beach. After setting our boards in the sand, Finn walks me through all the basics of surfing. He has me lie flat on the board, gripping both sides, then shows me how to master the "pop-up" to get up on my feet. We do this several times, and I have the sneaking suspicion that while this seems way too easy, it's going to be a whole different ball game once I'm actually out on the water.

We head out toward the surf, and Finn shows me how to get a running start, then jump onto my board, lying flat on my stomach. We paddle out, floating alongside each other, and I realize exactly what I've asked Finn to do as I watch his face.

"Finn, I'm sorry, this was a bad idea. Let's go back in." I start to paddle back toward the beach that is now much farther away than I realized.

"No way you're getting out of it that easy. Besides, you talked me into this, you're getting your lesson." He sits up on the board, straddling it between his legs, and flips it around to face the shore. "Your turn," he says. Like he actually believes it's something I can do.

I literally grunt. Out loud. Me straddling the board like he does is highly unlikely, thanks to my height and awkward limbs that have zero control now that we're out on the water. But I try it anyway and fall right off. The board shoots forward and the leash I have strapped to my ankle tugs at my leg. Finn steadies the board as I slither my way back on none too gracefully.

I finally manage to get my board turned in the direction of the beach, and I realize it's sapped about all my energy. Around us, there are a few other tourists taking lessons, so at least I don't feel so nervous.

"Okay, we're watching for a decent set to make its way in. This is Waikiki, so we're not talking anything big. But something with a little cap to it. Once we see it, you need to start paddling hard toward the shore. When the wave gets just behind you, pop up like you practiced on the beach, okay?"

"Just pop up like I practiced, huh? *Yeah*," I mutter. I get the feeling he has a lot more confidence in me than I do in myself.

"Okay, this looks like a good one. You ready? Let's go!"

We both begin paddling. As the momentum of the wave catches us, I watch Finn easily hop up, but I stay solidly rooted to my board as if I'm glued there. His feet do most of the work, prodding him in the direction he wants to go. It looks so effortless, but when he glances over his shoulder, he finds me still laid out flat, like a harbor seal on dry land.

"Yeah, I don't quite think that qualifies as surfing," he says as he makes his way back to me and we paddle out again.

"I swear, next one for sure, I'm totally standing up. Maybe." Which I kinda do. Sorta. Mostly my feet become tangled in each other, and I go flying off the board as it shoots out from under me, yanking at my ankle once again.

But now I have a taste for it and I want more. Because while I'm getting really good at the falling-off part, I want to stand at least once. *Once.* That's all I'm asking.

Finn spots a good set, the best one we've seen yet, and hollers at me to start paddling. I do exactly that, and as the wave chases me down, I stand up. And I don't have a single clue what I'm supposed to do next.

Finn rides the small wave right next to me and holds out his hand for a high five. I slap it, and my board careens into his, wiping us both out. I come up shooting water from my mouth as he laughs.

"Nice! Looks like you might have some Hawaiian in you after all!"

"Only needed someone that knew what they were doing to teach me, is all."

We bob on our boards and wait for another decent set to come in. Which it turns out in Waikiki, can take a while.

"Thanks for doing this, by the way. Man, it's been forever since my muscles hurt like this." I stretch my arms and roll out my neck as I float on my board. "Can I ask why it's been so long since you've been surfing? I mean, before today? From those pictures, you look pretty amazing at it."

He rubs at the back of his own neck and stares out at the water.

"I'm sorry, never mind."

"No, it's okay. It's probably about time I told you anyway." He coughs to clear his throat. "Those pictures . . . they aren't of me."

I frown, because the guy in the photographs looks exactly like him. *Exactly*. "You have a brother?"

It takes a while before he responds. "Had. I had a brother, Quinn. He was a year older than me." He runs his fingers in the water, making small ripples with his hand. "He was the good surfer, not me. I raced motorbikes and played football and constantly fucked up. But Quinn, he surfed in competitions all around the world, won most of them, too. And according to my father, there wasn't anything he couldn't do."

I can't imagine what that would be like. Growing up with Penn, our parents never favored one over the other. Well, if they did, they never showed it. So I have no idea how to relate to that.

"But then one morning he went out to surf . . . and didn't come back." He shuts his eyes tight.

"Oh my God, Finn."

"There was a big storm getting ready to hit and the swells were insane, but that's exactly the type of surf Quinn loved to ride most. I'm not exactly sure what happened, but they think he took a bad spill and hit his head, knocking him unconscious." He slaps at the water, sending a spray of it away from us. "He drowned doing exactly what he loved, and I don't think he would've wanted it any other way."

The last part comes out almost in a whisper, but the meaning hits me loud, almost like he shouted.

"I was supposed to go surfing with him that day, but I wanted to go race motorcycles instead. So I packed up my bike and went. But Luce . . . Luce was there." He swipes water off the top of his board, like he can't believe it had the audacity to take up residence there. "She was the one that called 9-1-1, and she never set foot in the water again, not until I saw her with you in your pool. And according to my father, I'm the reason my brother is dead and my sister needed to see a shrink for over a year."

"Finn, I'm so sorry." I stop right there, because I don't know what else to say. I reach over and pick up his hand, bringing it up to my lips. "And I'm so sorry I made you come out here today. You didn't have to."

"Sloane, it's fine, really. You're right—I could've said no. But actually, it's been kinda nice being back out here; I'm having a good time." He looks over at me and squeezes my hand, still holding on to his. "I miss him . . . but he's gone now. And I can't do anything about that."

I can't even imagine what I'd do if I ever lost my brother. If something were to happen to Penn, I'd never be the same.

"I'm still really sorry, Finn."

He smiles but it doesn't reach his eyes, then he turns to stare back out at the water.

"I think that's enough serious crap for the day." As if Mother Nature agrees, she sends another decent swell our way, and Finn points it out. "Ready to give your legs another go?"

We spend the rest of the afternoon trying to make a frequent habit out of me standing, and I don't do so badly. When we finally return to the beach, I flop down into the wet sand next to my board, and Finn does the same.

"It looks so easy, but then the tiniest of waves comes along and proves you wrong!" I drop an arm over my eyes as I try to catch my breath.

"You did really well for your first time. It takes most people much longer to get up on the board. And technically, you stood up on your first real try. Granted, it wasn't for very long, but still." He smiles at me from under his own arm as he shields his face from the sun.

"Yeah, well, at least you didn't end up like Shep, so there's that. I honestly think he'd leave the Islands if he saw me holding a surfboard in his direction."

Picking up our boards, we head back to his room.

"So . . . any big plans for the Fourth?"

"Um, nope. What did you have in mind?" I really hope he has something in mind.

"Well, since my dad just left for Thailand, I was thinking about throwing a party here at the hotel. Actually, I've been thinking about it for a while. And I'm talking nothing but the good stuff—food, drinks, and definitely fireworks. You can't have the Fourth without blowing something up."

I turn toward him and nod. "Now *that* sounds like an awesome idea."

Seventeen

On the morning of the Fourth, I roll out of bed and instinctively grab my phone to text Mick. I can't wait to tell her all the details about the big party planned for tonight, because she's completely going to freak out. And I so wish she could be here.

It's always been tradition for us to text back and forth today—not only to touch base, but also to share whatever crazy excitement would be taking up our holiday. So I'm surprised when I don't see a text already waiting from her on my phone.

But then I fully wake up, and remember why.

I sag with disappointment as I delete my text without sending it. Chalk that one up to yet another BFF moment the two of us will no longer share.

I head off to take a shower, only to come out afterward to find a text from Finn. It's a picture of the barge off the beach of Waikiki that contains all the fireworks for the Echelon's celebration tonight.

And that's when I realize not even Mick can ruin today.

Because this party I've been helping Finn plan is going to be huge. Epic even.

It's all everyone's been talking about . . . and I mean everyone.

I finish wrapping the straps to my new sandals around my ankles and buckle them before standing, giving my mirror one last look. I have to admit, my mom does have great taste and I love the new denim skirt and fiery orange halter top she bought for me the other day.

I walk out to the living room where Penn and my parents are waiting.

"Look how great you look, Sloane! I knew that would fit perfectly!" my mom says, giving my forehead a kiss. "You two have fun tonight. But be careful, okay?" She gives us her stern mom look, but it doesn't stay in place for long. "And call if you need one of us to come pick you up."

Every year, all the hotels on the Waikiki strip put on this huge fireworks war against one another, trading off back and forth, taking turns lighting up the sky in colorful explosions. And there couldn't be a better location to watch it all than from the rooftop deck at the Echelon. Especially since their fireworks show is supposed to be the best.

When Penn and I arrive, Finn is waiting for us in the lobby. He takes my hand in his, then gives a key card to Penn.

"Suite 1601. Everyone crashes here, dude. You and Mia included." He winks at my brother. "She's already upstairs."

Unlike all the other partygoers who are directed by the staff to the normal elevators, Finn leads us to the elevator that goes up to his floor.

We stop in Finn's suite, and I disappear into his room to drop off my bag, then we make our way up a flight of stairs to the rooftop above, where the party is already in full swing. The coolest lighting effects cast the entire space in a vibrant shade of magenta with different shadow patterns that swirl and ripple across the floor. A few seconds later, the color fades and changes to a deep purple. Cabanas line the perimeter and are packed with milling guests, and a DJ cranks out loud music as bodies grind to the beat. There are dozens of kids in the rooftop pool, some dancing, some shooting hoops, and some even playing chicken.

"Oh, we'll be giving that another go, don't you worry about that," Finn says in my ear. He leads me over to a line, where I see Mia and a few others already grabbing beers. Shep is standing in the group with her, which I'm hoping is a good thing.

I can't believe this party has its own bar, considering we're all underage. Then again, it's not like this is a public event, and Finn does have the means to do whatever he wants. He squeezes my hand, and I squeeze his back.

"Luce is staying with a friend tonight, so you can crash in her room if you want. I can also get you your own room or you can always stay with me—your choice." He says it in a way that lets me know the decision really is up to me. And I like that. Because right now, even though the thought has crossed my mind a time or two, I haven't decided what I want to do—if I'm really ready to go there with Finn.

Beers in hand, Mia and Shep make their way over to where we stand in line, but she gives me a pleading look like she's begging me to help her shake him. I have to wonder if he hopes he has a chance at rekindling what they had, and I can only pray for the safety of my brother when Shep finds out Mia has moved on.

"This party is off the rails!" Mia squeals, giving Finn a sideways hug. He slaps hands with Shep, then speaks to the bartender to order our drinks.

"Hey, you! I see you finally ditched the cast?" Mia throws her arms around my neck and steers me away from the others.

"Yeah, it came off the other day!" I say, looking over at Shep. He's now in conversation with a group of guys waiting in line for drinks and doesn't seem to notice he's been given the slip. "Wanna tell me what that was all about?"

She cringes, shaking her head. "He won't leave me alone, Slo. He showed up at my house yesterday with flowers, and I told him it wasn't going to work and that I wanted to move on. He thinks I just need time. What do I do?" She stares across the roof at my brother. "It's hard enough that I want to make it clear we've broken up, but it doesn't feel right to throw it in his face that I'm together with Penn. At least not so soon."

"So he has no idea about Penn? Mia, he's gonna lose his shit when he finds out."

"I know." Mia bites her lip.

"You have to tell him. It's going to hurt but it's the truth, and he deserves to know the truth. You could even tell him that you and Penn got together last year and seeing him again has brought back all kinds of memories."

After all, I'm an expert when it comes to knowing how seeing someone can bring back memories.

"God, why does this have to be so hard?"

"I don't know, Mia, but I do know that he's going to find out soon enough that you're with my brother, whether it's from you or someone else. Don't let it be from someone else."

I pause for a second, wondering if that's the best advice I can give. Or maybe I just signed my brother's death certificate.

"You're right, Slo, I know you are. I just hope Shep doesn't do anything stupid." She hugs me tight. "I promise I'll take care of it tonight, but I think I should talk to Penn first—make sure we both agree." She lets out a shuddering sigh as she tries to pull herself together. "Man, this totally sucks."

"I know. But you're going to feel so much better once it's done and over with."

We stare at the view of the city around us, then out to the beach and the darkness that is the ocean beyond. Then Mia spots my tattoo and spins me around for a better look.

"No way! You lose the cast and get yourself a tat? What

does '*Memento Vivere*' mean?" she reads out loud, twisting her head sideways.

Aside from Finn and now Mia, no one else has seen it. Not even my brother.

"It's Latin for 'Remember to live.' Just a little reminder, is all."

Finn comes up behind us and hands me my drink. "Pretty awesome, don't you think?"

"Awesome? It's perfect! I love it, Slo!"

"I love it, too, although it hurt like a bitch. And if it wasn't for this guy, I think I would've chickened out." I motion toward Finn, and Mia hesitates, like she's trying to piece something together.

"Wow. Someone's rubbing off on someone here. About damn time. But if you hurt my girl in any way, believe me, I'll have your balls hanging from my rearview mirror in two seconds flat." Then she actually pats his shoulder and smiles sweetly.

"No need to worry about that." Finn smiles back, her comment not affecting him in the least as he leans down to kiss my temple. It's the first outward display of affection in front of our friends, and as Mia squeals, I know my face has gone solar.

Finn excuses himself to greet a few guests, one of whom I see is Gianna, who at least didn't come alone. As soon as he's out of earshot, Mia shimmies her hip against mine.

"So it's getting pretty serious between you guys, huh?"

I don't even hesitate. "Yeah, I think it is."

She watches me closely, then leans in and kisses my cheek. "Slo, I can't tell you how happy I am to see *you* this happy. Because I hate to say it, but you were pretty messed up when you first got down here."

"Ha-ha, thanks a lot." My smile stretches so wide across my face, it actually hurts my cheeks. "I thought I was happy with Tyler, you know? I never knew it could be better than that. Until it was." I take a sip of my drink and realize it's already almost gone. "And even though I have no idea what's going on between me and Finn, I don't really care, because I like it . . . whatever it is."

"So I guess Tyler's old news, then? It sounds like you've made up your mind."

"Yeah, I think I have." I can't believe how good that feels to say out loud. "I know it's easier because he's not here. But then again, I'm not sure that would make a difference now." I stir the ice in my glass, then finish off the last of it. "Come on, let's go get another drink."

We order another round, and I down it there at the bar before we head out to the mass of bodies dancing on the makeshift dance floor. I spot Maile and Stacey grinding to the beat, and they're pretty awesome together. I of course am not the only one who notices, as practically every guy within a fifteen-foot radius has stopped what they're doing to watch. Mia and I make our way over to them, and with my second drink down, I let all my cares go and join them.

"Wicked tat!" Maile yells loud over the music as she pulls back the side of my halter top to get a closer look. She's doesn't ask what it means, but instead continues to sway her hips in groove to the beat, then her hands trail down my sides and grab hold of my hands, raising them above our heads.

Maile's hands are replaced with ones that are much bigger, much stronger. I feel a different body pressed hard against my back, all muscle and male.

"Having fun?" Finn says in my ear.

"You're damn right I am!"

He brings my clasped hands down around his neck, then his own slide along my arms, and settle on my waist as we move as one to the music. A shiver races through me, even though it's hot, especially with everyone dancing so close around us. He leans in and kisses my neck, and I feel as if I might melt into a puddle right here.

We dance for several more songs, until my hair begins to plaster against my skin. The dance floor is packed, and there's barely any room to move, let alone breathe.

"Come on, let's go get another drink." Finn grabs my hand and leads me over to the bar.

He signals for the bartender to make another round as I settle in close to his side, his hand low on my hip. His fingertips graze the skin above the waistband to my skirt and goose bumps race each other down my arms.

"The fireworks are about to start," he says, and we take our drinks over to the railing.

The music changes, and the first of the explosions lights up the sky from a hotel down the beach. I don't know how the DJ is doing it, but his beats are in time with the show and it's spinning the dancers into a frenzy. Then another hotel lights up the sky, and then another one. It's crazy and beautiful all at the same time, and I lean back against Finn's chest to take it all in. Just when I think it's about to end, the barge in the water directly in front of us knocks them all out of the park.

"Oh my God, it doesn't even compare!" I squeal as the huge plumes of color burst and rain down around us. I watch in awe. It's so close I can almost reach out and touch it all.

"Finale," Finn says as the barge goes wild, unleashing a beautiful chaos into the night sky.

When the fireworks are over, the entire rooftop erupts in cheers, and the music only gets louder. Mia runs up to us and grabs both of our hands and pulls us in the direction of the pool.

"I hope you're both ready to lose, because you're going down!" She motions over to Shep, who's already waiting in the water. When I give her a look, she shakes her head. "We have unfinished business between the four of us, so I'm taking one for the team." She strips off her clothes down to her swimsuit and dives in, surfacing over near Shep.

One look at Finn and I know there's no way we're losing this time. I yank my halter top up over my head and shimmy out of my skirt. My sandals take a little bit more work. Finn is already out of his T-shirt and kicks his flip-flops to the side. And then we both dive in.

Seconds later, I'm rising up, high above the pool, as water rains down off me and onto Finn below. But it's no contest this time. Mia's arms flail as she and Shep teeter trying to stay upright, then they both crash into the water. Finn holds a hand up, and I slap it in a high five as Mia breaks the surface, her face the epitome of disbelief.

"What's the matter?" I pretend to pout. "It was easy taking advantage of an injured arm, but you're not so tough now that I have my cast off, eh? Come on and get back up, we're so not done here!"

Finn and I beat them three to zero. But then my brother has some redhead high up on his shoulders, and I'm not sure how he's keeping her there, since he's wasted and her hair— that she's busy swishing from shoulder to shoulder—far outweighs the rest of her. I'm surprised she's actually willing to get it wet.

"Think you guys are hot shit, eh?" Penn slurs. "Well, Misty and I beg to differ. Twenty bucks says we take you down, best of five. And I'm so telling Mom about that tattoo, Slo."

He sticks out his tongue in a playful gesture. "Oh you're so on, P. And make it fifty. But if you lose, not a word to Mom." As if he agrees, Finn squeezes both of my thighs.

I spot Mia as she climbs out of the pool, slapping Shep's hand away as he offers to help. I know she's mad about Penn and Misty, but I'm sure my brother wasn't too happy to see Shep as her partner, either.

Finn and I slowly make our way toward the tower of the

other two. I have no idea what Penn was thinking when he put her up there, because I barely even touch her and she's already squealing and falling off. The second round, she gives me a little bit more of a challenge, and I wonder if maybe she's holding back, but once again she goes down. The third round, she tries to play dirty and takes a swipe at my suit. So gross. Where the hell does my brother find these girls?

I reach out and grab both of her shoulders and shove her hard backward. The momentum is too much for Penn, and they both go crashing down. And just like that, we've beat them three to zero.

High fives go around the pool as others challenge Finn and me.

"Sorry, guys, I hate to disappoint, but this lady is done for the night!" I feign that my arm is starting to hurt, which wins me many sympathy votes, but really, it's because I've had my fair share of booze and God help me if I were to puke on Finn. *Again.* I'd never live that down a second time.

"Wow, even I almost believe you," Finn says with a smirk. He helps me from the pool and wraps a fluffy robe around my shoulders, then grabs one for himself.

I look around for Mia and Shep, but they're nowhere to be seen, and I really hope it's for the reason I think—that she's actually telling him the truth. We make our way over to a cabana where most of our friends are playing a drinking game and all of them give us a rousing round of applause.

"You guys wanna join?" Maile asks.

I look around at the many cups of beer set up on the table and realize this would be a very bad idea.

"Actually, I think I'm done for the night," I say, and look up at Finn.

He smiles. "Me too."

Our friends boo as we say good night. Weaving through the rest of the guests, we sneak in the back door and down to his suite.

"I had such a great time tonight. That really was one hell of a party."

"Thank you for helping me plan it all." Cupping my chin in his hand, Finn kisses me softly. He pulls away and looks down at me, and I know he's wondering if this is okay.

And it is.

I pull on the front of his robe and lead him toward his room and lie down on the bed. He lies down next to me and kisses me again, then his lips trail down my chin and along my neck. Moving aside my robe, he feathers soft kisses across my collarbone.

Then he pauses, cradling my face in his hands, and everything about him feels right. This moment feels right.

And thinking of nothing else, I let myself go.

Eighteen

Finn and I go back to our waterfall the next day. And even though we jump a few times, we spend most of the morning tangled around each other on the blanket.

My first time with Tyler was awkward and clumsy, but he had still somehow managed to make it special. Not to mention, I was in love with him, so nothing else mattered. Nothing.

But with Finn it's different. I can't keep my hands off him or pull him close enough to my body. Like I want to crawl inside his skin.

A little while later, I realize I must have nodded off, because I start when my phone buzzes. I roll over to see a text from Mia:

I so need your help, but have 2 work. Dinner 2 nite?

"Everything okay?" Finn runs a hand through my hair, and I lean into his palm.

"It's Mia. I have a bad feeling things didn't go so well last night after we left."

I toss my phone back into my bag and lie down, staring up at the sky.

"Hey, I'm sure everything's fine." He traces his fingertips along my forehead until they trail down and reach my lips. "Have dinner with me tonight. Let me take you someplace nice. Just the two of us."

He waits for me to respond, but before I have a chance, he tugs at my bottom lip and does his best attempt at my voice. "Why, Finn, I'd love to! I thought you'd never ask!"

I playfully jerk my head away from his fingertips and laugh. "Sorry . . . but I just told Mia I'd meet her for dinner. You think I can get a rain check?"

He looks disappointed at first, but shrugs it off quickly. "Of course. Damn, I knew I should've asked sooner." He pretends to make a snapping motion with his fingers, like he just missed it by that much.

An easy smile lights up his face, but then it fades and he looks at me with so much intensity, it's almost as if it hurts. His lips find mine, and one minute, he's kissing me with this raw passion I've never felt before, as if he can't get enough, and in the next, he slows, my heart racing wild like it does when we jump. He rests his forehead against mine and closes his eyes.

"You need to know . . . I've never felt this way about anyone before. I've never bothered with a serious relationship. Hell, I've never even spent more than a few days with the same girl." He cradles my cheek in his palm and stares at me. "You're just so different, Sloane. I don't know how to explain it." He shakes his head like he's trying to grasp at the words, and they aren't coming. "This isn't just a casual thing for me. Not with you."

"I feel the same way, too." I don't know how to explain it, either. For the first time, I really, truly feel like I've moved on from Tyler. And while I know he'll always have a piece of my heart, now it's all about Finn. And that's what I want. I brush his hair off his forehead and stare into the bluest eyes I've ever been this close to. And I want to keep staring until I memorize every shade of blue there is.

We're on our way back when Finn's cell phone rings. He takes one look at the caller ID and curses loudly. Oh, I've been there before, my friend.

With a heavy sigh, he presses a button on the steering wheel to engage the call over the speakers in the car. "Father."

"Phineas. Please clear your schedule this evening, I'd like to have dinner with you and your sister, seven P.M." It's said

216

in such a matter-of-fact tone, as if Finn simply could not have any other plans.

Finn takes a deep breath. "When did you get back into town?"

"Early this morning, and please, don't change the subject," his father says. "So tonight, seven P.M. I'll see you then." The phone disconnects before Finn has a chance to respond.

"Son of a bitch." He slams his hand on the steering wheel, the muscles in his jaw flexing into a hard line.

"Hey, I'm so sorry." I know how horrible this evening will most likely play out for him, like they always do whenever his father is involved. I lift his hand to my lips and kiss his knuckles. I want so badly to make this all go away. "What can I do?"

Blowing out a breath, he continues to stare at the road. "Go with me. Other than that, there's really nothing else."

"I'll go." The words are out of my mouth before I even think about what I'm saying, because if there's any way I can help, I will.

"Sloane, I was totally joking. You already have plans with Mia. I'll be fine, I promise. I've done this before."

"Finn, it's okay. Mia will understand. And if you think me being there will help, then count me in."

"It definitely won't hurt, that's for sure. He'll be less likely to ride my ass if you're there."

I pick up my phone and text Mia before Finn can tell me not to. I ask her if she's okay with meeting a little later tonight than originally planned. She doesn't respond, but I know she's at work and will when she can. "Already done."

"Thank you. You really didn't have to do that, but thank you. I'll pick you up at six thirty, okay?"

He drops me off and leaves to get ready. I have a little less than two hours, which normally would be plenty of time. But the fact I'm doubting I have anything suitable to wear is only one of the problems. I mean, it's dinner with his father, who showed up at the pool *wearing a suit*. Not to mention, Finn was also wearing one the last time he went out with his dad, so I know this isn't going to be a shorts-and-T-shirt kind of dinner. I race to my closet and pull the doors wide, then step inside and spin around, wondering what outfit I might possibly pull off tonight.

But then I spot it. The dress I wore to my spring formal that somehow found its way into my suitcase when I was doped up on painkillers.

The bodice is strapless and all sparkling silver sequins that fade to charcoal and down to black, and then transition into an all-black feathered short skirt. It shows a lot of leg, but right now, it's the only thing I've got. I also thank my lucky stars that among all the things my mom has bought for me during this trip, a pair of strappy silver heels was one of her purchases. And they're perfect.

"Mom! I need your help!" I run to find her and explain that I need some sort of wrap for my shoulders.

"I've got just the thing." She disappears into her closet

and comes out a moment later with a black pashmina. "Big plans tonight?"

"We're having dinner with Mr. McAllister." My face must say it all because my mom starts to laugh. "I don't think he likes me . . . or anyone else for that matter. So this should be fun."

"I'm sure that's not true. But if it is, I guess you'll just have to change his mind, won't you?" She walks over to her dresser and opens her jewelry box, lifting out a delicate chain with a large diamond solitaire hanging directly in the center. She drops it, along with a pair of matching stud earrings, in the palm of my hand. My father gave them to her after they were married.

"Thanks, Mom!" Kissing her cheek, I race off to get ready.

As I'm working on my hair, I get an odd text from Penn:

Can't believe you bailed on Mia tonight.

Nice, Sloane, real nice.

I stare at my phone, but don't respond. That isn't what happened at all. I didn't bail on Mia . . . did I?

I shoot her a quick text:

Sorry I can't make dinner.
But I promise I'll be over later tonight. K?

I tuck my cell into my clutch and am surprised when I walk out to the living room to find Finn already here. He's standing in the kitchen with his back to me, laughing with my mom. She lets out a whistle when she sees me, and when Finn turns around, he stops, as if frozen in place.

I have no words for how to describe him, because just saying he looks hot is not nearly good enough. It's not even close.

He's wearing a dark charcoal pinstripe suit that fits every inch of his body as if expertly tailored to fit. Probably because it is. He even has on the matching vest underneath, his tie tucked snugly inside. My mom stands behind him where he can't see her and points, while mouthing, "Oh my!" and I'm forced to bite back a giggle.

"Hey, you look great," I muster, coming up to his side. "Where's Luce?"

"She went with my father." He lightly presses his fingertips to my arm, then slides his hand down to take mine. "And *you* look amazing."

We say our good-byes, and Finn walks me to the car. I knew he wouldn't have taken the bike, but thought for sure it would be the Jeep. Instead, one of the black SUVs from the hotel is waiting in my driveway. And I have to admit, it's nice having Finn sit with his arm around me.

"My dad isn't particularly fond of the Jeep. And don't even get him started on my bike."

We ride in silence for a few minutes, until Finn presses

the button for the center partition to close between us and the driver.

"Thank you for coming tonight. I can't tell you how much I appreciate it. Not to mention I'm really looking forward to what my father has to say." It's said with total sarcasm, and I can already feel the tension he's giving off. "My apologies in advance, because I know what's coming. I feel bad that you don't."

"Finn, as long as you're okay with this, I have no problems being here. And I'm sure it won't be that bad." I'm trying my best to sound confident, but after what I've seen so far of his father, I'm not so sure that I'm right. "This is important and I don't want you to feel like you're alone, because you're not."

He lifts my hand to his lips and presses a kiss along the top. "You're kind of the greatest thing ever, you know that, right?"

"Only 'kind of'? Guess I'll need to work on that." I playfully elbow him in the side.

We pull up in front of the restaurant, and I'm surprised to see it's one I've been to before. My mom met the head chef and owner several years back when his daughter broke her ankle playing soccer. She needed surgery, and my mom was the surgeon he came to. Bob has also done some work on his wife, but getting new lips and boobs isn't exactly something that's talked about.

As soon as we're through the front doors, we're greeted by the hostess, and I can instantly tell when Finn's demeanor changes. It's like he's an entirely different person. And I realize if there's any chance I can help deflect, I'm really going to try.

"Mr. McAllister, your father and sister are waiting at your usual table. This way, please." We're led through the main dining room to a private table, secluded from the rest of the dinner guests.

Finn's father stands as soon as he sees us and immediately Finn steps forward to shake his hand. Luce also stands. She's sucking in both of her lips and looking down at the table with her hands tucked behind her. She looks incredibly uncomfortable.

"Father, you remember Sloane."

"I do. I just didn't know she'd be joining us tonight." He eyes Finn, and I wonder if that will be a conversation saved for later.

"Sorry to once again disappoint, but Sloane and I already had plans this evening, before you called," Finn replies.

Yes, it's a lie, but I understand why he says it. I stick my hand out to shake with Mr. McAllister, and I'm surprised when he takes it. Especially after what he just said. His handshake is firm and deliberate and his eyes search me from head to toe, before I see the nod of his approval.

"Miss McIntyre, so glad you could join us. Please, have a seat." I turn to sit down, and Finn is behind me, helping me with my chair before he takes his own.

Mr. McAllister signals one of the waitstaff. "Please

increase our dinner tonight to four," he says to the waiter, as another setting is placed in front of me.

A bottle of wine is already at the table and as one of the servers fills up our glasses, Mr. McAllister frowns in my direction. I think it's because the wine probably isn't supposed to be for us. So it surprises me when instead he says, "I've already taken the liberty of ordering. The menu here is prix fixe, so you don't get to choose what you want—and they don't serve chicken fingers and French fries."

Ha! I realize two things very quickly: One, he thinks I have no idea what the term "prix fixe" means. And two, I'm not about to lose to this man.

"Oh, I know. Chef George does an amazing job with the menu here. It's wonderful. And I have no aversions to any type of food. I love to try everything." Even though I say it all with an easy, steady tone, I take a sip of the wine, hoping it will help with my nerves.

His eyebrows actually raise just a hair. I believe this might be his surprised look. Because something tells me he doesn't quite believe I've been here before. Like Finn couldn't possibly be hanging out with someone that has.

"So tell me, Miss McIntyre, what do your parents do?" As he says this, our first course is set down in front of us, a seared ahi tuna with Aleppo pepper aioli over basmati rice. It looks amazing.

I get the distinct feeling he's sizing me up, and that's fine.

I'm rather proud of my mom and dad. Finn takes my hand under the table and gives it a reassuring squeeze. I squeeze it right back to let him know I'm okay. Luce looks like she'd rather be anywhere else but here.

"My father is a litigation attorney in Seattle. And my mother is an orthopedic surgeon here in Honolulu and owns her own practice. My stepdad is a plastic surgeon here as well."

"So your parents are divorced, then."

It's not really a question, but more of a statement.

"Yes, they got divorced when I was in the fourth grade. I live with my dad during the school year, but have been coming down here to stay with my mom every summer." I take another sip of wine and decide to turn the tables. "So aside from all your hotels, I hear you also have interest in the LA Dodgers?"

Both he and Finn seem surprised that I know this. Thank God for Google.

"I do actually. Are *you* a baseball fan?"

"Yeah . . . I mean yes. And had the Dodgers stayed in New York, I'm sure I would've rooted for them. But instead, I'm a Yankees girl, through and through." He once again raises one very curious eyebrow in my direction, a look not unlike the one I've seen from his son. "My father is Brooklyn born and raised, and my grandfather was a die-hard Brooklyn Dodgers fan. I grew up hearing stories that he cried for days when they moved to LA, so he raised my dad to love the Yankees instead. It was kind of impossible for me to not love the Yankees, too." I take another sip from my glass. "Oh, and we also root for the Mariners. Although they really need to beef up their offense if they're going to have any shot at the pennant."

Luce beams at me while Finn coughs into his napkin, and I can tell he's fighting back a smile. I'm kinda proud of myself, too. Maybe it's the few sips of wine I've had or maybe I want Mr. McAllister to realize I'm not afraid to speak my own mind. Even if maybe I kinda am. But he doesn't know that.

Besides, I feel like some of the tension has lifted and has allowed Finn to relax a little.

My phone buzzes with an incoming text, and I slide it out from my purse, under the table so no one sees. It's from Mia.

> If u can make it over later, fine. If not, don't bother.

Crap. She's totally pissed. So I respond back immediately.

> Mia, I'm so sorry I had to move out the time.

> When u didn't respond, I thought it was okay. That's my bad.

> I'll be over as soon as I can.

I feel horrible. She needed to talk to me, and I totally flaked.

The waitstaff clears our plates, and our second course is settled on the table. It's a small dish of foie gras and toast points, and with it comes a different glass of wine.

"Well, I'd have to say I'd be a little disappointed if my son is swayed toward the Yankees, especially after he starts at Yale." He lifts his napkin and dabs at his mouth. "Speaking of which, did I tell you I spoke to the dean of admissions a few weeks ago? With as much money as I've donated over the years, they won't be turning you down."

Finn's face falls slightly, and I realize I've done all I can in keeping the conversation off him.

"Father, I've already told you. I'm still considering my options, but I think I like MIT the best. UC Berkeley might be my second choice." I can tell this is a conversation they've had plenty of times by the exasperated tone in his voice.

"Phineas, there's nothing to consider here. Three generations of McAllisters have gone to Yale, and your brother would've been next—there was never even a question about that." He scoffs, irritated with Finn, as he shakes his head. "Quinn would have never thrown such an opportunity away. And I'll be damned if you think you will."

"Dad, maybe we can talk about this later?" Luce asks. She doesn't look at him when she says it, but I know she's trying to help.

"Luce, this is between your brother and me."

"I know. I just thought maybe we could talk about something else for a change. Like . . . like the fact that Sloane is teaching me how to swim." She eyes me over her glass of water as she takes a sip, but I don't miss her smile. "It's awesome, Dad. And I'm getting good!"

Mr. McAllister clears his throat. "You're back in the water? When did that happen?" He doesn't wait for her to respond, but I love the fact that Luce was able to change the conversation just like that. "Does Dr. Klein think this is a good idea?"

"As a matter of fact, he does. He's even the one that suggested it. Besides, I'm learning a lot, and Sloane's a really, really good teacher."

Mr. McAllister slowly turns to me; a scowl creases his forehead. I can actually see him processing what he'll say next and how he's going to say it. And now I know exactly how his kids must feel every time they sit here with him.

"So what exactly makes you qualified to be teaching a minor how to swim? Are your parents there? I don't remember giving permission for this."

I'm a little taken aback by his tone, not to mention his words.

"Actually, I'm certified in Seattle and have been giving lessons for years. And—" I go to say more when my phone buzzes with a text. My mistake is when I glance down and see that it's from Mia and it makes me lose my train of thought. "I . . . anyhow, yes, I am qualified."

"And I'm the one that said it would be okay," Finn interjects.

I'm not sure if that's enough, so I'm surprised when his father doesn't probe any further. That, or he's already thought up the next topic he'll be grilling his kids on.

My phone buzzes again. I take a deep breath, but don't look at who it's from.

"Speaking of being out in the water, would you like to tell me why I saw the surfboards left out?" This question is directed back toward Finn. "It wasn't enough for me to lose one son, but now you're back at that ridiculous hobby again?"

"We were just tooling around off Waikiki. I'm not *back* at anything." I can tell Finn really wants to roll his eyes, but he refrains. "And just because something happened to Quinn, doesn't mean it will happen to me. Especially not in the two feet of wild Waikiki surf."

His dad doesn't miss Finn's sarcastic tone, and I'm pretty sure it's made things worse. "I'm assuming the 'we' in this situation is the two of you?" He motions between Finn and me. "You seem to be having a *very* interesting influence on my children, Miss McIntyre."

His comment slides down my back like ice. But then he turns back to Finn.

"And I don't care if you're surfing in the bathtub. I don't like it, and I don't want it to happen again. Have I made myself clear?"

My phone buzzes once more. I feel like I'm being torn in a million directions, and before I can stop myself, everything breaks wide open.

"Wow, I can see why your kids love having dinner with you." The entire table goes mute. "What? I'm only pointing out the obvious. We all know this is downright miserable. And you don't even know me, so what gives you the right to speak to me this way?"

Mr. McAllister's face turns stony, like hard cement. Luce looks like she might actually get sick. And Finn . . . I wait for him to defend me—to back up what I've said, because I know deep down he feels the exact same way. So I'm shocked when he just stares at me in disbelief. In fact, of all things, he looks disappointed. And suddenly my heart goes still.

"So he can say whatever he wants, but when I do, I'm the one being rude?" I grab my phone and my handbag. "Thank you for dinner, but please, you'll have to excuse me."

I shove back from the table and rush toward the bathroom, but Finn catches my arm and spins me around before I get there.

"What the hell was that?"

I blink, stunned. "Huh, that doesn't quite sound like an apology to me."

"You actually think I should be the one to apologize after what *you* just said back there?"

"After what I just said? What about your father?"

"You're not the one who has to deal with him at the end of the night!" He rubs a hand angrily down his face, leaving red track marks behind. "Thanks a lot. . . . No really, thanks. Of all people, you're the one that's supposed to understand."

"Wait a minute. Did you really expect me to just sit

there and not respond to any of the rude things coming out of his mouth? Did you expect me to be okay with how he talked to you, to Luce, to me?" I stand tall and run my hands over my dress to smooth it out. "I was trying to defend you. Everything I've done tonight was for you. I got all dressed up and came to dinner for you. I canceled my plans with Mia for you. All of it . . . for you!"

And then it hits me. I didn't see it before, or maybe I didn't want to, but I'm right back where I was with both Mick and Tyler. Giving everything up for someone else. I even canceled plans with Mia, my best friend on the planet right now—who told me she needed me—for him.

God, how could I have not learned my lesson the first time?

"I'm so stupid. This entire night was stupid. But believe me, it won't *ever* happen again." I don't even let him respond before I turn and storm out of the restaurant.

Nineteen

I'm a complete mess during the cab ride back to my house, as I replay everything over in my head. I'm beyond pissed at Finn and how he reacted, and I can't believe I ditched Mia for that asshole. What the hell is my problem? Why am I constantly getting so wrapped up in someone else that I stop seeing what's important to me?

I pay for my fare and stumble into the house, tearing my heels off as I go.

"Penn, is that you?" My mom comes out from the living room, a glass of wine in one hand. "Oh, Sloane, what happened?"

"It was a disaster, Mom—a complete disaster."

I tell her everything, including what I said to Mr. McAllister, and I watch as her eyes go wide.

"Huh. Well, it sounds like you didn't hold back, did you? But it also sounds like it's about time someone told that man the truth."

"You should've seen their faces, Mom. It was bad. And maybe I shouldn't have said some things, but honestly, out of everything, I feel the worst about bailing on Mia. God, I'm such a shitty friend."

"No you're not, Sloane. You just did what you thought was right for another friend, that's all. But you should go see her. Tell her what you just told me. She'll understand."

It's amazing how quickly things can change. Today started off on a total high, but ended in complete disaster. Hopefully I can at least still fix things with Mia. I send her a text that I'm on my way over and go to my room to change.

I'm about ready to leave when my phone rings. I grab for it, thinking it might be her, but I'm surprised when the caller ID shows that it's Tyler. It's really late in Seattle, past one in the morning. And I'd bet my entire summer's salary he's drunk, so I don't answer it. I'm not in the mood.

I wait for him to leave a voice mail like he always does. But this time, he doesn't. And a few seconds later, he calls again.

Frustrated, I turn off my phone and grab my bag, when Penn comes into my room. He doesn't need to say a word for me to know that something isn't right.

"What is it, what's wrong?" I ask.

"Slo, you need to talk to Tyler." He hands me his phone, but I'm not sure if I'm ready to hear his voice. "Sloane, *please*, trust me, you need to take this."

I grab his phone but only because I know my brother

wouldn't ask if it wasn't important. Taking a deep breath, I hold it up to my ear, my eyes never leaving Penn's.

"Hey."

"Sloane . . . it's . . . it's McKinley."

Instantly, I'm on alert, because I can tell by the tone of Tyler's voice that something is very, very wrong.

"Tyler, what is it? Where is she?"

I hear the unmistakable suck in of breath, as if he's trying to contain himself, contain his emotions.

"There's been an accident. I'm at the hospital, but I have no idea what's going on. No one will talk to me." He falters for a second and takes another breath. "God, you should've seen her car. There's nothing left."

My heart feels like it's going to break out from my chest.

"Wait, what? What the hell was she doing driving? She doesn't even have her license, Tyler! And why won't anyone tell you what's going on?"

"They won't talk to me because I'm not family. But I think it's bad . . . it's gotta be bad if they're not saying anything, right? Please, Sloane, you need to come home. I don't know what to do."

I don't even hesitate. "I'll be on the next flight."

I throw a change of clothes in my backpack. Anything else I need will be at my dad's place. I rush out to the living room, and Penn must've already told my mom and Bob because they're all there, waiting for me.

My mom is on the phone, but she covers the mouthpiece

as soon as she sees me. "I'm on with the airlines now." She hugs me tight. "I'll call you as soon as I have your flight confirmed."

Penn drives me to the airport, and I realize I need to call Mia and let her know I'm not making it over. She picks up on the second ring.

"Yeah?"

"Mia, I'm so sorry. There's been some kind of accident with Mick. . . . God, I have no idea what's going on. But Penn's taking me to the airport now to catch a flight home." I don't miss her hesitation at the mention of my brother. "Mia?"

"Go, Sloane. Don't worry about me. I'll be here when you get back. I'm so sorry. I hope . . . I hope everything's okay."

"Thank you, Mia. I'm really sorry about tonight. I totally fucked up, please don't be mad."

"Sloane, don't worry about that—I understand. Go do what you need to do and call me when you can, okay? Love you."

"Love you, too, Mia." I disconnect the phone and immediately it rings again. My mom tells me I'm booked on a red-eye flight and gives me all the information. She also called my dad. Unfortunately he's out of town at some work conference, but he's trying to get home on the next flight that he can. I end up texting Tyler and ask if he'll be able to pick me up. His response is immediate:

I'll be there, 8:30am sharp. Thanks for coming, Slo.

So much is swirling around in my head right now, I don't know what to focus on first, where to start. I feel like things are beginning to close in on me, and I feel my breathing start to waver. I take a puff from my inhaler and suck in a long, deep breath, then push myself to concentrate on one thing at a time, and that starts with what's right in front of me.

"I take it things aren't okay with you and Mia?"

Penn glances at me sideways, his focus still on the road in front of him.

It takes about five seconds for me to catch up. "Oh, God. She told him, didn't she? Mia finally told Shep?" I realize the last time I saw my brother was last night in the pool, when he had Misty high up on his shoulders playing chicken. After everything that's happened today, that feels like such a long time ago.

"Yeah, she told him and Shep and I are cool. He's not the problem."

He coughs to clear his throat, pausing for a few seconds longer, before saying anything more.

"I have no idea what the hell's going on, Slo. I don't even remember what happened last night. All I do know is that I woke up with a very naked Misty in my room this morning, and I was hungover like nothing else. So of course why wouldn't that be the exact moment Mia showed up?"

"Oh, God." I feel sick to my stomach. That had to have been when she texted me this morning.

"I went over there this afternoon to try to talk to her, but she blew up at me, saying all this shit about how both of us suck because you bailed on her and I can't keep my junk in my pants. I tried to explain what I could about Misty, but she wants nothing to do with me. And now she won't answer the phone. So until I can find out what the hell happened, well, I'm as lost as you are."

He flips on his blinker and begins easing his way over lane by lane for our upcoming exit. I try to absorb everything he just told me, but based on what he's said, there could be a million different scenarios that happened last night.

"I'm sorry, Penn. I really am. If there's anything I can do, I will. I promise."

"Don't worry about that right now." He pulls up to the curb and turns to look at me, his face completely serious. "I have to figure this out myself. Besides, you've got bigger problems to deal with."

"I'll call you as soon as I land, okay?" I hug Penn tight. "P., I hope you figure this all out. I'm sorry I can't be here to help. And also . . . thank you for making me talk to Tyler."

"Don't worry about it. Have a safe flight."

I jump out of the car and run inside to the ticket counter. The agent can obviously see I'm upset, and when I explain there's been a family emergency at home, she reassures me that everything is taken care of and hands me my ticket. My flight departs in thirty minutes, so I need to hurry.

And with that, I'm racing through security. The ride on the Wiki-Wiki shuttle bus to my terminal takes forever, and for a second, I think I'm not gonna make it. When I get to my gate, I'm the last passenger to board the plane, and they seal the doors shut behind me.

I'm trying to finagle my backpack into an already full overhead compartment above my head, when one of the flight attendants comes to my aid. Of course that's also the same time I shove someone else's bag to make room for mine, and I watch helplessly as it slides just out of my reach and smacks her in the shoulder. A Costco-sized box of chocolate-covered macadamia nuts decides to jump with it and lands on her feet. She lets out a grunt.

"Oops . . . sorry."

I attempt to help grab whatever I can in the now cramped aisle, when I hear her deep intake of breath. Scowling, she points to my seat, and I do as I'm told. She settles everything in the overhead bin and moves on to the row behind me.

Buckling my seat belt, I realize I need to call Finn and let him know what's going on. I'm still pissed at him, but suddenly everything that happened at dinner seems so stupid.

I pull out my phone to dial his number, but then my favorite flight attendant returns.

"Miss, you're going to have to turn that off and stow it until after we've landed in Seattle." I want to tell her that I'll make it quick, but the look on her face is nothing but serious. "I'd have no problem confiscating it if I have to."

"Yeah, I was just making sure it was turned off." She stands guard as I power down my phone and tuck it in the seat pocket in front of me, like she doesn't believe me.

I guess Finn will just have to wait until my flight lands tomorrow morning.

Which seems like it takes forever.

It doesn't help that I can't shut off my mind from all the crap that's happened in the last few hours. And I try not to imagine what could have happened in the time that's passed since I've been on the plane. I try not to think about all the worst-case scenarios, scenarios like the one where Mick doesn't make it.

Or worse, the scenario in which I'm already too late.

Tyler is waiting for me when I land, and without even thinking, I hug him tight. I look up at his face for confirmation that Mick is okay, and while it's grim, I still see hope there.

"Is she still . . . ?" I can't bring myself to say it.

"She's serious, but stable. I was finally able to talk to her brother for a second, but I don't know much. I guess she's been in surgery for most of the morning. They moved her to recovery about an hour ago. I'm sorry, Sloane. They're only allowing family in to see her right now."

"Well, when *can* we see her? Did Bryson at least tell you that?"

"I'm not sure. He only said he'd call later with an update. I guess I'll take you home and we can wait for him to call."

He snags my backpack from my shoulder, and we walk in the direction of the parking garage.

On one hand, I'm relieved, because stable at least sounds

hopeful. But it still doesn't explain how she ended up in the hospital to begin with.

"Jesus, Tyler. What the hell happened?"

Throwing my bag in the trunk, he unlocks my door and holds it open, then goes around to the driver's side and gets in.

"Jansen threw a rager last night. The entire school was there, and everyone was wasted. You know how his parties are." Jansen is one of Tyler's football buddies, and ever since the ninth grade, he's been known for these parties at his parents' lake house. "Mick snuck out and took her mom's car."

I suck in a deep breath of air.

The fact Mick snuck out is one thing, because even though she's done that with me, I've never seen her do it by herself. But the bigger deal is that she took her mom's car . . . without having a license. And that doesn't sound like her at all.

"Of course as soon as I saw her, I told her she shouldn't be there . . . you know, with the baby and all. And we totally got into it. Fuck, she was a mess—screaming at me and crying, saying I'd ruined everything for her. I tried to calm her down, but hell, Sloane, I was blitzed myself. She took off before I could stop her."

His knuckles turn white as he grips the steering wheel tighter. "She hit an SUV head-on, and both she and the other driver were airlifted to the hospital. I don't even know how they pulled her out of her car, it was so bad. She's lucky to be alive."

There's more I need to ask, more I need to know, but my

phone rings and it's my dad, so I answer. I update him with what little news we have, but when I ask when he'll be home, I find out his conference is in Miami and a stupid hurricane is headed to shore.

"I'm so sorry, Sloane. Why we'd have a conference in Miami during hurricane season is beyond me, but I'll be on the next flight out, I promise. I'll see you soon."

It's early, but I call Penn anyway to fill him in and ask that he tell Mom and Bob, because I'm too exhausted to talk anymore. But there is one more person I need to call. When I dial Finn's number, it goes straight to voice mail, and I don't leave a message. It's six thirty in the morning there, so he's probably still asleep.

Tyler takes my bag from the trunk, then follows me up to the house. It's hard not to remember what happened the last time we were both here. But I need to get past that. I need to move on.

I unlock the front door and hold it open. "Come inside. I'd like to be there when Bryson calls you."

He hesitates, but only for a moment, then steps through the door and shuts it behind him. We head up to my room, and he tosses my backpack on my desk chair. It's weird being here, with him, but it also feels familiar.

"So you don't have to tell me if you don't want to . . . but what about the baby?"

His eyes well up with tears, and I know the answer without him having to say anything. While the baby may have been something he didn't want before, I realize now it's no longer a choice. My heart sinks into my toes.

God, how fucked-up everything's gotten. I have no idea how I let it get this bad. Or how I get it to go back to the way it was before.

I need to fix this. We all made mistakes, but I need to make it better. I just don't know where to start.

"I'm really sorry, Tyler. . . ."

"It's not your fault." He doesn't say anything more, but when he rakes his fingers down his face, I can see how exhausted he really is.

"I think we both could use a nap. You can crash in Penn's room if you want." Nodding, he takes that as his cue to leave, but I grab his hand. "I really am sorry, Tyler—about everything. If there's anything I can do, please tell me."

There's a desperation in his eyes mixed with uncertainty, like he's not sure if I mean what I'm saying. Hell, I have no idea what I'm saying myself.

He lets go of my hand and sits on the edge of my bed with his elbows on his knees, his face in his hands. I stand next to him, my fingertips finding their way to his hair, and I comb them along like I've done a thousand times before. Both of his arms wrap around my waist, and he pulls me to him, resting his forehead against my stomach.

We sit that way for a while, and then he stands and his eyes search mine. He lowers his head, pauses . . . and then he kisses me.

He's the only one that understands exactly what it is I'm going through, because he's going through it himself. And while I know this is all sorts of wrong in so many ways, I need to kiss him, too.

So I do.

But then my mind flashes on Finn, and I pull away.

Tyler stands back to look at me—*really* look at me. And yes, he's done this a million times before, but something in the way he does it now is different. Like we're different.

Because we are.

"I'm so sorry I ever hurt you, Sloane."

He gently, tentatively, kisses my forehead, then lowers himself onto my bed and lies back. When he folds his hands in his lap, I know he's telling me it's safe—he's not about to try anything. Grateful, because I am way too tired and scared and confused to deal with any of this, I lie down next to him, my left side against his right.

I don't know what he is to me now, but I know that, with everything going on, having him here is comforting. And in this moment, that's about as far as I can think it through. So instead, I lean into him, close my eyes, and fall asleep.

Twenty

I hear the sound of a cell phone buzzing with an incoming call. It's hours later, the sun still out, but much farther along in the sky than it was before.

Tyler reaches for the phone.

"Bryson, how is she?" he whispers. I can tell he doesn't know I'm awake. "Oh, sorry about that." Pause. "She's sleeping, but I'll let her know you . . . hello?"

He disconnects the call, sets my phone back down on the nightstand next to his, and stares at it.

"Shit." He rubs at his eyes, then runs his fingers up the back of his head, skewing his hair in different directions.

Before I can ask who it was, Tyler goes to use my bathroom. When he comes back out, he sees that I'm awake, lying on my stomach facing him with my arms tucked under my pillow. He sits down on the bed next to me. Sliding the strap of my tank top to the side, he traces along my tattoo, and then his hand moves up to my hair and twines a strand around his finger.

"You've changed so much, Slo. The old you would've never done this to your hair. And you hate needles more than anything."

I take a deep breath. "I still hate needles. But I guess I wanted to try something new, do something different." I glance over my shoulder at the tattoo. "And I happen to like my hair, thank you very much."

He smiles and shakes his head. "I like it, too, Slo. That's just it. You look amazing. You have this confidence now like nothing and no one can stop you."

"And I didn't have that before?"

"No, you did, just not quite . . . I don't know, not quite as much." He traces my tattoo again. "What does it mean?"

"Remember to live."

He glances at me, then shakes his head. "But when did you forget?"

I look him in the eyes and hold his gaze as he waits for my answer.

"The day my best friend told me she'd slept with my boyfriend and she was pregnant. Only to find out an hour later, she'd actually slept with him twice."

He cringes and hangs his head, his eyes closed.

"I can't believe it's already been a month," I say. "And, God, it didn't feel like it then—and sometimes it still doesn't now—but I think everything that happened made me finally wake up. Made me take a new look at what really matters, or better yet, *who* really matters. Because you can't imagine how it feels when the people you love the most end up being the ones that hurt you the most."

I realize I'm not yelling at him, and I'm not crying, either. And while this is such a different conversation than ones I've had with Tyler as of late, there's still something I need to know. Something I need Tyler to answer.

"I know you said no when you were in Hawaii, but I need you to really be honest with me. Did you . . . do you love her?"

He stares down at the floor and shakes his head slowly. Then his eyes drift up to meet mine.

"No, other than as a friend, no. It was a stupid mistake, Slo, and if I could go back and change it all, I would. I don't know why I was so confused when she told me she had feelings for me, because that never should have mattered." He touches my tattoo again. "But I know that's all a little too late. What I did . . . what Mick and I did, it changed everything. I know you've moved on. I can see it all over your face. And I could feel it when I kissed you." He takes a breath. "You really like him, don't you?"

"I do." There's no hesitation when I say it, because it's the truth. And suddenly, I know I need to talk to Finn, tell him how much of a mess dinner was, and apologize for going off like I did.

"Sloane, I'm really sorry, but he called you earlier."

I sit up straight. "Crap. That was him?"

Tyler nods. "I heard the phone and I thought it might be Mick's family, so I answered it. And he didn't sound happy. At all."

He hands me my phone, then brushes my hair back from my forehead. "You should probably call him. I'll go see if I can find us something to eat."

He shuts the door, and I stare at it. I can't believe he actually told me Finn called. That he's suggesting I call him back. Maybe Tyler's trying to move on, too.

I swallow hard and call Finn. He doesn't answer right away, but when he does, I hear laughter and voices in the background and the unmistakable sound of a girl's voice nearby. A girl with an accent.

"I said I'll be right there, Gianna. Hello?" he snaps into the phone.

"Wait, you're with Gianna?" I can't keep the disbelief out of my voice.

"And you're with Tyler."

Touché.

"That didn't take long," he adds. "Hopped the first plane back to Seattle, huh?"

"Finn, are you kidding me? I tried to call you earlier. Do you have any idea what's going on here?"

"Nope. Only that you ran home to fucknuts as soon as things got rough here. Imagine that. Gotta go."

And with that, he disconnects the call. Just like his father.

I stare at my phone in utter disbelief. *"Nope"*? What the hell does he mean by "nope"? I start to call him again, but stop when I realize two things. One, he'll probably not even bother to answer, and two, there's nothing I can say that will make him listen, at least not right now.

Not even five seconds later, I try calling him anyway. I can't leave it like this. But this time it rings a few times and, unsurprisingly, goes to voice mail.

As it turns out, there isn't anything for us to eat in the house. The refrigerator holds nothing but a half carton of milk, one egg, a container of take-out leftovers, and a jar of olives. The cupboards are just as bare. I take one sniff of the leftovers and throw them out. They've probably been sitting in there since I left. I can't believe this is how my dad lives when we're gone.

"Come on, let's go grab a burger, my treat." Tyler places a hand on my head and turns me around from the kitchen toward the front door. "So were you able to get a hold of Fink?"

He looks at me sideways and smiles. We both know he knows his name. But when he sees my face, his smile straightens out and disappears. As he throws his car in reverse and backs it out from my driveway, I stare out my window, chewing on my thumbnail.

"He was with another girl." I don't miss his audible intake of air. "God, what the hell is wrong with me?"

Tyler drives for a few moments, not saying anything. He grips the steering wheel tightly and stares straight ahead as we come to a stop sign, but then he turns and looks me square in the eye.

"Sloane, there's *absolutely* nothing wrong with you. It's all us douche bags that can't seem to realize the good thing we have when we have it."

Even though this all started because of her, I wish Mick were here. The Mick from before. More than anything in the world. She would help me figure this whole mess out.

How could everything have gotten this bad? There's so much wrong right now, and it's not just in my life. We've all been caught up in this ever-expanding spiderweb of bad decisions.

Instead of going to our favorite hangout, Tyler drives a little farther out of town, and I don't even need to ask why. I can't find it in me to pretend I want to talk to anyone we know, especially with the abundance of topics for them to choose from. I guess Tyler is feeling the same way.

We sit down in a corner booth and Tyler slides a chocolate milk shake and a cheeseburger wrapped in orange paper my way. He dumps the fries out between us on the paper liner from his own burger, then begins to dig in. Well, Tyler digs in. I move some fries around from one side to the other, then back again.

I think about Mick lying in the hospital, with God knows how many tubes and machines attached, keeping her stable. I think about how many times she reached out to me and I ignored them all. I ignored her.

I stare at Tyler as he fiddles with his straw and spaces off somewhere else. I never would have thought three months ago I'd be sitting right where I am. Trying to figure out, pinpoint exactly, when Mick decided she was in love with my boyfriend. Wondering if there was anything I possibly could've done to have stopped it from happening. And I can't help but think about how different everything could've been if I had.

I would've said good-bye to my best friend and my boyfriend and gone to visit my mom like I always have. I would've still met Finn, but because Tyler and I would have been together, nothing more would have happened. Summer would end, and I'd come back home and start my senior year with nothing but a great tan to show for the last few months.

I actually laugh out loud, and Tyler stares at me. But then I can't look at him, and I dig the heels of my palms into my eyes, like if I can't see him, he can't see me. I plant my elbows on the table and stay like that, hidden from everything.

I can't believe Mick almost died in a car accident. I can't believe less than an hour ago I was sleeping next to Tyler, and that we kissed. And I can't believe Finn was with Gianna and that he actually hung up on me. I can't believe any of it. It all feels like it's been a really sick and twisted dream and at some point I'll wake up.

But who am I kidding? It's all real. Everything is.

We're headed back to my house when Bryson finally calls. Tyler hands his phone to me to answer.

"Hey, it's Sloane. How's Mick? What's going on?"

"Hey, it's good to hear your voice. Tyler mentioned you were headed back to town." There's a slight rustle on the line as Bryson speaks to someone there in the background. "Sorry about that, I only have a minute. . . . It was my turn to make a food run, so I thought I'd try to catch you guys while I was out. Reception inside the hospital is pretty much nonexistent."

He thanks whoever is helping him.

"So . . ." He pauses to take a breath. "Things are still really iffy right now. Her condition is serious, but at least she's stable. She was in surgery most of the morning and has a lot of internal injuries affecting both her pelvis and spleen. It took them a while to find the source of the bleeding and get it to stop. That's on top of a busted-up leg and arm and a pretty serious concussion. She's still heavily sedated right now, so she's not awake, but we're hoping she's through the worst of it. Her doctor says that if all goes well through the night, there's an eighty percent chance of a full recovery."

I realize he's waiting for me to say something, but I can hardly absorb what I've heard.

"If . . ." My voice cracks. "If all goes well through the night? Is there a chance that it won't?"

"Honestly, I don't know. You know how cryptic doctors can be. But I've got to believe everything's going to be okay. Although she's not going to be happy once she wakes up and hears how long she'll need to stay here."

"Why, how long do they think she'll need to stay?"

"Right now they're saying it could be anywhere from several weeks to maybe a couple of months. It all depends on her recovery. And she'll need to be in physical therapy for a while after that."

Everything, all of it, makes me feel numb to my very core. I try to piece it together. Try to understand exactly what it could mean. But there's too much. Or maybe there's not enough. And I realize seeing her is the only answer.

"Is there any chance I can see her? I promise I won't stay long."

He hesitates for a moment, and I think he wants to tell me no. "We're hoping they'll upgrade her condition tomorrow. If they do, then she can have visitors." He pauses for a second. "Look, Sloane, to be completely honest, I'm not sure my mom wants you or Tyler to see her. You know how she can be."

I don't miss the meaning in his words. Mrs. Peterson blames me, blames Tyler, for breaking her daughter.

"Yeah, I know how she can be."

"Hey, I'll do what I can. I'll come up with something. Just wait for me to call you in the morning. I'll know more then. I gotta run, Sloane, but it was really good talking to you and I promise, tomorrow, okay?"

"Tomorrow. Thanks, Brys." I'm not sure if he hears me because the phone disconnects.

I try to put on a happy face as I turn toward Tyler, but

I know he can see right through it all. I tell him everything Bryson just told me.

"That bitch." He punches the ceiling of his car. "She honestly believes Mick had *nothing* to do with anything that happened? That all of this is our fault?"

"I guess so. . . . I don't know. She's probably freaking out, Tyler. She's probably just looking for anyone to blame."

I reach over and take his hand in mine, and he grips it something fierce.

"She's not entirely wrong, you know. If I had just talked to her once, just *once*—maybe we wouldn't be sitting here right now." I look up and see the same guilt I'm feeling flash in his eyes. "If I could go back, I'd do so many things differently. I'd do it all so differently."

"Me too," he whispers. "You have no idea."

My dad calls to let me know he'll be on the first flight out tomorrow morning and will be here sometime around noon. Tyler spends the night, but only because I don't want to be home by myself, and we stay up telling stories about Mick. We laugh at different memories, one in particular of Mick and me sneaking out of my house to go pick up Tyler and a few of the other boys.

I cover my mouth, holding back a laugh. "She kept telling me I had to keep it down, but then she was the one that totally slipped and tumbled down the entire staircase, *on her ass*, and woke up my dad and half the neighborhood!"

"I know, right? I thought for sure you both were going to be grounded for life! You're lucky your dad is so cool."

Oh, how true that is. Because had it been Mick's parents that caught us, it would've been an entirely different outcome, even for me.

"Or that time when the police caught us after we'd TP'd and forked your house? Shit, we were digging a hole in your front yard and sticking a For Sale sign in the ground when they pulled up!"

I laugh until the tears come, and then I can't remember anything funny anymore. All I know is that Mick has to get better. She has to pull through.

Twenty-One

Tyler and I are out having breakfast the next morning when Bryson finally calls. My heart leaps when I hear the phone, and then I feel both disappointed and totally ashamed when I see who it is. Because I'd immediately pictured Finn, and now I can't believe I'm that self-centered. I take a deep breath. I'm almost afraid to answer it, but I do.

"Hey."

"Hey. So listen. Mick woke up shortly after I spoke to you yesterday, and although she was still pretty out of it, she had a really good night. She's not in the clear yet, but she's definitely feeling better this morning. So I convinced my dad to take my mom out for lunch later today, and they should be gone for at least an hour. Think you guys can be here around noon?"

I let out a breath I didn't realize I was holding. "That's . . . that's great news, Bryson. And of course we can be there at noon." I glance down at my watch and see that we have a little over an hour and a half. "Thank you . . . for what you're doing. Just . . . thanks."

"Don't sweat it. I'll see you guys later."

An hour and a half seems like a lot of time, until you realize everything from the past month is about to come flooding back. And then it doesn't seem like enough time at all. Before I even really have a chance to digest what I'm going to say or how I'm going to say it, Tyler is already pulling his car into an open spot in the hospital parking lot.

"You ready?"

I wipe my hands down the top of my thighs. "You know what? I am."

I make a quick pit stop at the hospital gift shop. The selection is bare, which is never a good thing at a hospital. I end up with a bouquet of sad-looking flowers and a stuffed bear that has his arm in a sling and a Band-Aid on his head.

Bryson is waiting for us in the lobby. "My parents just left, so we have a little less than an hour. But, um, you guys should know. Mick received some not-so-great news this morning—I'll let her tell you yourself. Oh, and she doesn't know you guys are coming. I was hoping the surprise would help put her in a better mood."

I glance at Tyler, and we trade the same look. I'm not sure if it's a good or bad thing she doesn't know we're here.

The doors of the elevator open on Mick's floor, and it's the smell that hits me first. Antiseptic and sterile. The

255

beeping of various machines are next, and I realize I really don't like hospitals at all. We sign in at the nurses' station and follow Bryson to her room.

I stop outside the door and shake out both of my hands, then rub at my eyes. I can do this. I can. Because it's Mick. The girl I've known since I was two years old. And I can honestly say I know that if the roles were reversed, she wouldn't even think twice about being here.

"I'll wait out here. Let me know if you guys need anything." Bryson grabs a magazine and goes to sit down as Tyler pushes open the door.

Mick is lying there on the bed, her face pale. Wires run everywhere, and she looks so fragile hidden beneath it all. There are a million bruises and cuts, her skin a patchwork quilt. Her arm is in an all-too-familiar-looking cast and her leg has one to match. Cuts zigzag across her forehead and down one cheek, and she looks as if she's sleeping.

I set the flowers and stuffed bear on the rolling table next to her bed. When I turn back around, Mick's eyes are open, and she's watching me.

"Hey, you. How are you feeling?"

"Huh. Can't say I was expecting to see the two of you here. *Together.*" She zones out on the flowers and the bear for a long time, then finally looks back at me. "What do you want, Sloane?"

"I'm sorry?" At first I don't think I hear her correctly.

But then she lets out this laugh that's not at all a reaction to something funny.

"You heard me, what do you want? I didn't ask you to fly home. Not that you would've responded if I had."

"Mick, that accident almost killed you. Of course I came."

Shaking her head, she looks away, disgusted. Like I truly have no right to be here. But then she focuses her gaze on Tyler. "And I know for a fact I didn't ask for *you* to be here, so you can just leave."

"Come on, Mick, don't be that way." Tyler takes a step toward her bed, but the icy look on her face makes him stop.

"I said get out. Or do you only understand things when someone breaks your nose?"

Tyler throws up his hands with a heavy sigh. "Whatever, McKinley. Sorry, Sloane. I'll be right outside." I watch as the door shuts behind him.

"Yeah, he says he's sorry, but I'm sure you've heard that a million times by now."

"Mick, what exactly is your problem? I flew home as soon as I heard. I've been waiting to see you. And I know I didn't respond to any of your messages, but that was only because I couldn't. I needed time to think about everything. I needed time for me. But now I'm here and you're acting like all of this is my fault. Like I'm the one that made you get in that car and caused the accident."

"You're unbelievable." She stares me down as best she can with one swollen eye. "You do realize you left me all alone when I needed you the most, right? You stopped talking to me when I had no one else to talk to. I have no one, Sloane. *No one.* All our friends? They won't even look at me, except to point and whisper about how much of a bitch I am for what I did to you.

"And then I find out I lost the baby. The one thing that started all of this and now that's gone, too." She wipes at her face with her good hand, but somehow still manages to keep it together. "But the worst thing? As if all of that isn't enough? Is when they told me this morning that my leg is so messed up, they don't think I'll ever be able to dance again. Kiss Juilliard good-bye. Kiss it all good-bye."

"Oh my God." I cover my mouth with my hand. "Mick—"

"But then you show up here thinking everything's all right, that everything's going to be the same as it was," she interjects. "That you can just be here and all of a sudden I'll be okay with it all, that we'll be BFFs like nothing ever happened. But it's never going to be the same."

"Wait a second. I do *not* think everything's all right. In case you've forgotten, this all started because you couldn't keep your clothes on around *my* boyfriend. Ex-boyfriend, whatever." I cross my arms over my chest. "Oh, that's right, and it happened more than once."

"Fuck you, Sloane. I told you how sorry I was for all of that, for everything. I called, I e-mailed, I texted, I even wrote letters. But what? Only Tyler gets to be forgiven? Or did I need to get on a plane and fly all the way down to Hawaii for that?"

"I never said I've forgiven Tyler," I whisper. "You have no idea what's going on there."

"Maybe I don't. But maybe you could've at least thought about that before showing up here *together*."

"And maybe you could've—at any point in time—told me you were in love with him." It slips out before I even realize what I've said.

And out of everything, that's what catches Mick off guard. That's what makes her face fall. She had no idea I knew.

We both stay silent for a long time. When she finally speaks, it's not what I was expecting.

"You know I read somewhere that envy is when you want something someone else has, but jealousy is when you don't want them to have it, either. Well, I've never been so jealous of someone in my entire life."

"What are you talking about, Mick? When have you ever been envious or jealous or whatever, of me?"

"You're not even listening to what I'm saying. I hated that you had Tyler and I had nothing. I hated that he loved you so much and could've cared less about me. Even after he found out I was pregnant, all he cared about was you. I hated it all. And I tried to get over it, Mack. I really did try. Just check your in-box or your trash folder and you'll *see* how hard I tried. But you just fucking ignored me. So guess what?" She takes in a broken breath. "Now I realize, I hate you, too."

I stare at her, my mouth open, as I try to wrap my brain around what she's saying. "Don't say that, Mick. You don't mean it. It's just the meds."

"No, no it's not. For the first time everything is so clear. It's your fault he wants absolutely nothing to do with me. It's your fault he doesn't love me back. And now I've lost the baby. And I won't be able to dance, ever again. *I've lost everything.*"

She smacks at the vase of flowers with her cast, sending it flying against the wall. I gasp as it shatters and shards of glass scatter everywhere.

"What's worse, is that you don't even want him now and he *still* doesn't want me. But please, tell me Sloane, what have *you* lost?"

I have no idea who this person is in front of me. The Mick I knew no longer exists. But whoever this angry, broken girl is, just my being here is upsetting her, and that's not what she needs right now.

"I lost my best friend, that's what I lost," I say finally. "But I hope she finds her way back someday."

Without waiting for her to ask me to leave again, I turn and go, shutting the door behind me.

I mumble my thanks to Bryson and walk away.

******

Instead of taking me home, Tyler drives the two of us to one of our favorite spots near Lake Washington. The summers here in Seattle are gorgeous, and today doesn't disappoint, regardless of what else has happened.

We walk along the lake for a while, side by side. His presence next to me is so familiar, almost like he never left. For the longest time, he was all I ever really knew, and even before we decided to be boyfriend and girlfriend, he was one of my best friends. We finally sit down on the grass together, my left side brushing up against his right.

"I guess things didn't turn out like we expected, did they?" He rests both elbows on his knees, and looks out at the water.

"You could definitely say that. Then again, a lot of things where Mick is concerned haven't exactly been as expected."

It's a busy day out on the water. Boats and Jet Skis skip across the lake like a handful of stones, their throaty engines echoing from our shore to the banks of Mercer Island across the way. For a long time, neither of us says anything.

"I know I've said this before, but I really hope you know how sorry I am, Sloane. For everything. And I don't expect you to ever forget what happened, or what I did to you. . . ." He pauses and takes in a deep breath. "But I hope one day you'll be able to forgive me."

I consider everything he's saying.

The moment I talked to him on the phone the other night, I somehow forgot that Tyler had a part in all of this, too, forgot he was half the reason why my summer started off so shitty. Then again, I was so caught up in everything that was going on with Mick, and somehow being with Tyler over the past couple of days helped me in a way I didn't know was possible.

"I'm not sure if I can ever completely forgive you for what you did, and I know I'll never forget it. But . . ." The tense muscle in his jaw softens slightly. "Things between us are definitely better than I thought they'd be."

While I know it wasn't everything he wanted to hear, I immediately can feel the effect my words have on both of us. I almost feel relieved.

Or maybe it's better than that. It's like my body has unfurled all my limbs from this tight little ball I've been curled in this entire time, and now they're finally free.

He bumps his shoulder against mine, and that smile of his is there. That smile that for years could fix the world for me. He looks down at my lips, then away, then back again. Slowly, he leans in, and our noses brush against one another. I close my eyes. His mouth touches softly against mine, and then he pulls back slightly, hesitantly, then it presses against mine again. The kiss is soft and sweet and everything Tyler and I always were. But then, just as quickly, it's over. And in a way I know this is the last time.

After that moment, he doesn't try to kiss me again. Not until he drops me off at my house, but then it's a simple peck on my forehead.

We both know we're in a better place than we were before, but when he says good-bye, there's a sadness there I can't quite explain. I think maybe it's because Tyler and I are saying more than good-bye to each other—we're saying good-bye to us.

Twenty-Two

My dad is home and waiting for me by the time Tyler drops me off, but he doesn't say a thing when all I want is to go up to my room and crawl into bed. I stare at my phone and don't realize until I hear it ringing that I've dialed Finn. I don't know why I'm surprised when all I get is his voice mail.

"Look, Finn . . . We really need to talk, but I don't want to do this over voice mail. Please, just call me so I can explain."

I call Mia next.

"Hey, lady, I'm sorry it's taken me so long to call."

"Please, no worries. I know you've had your hands full. But tell me, what's going on up there? How's Mick? Is everything okay?"

I give her a brief rundown of everything that's happened over the past forty-eight hours.

"Wow, that's how she's gonna be? Jesus, Sloane, I'm sorry. I mean I'm glad she's going to be okay and all, but that still sucks."

"Yeah, sucks is a good way to put it. Anyway, what about you? How are you doing?"

I hear her blow out a breath. "Yeah, it sucks here, too. I don't know what to do, Sloane. Your brother, that hooch he was with, all of it. The only good thing that happened is Shep. When I told him the truth, he definitely seemed bummed, but he was honestly okay with everything—said if I had to be with someone else, at least it was with a 'good guy' like Penn. Ha. If he only knew."

"I don't know what happened between my brother and Misty, Mia. And based on our conversation the other night, he doesn't have a clue, either. I wish I had better advice, but me telling you to give him a second chance would be totally hypocritical, especially after everything that's happened. God, boys can be so stupid, huh?"

"Yeah, you can say that again. Speaking of boys, what's going on with you and Finn?"

That whole mess takes another ten minutes to explain.

"Slo, I'm sure he'll understand as soon as you get the chance to talk to him in person. There was so much going on, it's amazing you've been able to stay sane."

I laugh, which doesn't help my defense where sane is concerned. "So I'm flying back down in the morning. If I haven't screwed things up too much, I'd really love to hang out this week."

"Oh, you have a deal. Call me when you get settled, okay? And, Slo, I really can't wait to see you."

"Me too, Mia."

I disconnect the phone and toss it on my nightstand. As soon as my head hits the pillow, I'm out.

It's not until sometime later that evening that my dad knocks on my door. I sit up, propping myself against my pillows as he walks in and sits on the edge of my bed, setting a bottle of water down on my nightstand.

"Are you hungry?"

"Starving." I eye the bottle. "Not sure water is precisely what I had in mind."

"Ha-ha. I know, I need to go to the store. I wasn't exactly expecting anyone. So I ordered us a pizza. Think the water can tide you over for the next thirty minutes?"

"Possibly."

I jostle his shoulder, making him laugh. When I see him this way, it's hard to believe what happened between him and my mom ever really happened, but I realize there's something I need to know. Something that will hopefully help make what's happening in my life a little more clear.

"So Mom told me everything about the divorce. I guess . . . I guess I just need to know why, Dad? What made you do it?"

His face falls ever so slightly. "Your mother and I . . ." He grips the back of his neck and the lines of his face go taut. "Sloane, I have no excuse for what I did. And I have no reason for it, other than pure weakness on my part—which I know

is not a good enough reason. You need to know I loved—"
His voice catches and he clears his throat. "*Love* your mother
and you kids, more than anything. *Anything* in the world. But
there's absolutely nothing I can do now to change what I've
done. Apologies aren't enough and I know that."

To hear him say that he *still* loves my mom catches me off
guard, and it makes me feel so sad. He turns to look at me,
and I can see the shame all over his face. In that moment, I
know that if there were any way he could go back in time and
change it, he would.

"I made a really big mistake." He looks at me, but I'm
not sure what I should say to that, or if I should say anything.
"I made mistakes and your mom rightfully couldn't forgive
me. But in time, even though we couldn't save our marriage,
your mom somehow learned how. And I'll forever be grateful
to her for that. Because I firmly believe I would've handled
things differently had she not. Or not handled them at all."

I don't know exactly what he means by "not handled
them at all," and I'm not sure I want him to elaborate.

"Anyhow, if there's any chance you can find it in you
to forgive, I hope you'll at least think about it. That doesn't
mean you'll ever forget . . . some things can never be forgotten. Believe me, I know," he mumbles. "And I don't know
if this helps with what you've been dealing with, but it at
least might be able to change how you deal with things going
forward.

"A wise woman once told me, right before she boarded a

plane back to Hawaii, that everyone is responsible for their own actions and it's ultimately up to that person on what it is they want to do. We all have a choice, so what are you going to do?"

Everything he says makes me grateful that Tyler and I had the chance to talk—to *really* talk and not just react and scream and cry. I'm glad that we left things at least on a better note this time than when I left for Hawaii last month.

But it still doesn't help with Mick.

I tell my dad what happened at the hospital and most of the words that were exchanged.

"A few days ago I never would've thought I'd forgive Mick, but then the accident happened, and all I could think about was how I would feel if Mick didn't get better, if I'd be okay with not having the chance to talk to her . . . or forgive her for what she did.

"But then she said everything she said, and at first I thought she was just strung out on pain meds and pissed at hearing the bad news about not being able to dance anymore . . . about losing the baby. But there's something more there, Dad. She's not the same person I left standing in that park over a month ago. I don't know if I'll ever forgive her, but honestly . . . I don't know if she's ever going to forgive me, either."

"Well, all I can say, Sloane, is that people do change. Traumatic situations can make it even worse, and Mick is dealing with a lot of that right now. Maybe she just needs time. You of all people should understand that."

"I don't know, Dad. I think she needs something more than time. And maybe I do, too."

He stares at me, I mean really stares at me, and I know what he's about to say is serious.

"You need to do what's best for you, Sloane. If that means moving on, then so be it—at least you can't say that you didn't try. Like I said, everyone is responsible for their own actions. Every single one of us, including Mick."

Twenty-Three

I leave for Hawaii the following day. The flight back gives me several hours to think—about everything and everyone—and it makes my head hurt like I've had a headache for days.

But then I land in Honolulu and the scent of flowers and the heat of the tropical sun washes over me once again, and now Tyler and Mick both seem so far away. Like a thing of the past.

I called Finn before my flight took off, but didn't bother to leave a message this time. I know it's impossible, but as I head down toward baggage claim, a part of me hopes Finn will somehow be there to pick me up. Like he'll just know I'm back.

Sadly, I'm a little disappointed when I see Penn standing there instead. The two of us wait quietly as we watch the luggage spin around the carousel. Even though I went home with only a backpack, I took advantage and packed a new bag while not under the influence of narcotics.

I get the easy conversation out of the way first and fill Penn in on what happened between Tyler and me. I tell him that I think, maybe in time, Tyler and I can go back to being friends. His relief is immediate, and I know that's because he misses his friend, too.

I also tell him what happened with Mick and how differently things ended there. But I change the subject before he has a chance to respond.

"So how are things with Mia?" I pretty much already know the answer to this, but I want to hear it from him. I look up in time to see the lines of his face harden.

"She still hasn't forgiven me for the Fourth. But in my defense, I was pissed that she was with Shep all night and I was drunk on top of that . . . and honestly? I have no idea what went down. Misty and I were in the same room, but while I was in the bed, she was passed out on the couch. I don't think we did anything, but I don't know for sure. I've been trying to find her, see if she'll tell me what happened . . . or hopefully, what didn't." He kicks at the front of the baggage carousel, and I know he's mad at himself. "Then maybe Mia will forgive me."

Then it's Penn's turn to change the subject. "So . . . have you talked to Finn?"

The linoleum floor has suddenly taken on an interesting appeal. The dark tiles hide the millions of scuffs I'm sure are there. Sometimes I wish it were that easy to hide my own flaws.

"He won't talk to me. It's . . . it's a long story." And then it all comes spilling out as we collect my bag and head to the car. Everything from the horrible dinner with his dad, to Tyler picking up the phone when he finally did call. Before I realize it, my brother is pulling the car into the garage at the Echelon.

"What the hell, Penn? Why are we here?"

"Oh, didn't I tell you I have to work today?" He pokes the inside of his cheek with his tongue. "That and I figured badass Sloane with her bitchin' tattoo might have a few choice words to say to a certain someone? I mean, are you gonna let him leave it like that? *Please*." He throws me the keys. "Don't worry about me, I'll find another way home. See you tonight." He disappears, leaving me standing at the car.

"Yeah, badass Sloane. Ha." I make my way out from the garage and try Finn's cell. Of course he doesn't answer. I turn in the direction of the pool. After all, it's early afternoon and usually a lounge chair is where he can be found this time of day. I say hello to Logan and a few of the other guards, but Finn is nowhere.

Okay, so I'll try the beach.

I maneuver my way through slathered bodies that smell like hot, sticky coconuts, and scan the waves. Although based on the conversation with his dad at dinner, I'm not sure Finn would bother with surfing, at least maybe not here in front of the hotel.

Making my way back to the hotel, I decide to give his phone another try. When he again doesn't answer, I realize I've somehow made my way to the elevator that goes up to his suite. He gave me the code a few weeks before, so I let myself up.

I don't know what I expect to happen when I finally end up finding him. After all, I got a lot more than I thought when my meeting with Mick finally happened. Maybe it's better I go into this one with no expectations at all.

The elevator doors open, and immediately I hear the TV on in his bedroom. I also hear voices. Laughter. I'm hesitant at first, but decide since I'm already here, I might as well knock.

"Come in," he says in between muffled laughter. I'm not sure if it's the TV or someone else that has him laughing. But when I open the door, I find him lying on his back, his hands folded behind his head, and Gianna is curled up next to him.

She has the audacity to look at me like *I'm* the one intruding. Her disgust is almost palpable as she eyes me from head to toe. And no matter what my brother just said to me, this is one situation even badass me can't fix.

In the back of my mind, a small warning starts to blare, letting me know I'm holding my breath, trying to keep it under control.

Finn sits up, surprised. "You came back."

"God, you have *got* to be kidding me," I whisper. It's all that comes out of my mouth, because I don't know what else to say. I turn on my heel and slam the door. I'm back at the elevator, jamming the button with my thumb, gasping for air, before I even realize he's behind me.

"When did you get back?" He's standing so close, his

breath moves the hair by my ear. "Sloane, I didn't think you were—"

I spin around, and before I know what I'm doing, I shove him hard. So hard and so unexpectedly, he actually stumbles backward.

"I called. Several times. Which is more than I can say for your sorry ass." I hear the elevator ding open behind me, but I'm only just getting started, so it will have to wait. "I've had more than my fair share of shit to deal with over the past month, not to mention the past few days. And while I thought we had something great going on, it's obvious I couldn't be more wrong." I take a step forward, and he actually takes a step back.

"I went home to Seattle because my once best friend was almost killed in a car accident. I sat there, for hours, and wondered if she was actually going to make it. And so many things were clouding my mind, but still, I had the time to think about everything I've messed up, including *you*," I say, looking away, my voice catching. "I thought about what happened at dinner with your father, about the things I said, about causing grief between the two of you, and I felt so stupid. I realized, after everything else that's happened, how *stupid* it all was, and I was going to apologize. And then, I come here, and . . . and . . ."

Finn holds up his hands. "Sloane, I had no idea. I didn't know about the accident, I didn't know about Mick."

"Of course you didn't know. How could you? You

wouldn't talk to me. You didn't answer any of my calls. You didn't let me explain."

My breathing spirals out of control and I try desperately to rein it in, get myself in check.

"Did you . . . did you sleep with her?"

His face goes dark as he looks back toward his bedroom door, and that alone answers my question. I bend over and clutch my stomach, my surroundings turning fuzzy around the edges. Ohmygod. How can this be happening? *Again?*

"I can't believe I'm such an idiot! I thought you were different! But how could I have ever thought I'd be enough? I wasn't enough for Tyler, and clearly I wasn't enough for you." I turn around and make my way to the elevator, struggling to control my breathing. My thumb jams against the call button yet again. "I hope you realize you're the one that walked away from us. Not me. I never would've done that, I never would've done what I know would've hurt you the most."

The doors open, and I stumble in, gasping for breath as I clutch at my chest with one hand and press the button for the lobby with my other without turning around. There are so many things I can't do right now, and looking at him is one of them.

"Sloane, are you okay?"

I shut him out and try to envision my pool. Slowly, it comes. The lanes, the water, the crowd.

But this time, as the doors slide shut, it doesn't help.

Twenty-Four

It's the beginning of August, and I'm giving Luce her last swim lesson. I want to finish what I started, even if Finn and I are no longer talking.

Over three weeks have passed since I last saw him. I thought I'd get fired from the Echelon after the words I had with Kent McAllister, but I was wrong. Because I quit. I couldn't work there anymore anyway because I was constantly afraid I'd run into Finn. And I want nothing to do with him, not after knowing he's been with Gianna.

He actually called a few times, but taking a cue from him, I sent him straight to voice mail. He also tried to talk to Penn, but my brother asked that he be kept out of it.

He came over a couple of times, too. But I never answered the door, and I promised my brother I'd be willing to risk another cast if he even thought of letting Finn in.

I hope he's having fun with Miss Italy.

"You're doing great, Luce!" I shout as she swims from one end of the pool to the other without stopping. I'm amazed at how she's overcome her fear of the water. How she's let it go and moved on. I think there's something I can learn from that.

She stops at the shallow end of the pool and stands up. Yanking her goggles off her head, she takes in several deep breaths.

"Did you see that, Sloane? I did it!" She hops up and down in the water and grins from ear to ear.

"You bet I saw you! Didn't I promise I'd have you swimming laps in no time? Didn't I?" I reach down and give her a high five, but then she hops out of the pool and wraps her arms around me tight.

"Thanks for everything." She tucks her head down, but I can see her suck in both lips as she looks away. "I'm really sorry my brother is being such a jerk, but I hope that doesn't mean we can't still be friends."

We've somehow managed to avoid any mention of her brother over the past few weeks. But I'm guessing since this is her last lesson, Luce is afraid it will mean we won't see each other again.

"Luce, whatever is going on between your brother and me has absolutely nothing to do with us, okay? We're friends, no matter what." I tighten my grip around her shoulders. "No matter what, Luce, I promise."

She smiles and a little color rises in her cheeks.

"He really misses you, you know. Every time I come home from one of my lessons, he asks a ton of questions— like if you bring him up, if you ask about him, stuff like that. Do you think you'll ever stop being mad at him? Because I think he really wants you to stop being mad at him."

I don't know what to say to any of that. Luce is so innocent, and she makes it sound so simple.

"I wish it were that easy, Luce. I really do."

She leaves for my room to go change and I meet her inside to walk her to the front door. Like clockwork, the car from the Echelon is waiting out front to take her home. I start to walk her to the car, but the back door opens and Finn gets out. He stands there in cargo shorts and a T-shirt, and we look at each other for a second too long.

But I can't do this, not in front of Luce. Not now.

I put my hand on her shoulder and look her in the eye.

"I'm so proud of you, Luce. You've been my best student yet, and I hope you don't ever give up on swimming."

She throws her arms around my neck. I can see Finn over her shoulder, watching us. Watching me.

"Can I still come over to swim even though my lessons are over?"

"You bet. Call me anytime." I let her go and stand back up. "I'll see you soon, okay?"

"Okay!" She heads to the car, skirts around Finn, and hops up onto the backseat.

He raises a hand in my direction like he wants to say

something, but I walk back into my house and shut the door behind me without another glance.

The following evening, Mia drags me out to the beach. Our beach, not the one down by the hotels in Waikiki. There's a small group of us gathered, minus Finn, and Mia's reassured me it will stay that way, at least for tonight.

Shep is also here. He and my brother are tossing the football around like nothing ever happened. I wish I knew how to do that.

I still don't know what's going on between Mia and my brother, because neither one of them is talking about it. But to be honest, I don't know if I really want to get in the middle of it anyway.

"Hey, you, we've missed you around the activities counter," Maile says, slinging an arm around my neck. I'm pretty sure she knows what's going on, for the most part, but she doesn't ask any questions. "You know a job will always be waiting, if you ever wanna come back."

"Thanks, Maile."

She kisses my forehead and lopes off to grab a beer from the cooler.

Mia hands me a bottle, but I'm not interested in drinking tonight, so I shake my head no. When she's busy threading her stick with a marshmallow, I catch my brother looking at her. And when Mia looks up at my brother, it's a second too late, and he's turned back to his game of catch.

I grab a bottle of water and make my way farther down

the beach, away from the others. The sand is so warm between my bare toes. I love how easily the golden swirls slide over the tops of my feet, making them disappear. Sitting down, I pull my knees to my chest, lift my chin to the last rays of the setting sun, and close my eyes. I'm going to miss this when I go home to Seattle.

I hear voices, but with how the hair on the back of my neck suddenly stands in alarm, I know it's not anyone already at the bonfire. When I turn, I see Shep and my brother headed our way, but they're with someone else. And, of course, why wouldn't that someone else be Finn?

His shirt is off, and he's spinning the football my brother and Shep were playing with between his fingers, very much like the first night I met him. They're laughing about something as Finn stares out at the ocean. And then his eyes lock on mine, and I watch something flicker there. It's like he was hoping I'd be here.

"Hey, I'm so sorry, Slo." Mia plunks down in the sand next to me and leans her shoulder against mine. "I'd heard he had other plans tonight. He wasn't supposed to be here."

"You're not responsible for him."

I hear them laugh again in easy conversation and watch as they make their way to the other side of the fire. From where he sits, he has a clear view of me. Mia bumps my shoulder, and I look back out toward the water.

"Slo, he's obviously doing this to get your attention. A guy doesn't bother with stares like that if he doesn't still care."

My laugh is short, clipped. "I think we're well past that now."

I manage to stick around for a few more minutes, but being mere feet away from him is more than I can take. I don't think I could handle it if he caused a scene here at the beach, in front of all our friends. So I stand, and Mia follows.

"I can't be here, Mia, sorry. This isn't gonna work."

"Let me get my stuff. I'll come with you."

I grab her arm before she can turn around. "Not that I wouldn't like to hang out tonight, but I think you've got some unfinished business with my brother that's more important." I nod in his direction, and she glances at him, then bites her lip. "Seriously, Mia, go talk to him. I'll call you tomorrow, okay? I'm gonna wanna hear all about how the two of you kissed and made up . . . well, you know what I mean."

She smiles and I go to the fire to retrieve my bag. I don't even bother looking at Finn. Instead, I gather my stuff and take off down the beach toward my car.

I'm almost to the parking lot when a hand grips my wrist and spins me around.

"Sloane, wait. Please."

I yank my arm away. "Don't touch me."

I drop my flip-flops, step into them, and make my way up the beach access path. His bike is parked a few spaces over from my car. I throw my bag into the empty passenger seat and get in, slamming the door shut behind me.

"Sloane, would you please wait?" He rests both hands on

my door as I start up the engine, my music blaring. "Can you turn that down?"

Turning it up even louder, I back out from the space and take off, leaving him standing there. Instead of taking a left toward my house, I decide to go right. Maybe a long drive will help clear my head.

Endless miles of beach are mere feet from the right side of my car. But as the road begins to curve, I hear the high-pitched whine of an engine screaming behind me, and I look up to see a single headlight in my rearview mirror.

Oh, you've got to be kidding me. Does he seriously think chasing me down will make me forgive him?

I get stuck following behind a minivan full of tourists driving ten miles under the speed limit, as one of them hangs out the window to take pictures of the setting sun. There's not a single car in front of them, but they're actually going slow enough that I can see Finn's hands shift down on the gears of his bike as he rides my tail. When the oncoming traffic lane finally clears, I step on the accelerator and speed around the minivan, then cut back over and take off. I don't wait to see if he's behind me, because I know that even though my car has an impressive engine, there's no way I can compete with his bike.

I fly down the road, until the traffic behind me fades and I wind around another curve. For a moment, I think he's given up. I slow down for a red light. The beach park to my right is vacating all its tourists for the day, as car after car pulls out and drives by me, heading back the way I came. I hear his bike again, clicking down through its gears as it slows and pulls up next to me.

Flipping up the visor on his helmet, he motions toward the emptying parking lot. "Sloane, would you please pull over?"

The light turns green and I take off, but all Finn does is snap his visor closed and keep pace with my car. Then he zips in front of me and his brake lights flash as he tries to slow us both down together. Pissed, I flip a U-turn in the middle of the road and speed back the other way.

It doesn't take long for him to catch up, and I can tell by the high-pitched squeal of his bike that he's driving the hell out of it. He follows close and mirrors every turn I take, pulling in behind me in my mom's driveway.

I'm up and out of the car in seconds, marching to the front door. Finn is immediately on my heels; I'm pretty sure he must've jumped off his bike while it was still moving. Before he can grab me yet again, I stop, turn, and level him with my coldest glare. He's so surprised he almost walks into me.

"I don't want you here. At what point did I not make myself clear?"

Without waiting for a response, I step through the front door and slam it behind me. I'm so tense I feel like I'm going to explode, and before I know what I'm doing, I find myself in my closet. My entire body is shaking violently, and I try to envision the pool in my head to calm myself down. Then I realize I've changed into my swimsuit and I'm standing there with my cap and goggles in hand.

I need to be in the water. Now.

Slipping the cap on my head, I tuck in my hair. I dip my goggles in the pool and rub both of the lenses before putting them on. I stand at the edge and stare at the water in front of me as I stretch out both of my arms. Immediately, my breathing slows down and I'm no longer shaking.

I dive in.

Each stroke is calculated, and I speed to the other side of the pool like a motor is strapped to my back. I make my turn, flipping over, then kick off from the wall. It propels me underwater for several yards as I glide along in pure silence. Then I rise up to the surface and start the process all over again. I'm not sure how many laps I do. I lose track somewhere around fifteen, which is something that never happens. I never lose track. But for some reason, I can't get myself to focus on the number.

It doesn't matter, though, because I know I'm swimming fast. Probably faster than I've ever swam. So I keep going, pushing myself harder.

It's when I'm about to make a turn that I see him standing there. But I don't stop.

I swim to the other side, flip, and am already on my way back toward Finn. I'm about to make my turn in front of him again, but this time, water and limbs are everywhere and my goggles get knocked loose. They rapidly fill with water, and

I scramble to stand, stripping them from my head as strong hands find my shoulders.

"What the hell, Finn?"

"Goddammit, Sloane, would you stop?"

"What don't you get? I have nothing to say to you!" I whip off my cap and fling it, along with my goggles, to the edge of the pool. "Why can't you leave me alone?"

I'm up and out of the pool in seconds. It's amazing what I'm capable of now that I have the use of both my arms. I storm toward the beach and the solace of the ocean beyond.

Finn is right behind me.

"God, just wait! Wait up! Please?" His breath is hot on my neck, and my chest is heaving something fierce. I'd be stupid to think it was only from the swimming, because his presence alone has this impact I wasn't even aware of. Or better yet, didn't want to admit. "If you would quit being so stubborn for just a second, maybe I could tell you what I never got to say before."

I've made my way to the sand, and I spin around to face him, closing the short distance between us. But before I can give him a piece of my mind, he yanks me into his arms and kisses me hard.

I shove against him, but this time, I'm the one that stumbles backward because he was prepared. Then I take a step forward, jamming my finger against his chest, and look him straight in the eye.

"No, you don't get to tell me how you think *I'm* being and then kiss me like that!" I shove him hard in the chest again.

"Let's get a few things straight. You were pissed because you never had the guts to stand up to your father, so when I did, you shut down. And then you completely lost it because you thought I left you and went running back to Seattle, when that's not what happened at all, which you would have *known* if you had *bothered* to answer any of my calls." With each syllable, I poke him hard to enunciate my point. "And then I'm at home and, yes, Tyler was there. And yes, he kissed me. But that's all that happened. He was there for me when we didn't know if Mick was going to make it. And he stood by my side when she rejected us both. It was nothing more than that. *Nothing.* Because in that moment I realized all I wanted was for it to be you, and Tyler could see it all over my face. I wanted it to be you, not him. *You.*"

I turn back around and face the ocean and clench my eyes tight, trapping my fear, my anxiety, my everything.

"But then you go and screw Gianna and God knows who else—for what? Trying to make a stupid point? Trying to rub it in?" My hands automatically find their way to my chest and press hard against my skin there. I will not lose control. Not this time.

I already see the pool in front of me, and it's filling with water, like it should.

He comes to stand in front of me, and when I don't look at him, he tilts my chin up until I do.

"Sloane, I didn't sleep with Gianna. I haven't touched another girl, not one." His fingertips lightly brush my forehead, and he tucks a strand of loose hair behind my ear, and I want to believe him. I do. But I trusted Tyler, and look where that got me. "And you're totally right about the whole thing with my dad. I realized I was pissed for no reason, but then when I called you the next day and Tyler answered the phone? Yeah, I kinda lost it. I couldn't believe you went running back to Seattle. That you went running back to him. That you'd actually *left*. Just like everyone does. I didn't think you were ever coming back."

All of a sudden, I understand. This is *his* fear. His mother left him without a word. His brother left him in the most horrible way possible. And then I left him after only one fight. At least, that was how he saw it. He thought I'd given up on him and flown back to Tyler. In the moment that Tyler answered my phone, he had no clue about Mick—no clue why I was really there.

"And then you showed up at my place and Gianna was there and I knew how bad that looked. But you were so pissed at me, you wouldn't stop yelling, and I couldn't get a word in. I didn't have a chance to tell you that nothing happened."

He runs a hand through his hair. "I'm sorry, Sloane, I shouldn't have automatically assumed the worst when you went home."

He slides a hand down my arm and grips my fingers in his. His other hand cups my cheek.

"And I definitely should never have thought that you'd walk away from me."

He dips his head, then hesitates, searching my eyes. I don't wait for him to figure out his next move. I pull him down until his lips are on mine.

It's frantic and desperate, like we're both searching each other for answers. Or maybe he's afraid he hasn't said enough and I'm still going to walk away. Or maybe I'm just so relieved he didn't sleep with Gianna.

Together, we drop to the sand, his legs intertwining with mine, his hands tangled in my hair. There's a part of me that can't get close enough to him, like even if there were a way to climb inside his skin, it still wouldn't be good enough.

His mouth pulls away from mine, and he trails light kisses along my cheek and forehead. But then he slows, his hands on either side of my face, as he gazes into my eyes.

"I'm so sorry, Sloane. Please tell me you forgive me?" he whispers, tracing one of my eyebrows with the tip of his finger. And those eyes, those brilliant blue eyes, are staring right through me. "Please. Tell me you don't want to walk away."

"Finn, I never wanted to walk away. I've never wanted to be with someone more. And I'm sorry, too. I'm sorry I ever made you think that."

As he leans in to kiss me again, I realize it wasn't so long ago I thought my entire life had completely shattered apart. But here, in this moment with Finn, I've never felt more complete.

Twenty-Five

Maybe all Mick needs is time. Or maybe she really will never speak to me again. At this point, I can't force her to do something she doesn't want to do—and honestly, why would I want that? Things will never be the same between us, not after everything that's happened. Not after everything that's been said. I'd be a fool to think differently.

I guess sometimes things just don't turn out the way you always thought they would. Or maybe they turn out exactly as they should, just not what you expected. Of course knowing what I know now, I would've done things differently. So much differently.

In some ways, I'll always feel guilty I didn't say something sooner to Mick. That I didn't respond to any of the many e-mails or letters or texts or voice mails she sent me.

Because Mick, Tyler, and I, we all made mistakes. Big mistakes.

But it wasn't entirely my fault. I didn't force Mick and Tyler to do what they did.

Like my father said, everyone is responsible for their own actions; it's just a matter of what they choose to do. And what we choose to do in response.

I finish getting ready and smile when Finn knocks at my door and pops his head in.

We're going to our waterfall today.

He looks amazing, even in swim trunks and a T-shirt.

He leans in and lands a soft kiss on my forehead, and a little flutter of nerves makes my stomach uneasy. God help me if I puke on the cute boy. *Again.*

Because today I'm letting him know I won't be going home to Seattle.

I've already enrolled at Punahou, and even though it's my Mom's alma mater, it still took a lot of finagling on her part to get me accepted. But I'm in.

Penn doesn't know what he wants to do—he and Mia are taking everything one day at a time, seeing where things might go. And while it's not perfect between the two of them, at least not yet, she's still a good reason for him to stay. But I know he's worried about leaving my father alone. Especially our last year before we both leave for college.

I struggled with all of that, too. I'm still struggling with the thought of not being home in Seattle for my last year of high school. Of not being with my dad. But I've talked to him and he's reassured me he understands. That it's the right thing to do.

Because when I think about everything I'd be leaving behind here, I know without a doubt he's right.

Hawaii is who I am now. Finn, Mia, Luce. *Everyone*. Not to mention my mom and the possibility for us to have something we haven't had in a very long time.

So yes, I've decided to stay.

And I'm doing *that* for me.

Acknowledgments

Like Sloane, I'm a firm believer that everything happens for a reason—even if it doesn't seem that way at the time. Had it not been for a particularly unfortunate 2013, I probably wouldn't be sitting here, holding a finished book in my hands. Had it also not been for an army of incredibly talented people behind me, the same thing could easily be said again.

To my agent, Lisa Grubka—my heartfelt gratitude for being on Twitter and #MSWL that wonderful day, pulling *Summer of Sloane* from the slush pile, and seven months later, giving me the best birthday news ever: sold! I'm so lucky to have you and the entire team at Fletcher & Company in my corner.

So much appreciation goes to my editor, Kieran Viola— our paths may have crossed in the most unusual of ways, but I'm so glad they did. Thank you for making *Sloane* better in every way and pushing me to go further than I ever thought possible. To my associate editor, Julie Moody—there isn't a doubt in my mind you made the entire Hyperion team see how beautiful Hawaii is, through the eyes of Sloane. So many thanks to Tyler Nevins for designing the most gorgeous cover an author could ask for; Jacqueline Hornberger for her line-editing prowess; Mary Ann Zissimos and Nicole Musich for their publicity genius; Emily Meehan—and everyone else at Hyperion—who helped make *Summer of Sloane* an actual honest-to-goodness book. And of course, to Lisa Yoskowitz—who loved Sloane and her story so much, she stood in front of an entire acquisitions team and convinced them that they did too.

I'm beyond lucky to call the following amazing women my critique partners: Heidi Sinnett, who relentlessly reads every single word I write—including the really bad ones—and still comes back for more; Bridgid Gallagher, who devoured that early draft of *Sloane* and left the longest and bestest voice mail ev-ver; Kris F. Oliver, who corrects any scientific facts I fail to get right—and there are a lot of them; and Sara Biren, who worried about all the technical ways to say something, so I could focus on telling the story instead.

I'm beyond grateful to the entire crew of the YA Buccaneers—I'm truly humbled to be surrounded by so much greatness. And of course to both the Sweet Sixteens and Sixteen To Read: I can't wait to be sitting on the shelves next to all of you!

As a writer, it's important to never forget how it feels to be on both sides of the book. It's because of this, I am eternally grateful to all the readers, bloggers, librarians, booksellers, and bookstore owners worldwide, for your unwavering support over the years, social media shout-outs, and overall enthusiasm. Sloane and I thank you from the bottom of our hearts.

To Mom, I wish you were here to see this beautiful journey unfold, but somehow I think you might have the best seat in the house. Save me a beer and some lau lau and poi, won't you? To Dad, who supported me every step of the way, and *always* believed—and thankfully taught me to not tuck my thumb in when throwing a punch. My sisters, Claudine and Nicole, and my brother, Eric, for providing the best childhood a girl could ever ask for. I'd gladly do it all over again, as long as the three of you are there.

So many thanks go out to my extended family and friends, of which there are too many to name here. I am truly grateful to every single one of you for your continued support and encouragement.

To the best companions ever: Ronin, who nudged my hand for pets and missed countless walks while sitting patiently at my feet; Ono, for curling up on my keyboard and reminding me to take breaks; Poke, for all the head bonks and giving me that "look"; and to all of my other four-legged kids that may no longer be here, but did their part in keeping me company on this otherwise solitary road called writing.

To my beautiful son, Kellan, who listened to every round of edits while in my tummy, as I read out loud—and not only kicked at all the right moments, but twirled at them too. I've always dreamed of becoming a published author, but my greatest accomplishment will forever be you. I love you with all my heart and soul.

And finally to my husband, Neal: for all the years you've stood by my side and never once laughed at any one of my crazy ideas—"I think I'm going to write a book" and "So . . . I've decided to quit my job to write full-time" being only two of them. My hole-in-one would have never been possible without you. I'll be cheering the loudest when you hit yours. Love you, Bubs.